MW01205013

RELEASED
BONNIE LACY

Dedication

Thanks:

To God. He is my Inspiration, my Source.

To my Dearly Beloved for believing in me and
providing for me so I could play.

To my precious family for believing in me
and encouraging me.

"The Spirit of the Lord God is upon me, because the Lord has anointed and qualified me to preach the Gospel of good tidings to the meek, the poor, and afflicted; He has sent me to bind up and heal the brokenhearted, to proclaim liberty to the [physical and spiritual] captives and the opening of the prison and of the eyes to those who are bound,"

Isaiah 61:1 Amplified Bible

CHAPTER ONE

"I ought to sue you! I can, you know!" Clarence Timmelsen screamed at the warden. He stiffened and shuddered. Tears of rage stung his eyes. "You're kicking me out of prison to send me to a nursing home?" He shook his fist and growled, "I'm gonna sue your ass!"

The warden hung his head as the cell door clanged shut. He turned to face Clarence through the bars, buttoning his black suit, his back rigid, emphasizing each word. "I'm sorry you feel that way. I have no control over the matter." Then he added, "It'll be better for you in the long run."

Clarence rushed the cell bars, white-knuckle-gripped them and glared. "In the long run? You mean till I die. That's what you mean. You're just kicking me out to get rid of me." His voice broke. "This is my home!"

He jerked away, but not before catching sight of inmates gathered behind the bars of each cell near his, across the commons area, upper and lower level. "What are you staring at?" Clarence bellowed. His deep gravelly voice ricocheted off the walls of the cellblock canyon.

The warden tapped his foot. "Good-bye, Clarence." He checked his watch. "All the wardens before me knew it would come to this." He cleared his throat. "Unfortunately, I'm the one on watch to carry out this final demand set forth in the proceedings by your judge."

Clarence stared at the warden. Ice shards crackled in his veins, just like when he'd heard the word "guilty" sixty years ago. "You mean that bastard judge set this up? Clear back then?" The visual of the judge's eyes burning with malice and the sharp rap of the gavel invaded his memory, just as it had every day of every year since then.

The warden slowly nodded and stepped away from the bars.

Clarence stumbled. He knew his eyes betrayed anguish as he stared at the warden. He gripped the bars, threw his head back and roared like a wounded, trapped lion.

Silence echoed off the entire cellblock until someone in the next cell snickered.

Clarence slowly rotated his head, following the sound. His eyes met Barred's. The rookie. Behind the rookie stood Dirk, the huge professional inmate.

Clarence locked eyes with Dirk.

Barred snickered again. "Ooo, the little ol' ladies'll like you." Another snicker. "You're f--"

Dirk rose up behind Barred, drew his fist back and pummeled him.

Clarence held his breath.

Dirk finally stopped, and the rookie crunched onto the concrete floor.

Three guards raced past the warden, sticks poised.

Keys rattled. Handcuffs clicked.

One guard pushed Dirk past Clarence's cell. The guard shook his head. "Stupid, stupid Dorko."

The inmate towered over the guard. "M'name's Dirk." A toothless grin spread across his face. "I got yur back, Clarence. See ya on the—"

The officer yanked on the cuffs and dragged Dirk past the cell.

Clarence's eyes shifted back to the warden's face. Old people's home. Wheelchairs lined up in rows. Vacant eyes. People forgotten.

The guards dragged an unconscious Barred past, one eye already swollen shut and purple. His slack jaw trailed blood.

Randy Gerald stepped over the trickle of blood and stood before the cell door. "Clarence." He dipped his head in greeting, smoothing a drab brown uniform over his big belly. He picked at a dark spot on his shirt. Looked like chocolate pudding. He lifted his head, his eyes direct. "I'm here to escort you to your new home."

Clarence glowered.

Randy adjusted his pants. Keys jingled from his belt. "We better get a move on. We have a long drive ahead of us."

Clarence braced himself.

"We can make this easy or hard—you choose," Randy said, hand on his gun. He turned toward the central station and waved at the guard. "You can open."

"Sure thing, Sir," blared the overhead speakers.

The lock on the cell door echoed as it unlatched.

Randy entered the cell and tossed a flimsy shopping bag onto the cot.

Clarence stared at him a long time. At the warden even longer.

His thoughts spun in a million directions: stay in prison, die, maim the warden, escape. None landed on the option facing him right now—a nursing home—his final resting place.

Maybe it was his age, or being caught in a new and unexpected situation, or both, but he wanted to bust out bawling. Only once before had he felt this helpless.

He stepped to the lavatory, intending to gather his belongings, but became distracted by the image in the mirror: steel gray hair combed back from his forehead and falling in waves to a black T shirt, a full beard mostly obscuring a deep scar on his right cheek, blue eyes glaring back at him, and wrinkles in places he didn't remember. Memories floated between reality in the mirror and the image of a much younger man, his hopes and dreams not yet shattered by life. The memories stirred emotion buried deep. Emotion Clarence long ago had declared not worth the pain and horror of digging up. So it had remained entombed, sealed with a capstone.

Until now.

"You ready to go, Clarence? Chicago traffic will be fierce this time of day."

Clarence swallowed, smoothed his old wool flap hat over his hair and donned his light tan jacket. He carefully pulled on his gloves and picked up the bag, gathering what was left of a toothpaste tube, the rest of his toiletries and his brush.

He scanned the cell one last time. Each cold concrete block, every crack, the stained out-in-the-open facilities, and the blue-white light overhead. It had held the years of his life, since ...

Clarence stepped to the cot, reached under the mattress and removed a folder. Stuffing it into the bag, he turned to exit the cell only to face three beat sticks in his face.

"Really?" His face burned, chin jutted. "It's been there sixty years, already."

The warden shoved around the guards, holding his hand out, fingers beckoning. "Hand it over."

Clarence's nostrils flared as he reached into the bag and produced the folder.

The warden opened it, revealing paperwork, yellowed newspaper clippings and an old picture of a young woman.

Another growl rose in Clarence's throat. He wiped perspiration off his upper lip.

The warden picked up the picture and studied it a long time. He slowly met Clarence's eyes.

Shoulders back, Clarence raised his head and looked him square in the face.

The warden carefully replaced the picture, closed the folder and held it out to Clarence.

Guards backed down, beat sticks replaced at their belts.

"Let's get going, shall we?" Randy stood aside to let Clarence through.

Clarence stepped onto the walkway overlooking the cellblock and froze. Inmates stood inside each cell across from his, both upper and lower levels, pounding on cell bars, stomping on the floor. Some saluted. Inmates, security guards, administrators, and board members lined the way out.

He swallowed, his jaw clenched. Lower lip threatened to quiver. "Let's make this fast, huh?"

"Yes, Sir." Randy caught hold of his bag and led him down the walkway.

Sir? He said Sir?

As Clarence followed, visual of the train station sixty years ago assaulted reality. People had lined the boardwalk then, like they lined the walkway now. His white-haired preacher appeared, shaking his head, judging from across time.

Randy glanced over his shoulder and hesitated. "You coming?"

Clarence hung his head and nodded. He waited with Randy at a heavy windowed door while the security guard gave the okay and the lock release buzzed. The door slid open, and as it did, his neighborhood paperboy appeared from the past—*the* edition of the newspaper crumpled in his hand.

Randy stepped aside to let Clarence through the door. He couldn't help looking back. An inmate paced behind the bars of one cell. His hand rapped against the bars, third finger of his other hand raised in salute, eyes burned into Clarence's.

Clarence shivered. A lot of men in this prison owed him because of legal favors, but not everyone would miss him.

Randy checked his watch.

Clarence nodded.

A young woman, still in a dietary uniform, rushed to his side and touched his arm. "Sir, good luck." She swallowed. "With your life." She brought something from behind her back. "I made you this. I hope it's okay. I mean, I hope you can use it." She practically curtsied and pressed a beautiful knitted scarf into his hands, all blues and greens with a scratchy brown fringe.

He stopped once more and bowed his head. Another vision popped before him—his old neighbor lady. Eyes expressed pain she felt for him, what her mouth could never say. Hand extended with a plate of cookies he couldn't take.

Randy pushed through the door.

Clarence sucked in a breath against the chilly air. A van waited at the curb. Brown, barren land stretched behind it.

One last person from his past appeared next to the van: Judge Green glared him down. He had gleefully and vengefully sentenced him. Clarence spat and yelled, "I hope you're rotting in hell, you old bastard!"

He stumbled, braced his hands against the doorway and backed into a guard.

Randy turned. "Hey buddy. Don't. Don't do that. Don't make this hard."

Clarence struggled against the guards surrounding him, growled, punched and pushed away from Randy.

"God, he's strong. Do we cuff him?"

Clarence snarled and spat as they each grabbed a limb and hoisted him off the ground, through the door, down the sidewalk.

"Don't hurt him. He's eighty years old. Careful."

"Are you kidding? He's a wild man."

Clarence struggled until he could fight no longer and shuddered a sob as the van loomed closer.

CHAPTER TWO

The drone of the van's engine pushed Clarence's rage to exploding point. His knuckles turned white against the restraints. Kill mode.

The van pulled away from the prison. He yanked at the shackles encasing his wrists and ankles. Even Dirk couldn't have escaped.

He scanned the inside of the van.

Clean.

Except for his bag. Socks, underwear, a change of clothes—courtesy of the prison. All he had in the world was in that bag.

He winced, remembering the last moments in prison. Tears threatened to break from his eyes as he squeezed them shut. He blew out a deep breath and shook his head.

A couple hours later, Randy pulled into a gas station and shut off the engine. "Clarence, we're gonna fill up."

"Why is it taking so long? We passed three old people's homes just now." Clarence leaned forward. "Where are we going?"

Randy glanced at Clarence in the rearview mirror. "They didn't tell you? Your hometown. Osceola, Nebraska."

Clarence gasped.

Randy pulled a credit card from his wallet. "That's why it's so far. Chicago to Osceola. I thought you knew."

He hopped out, swiped his card at the pump and started gassing up. He walked around the front of the van.

Clarence bounced back and forth on the bench seat, fingers splayed. "No! No! Not Osceola!"

The side door opened. "Sorry about the shackles. But man, you're strong. You gave us no choice." Randy reached down to unlock an ankle.

"Not Osceola. I can't go back there."

"Easy." Randy straightened and tilted his head, hand on his thigh. "It's your hometown."

"I can't go back there," Clarence said. "Those people ... they're the reason I got stuck in prison in the first place."

"I'm surprised they didn't tell you." He bent again to undo a buckle.

Clarence tensed. Poised.

Randy hesitated, grimaced and looked up at Clarence. "You're not. Not again. Listen Clarence, I've known you a long time. Longer than most of the inmates and staff. You can either ride here like an animal, all locked up, or act like a mature—"

Clarence flinched.

Randy flexed his arm muscles, his hands still on the shackles, brown eyes snapping. "Yeah, you're eighty. Act your age. Or at least act like someone ... never mind. Nobody in that prison acts like they have any brains. Including you." Randy slammed the door.

"No. No. Please." Clarence hung his head. He locked eyes with Randy through the window.

Randy folded his arms across his chest, his eyes piercing. He finally opened the door. "What'd you say?"

"I said please," Clarence whispered.

Randy raised his head, eyes squinted. He slowly climbed in the van. "Just one stupid—"

"There won't be any."

Randy held his stance.

Clarence focused on the shackles. "I mean it. I'm done." He held his breath, braced himself as Randy bent and unlocked one ankle.

Clarence kicked him in the shin. "Not Osceola!"

"Arggh. Fool! You ... are not only stupid ... but a liar." Randy struggled to restrain Clarence's leg. He whipped his stick around and delivered a blow to Clarence's knee. Then locked him down.

"Ow. Ow. F-n asshole."

Randy slammed the door so hard it shook the van. He limped to the gas pump and rubbed his shin.

Clarence fumed and cussed. He rocked the van right and left against the restraints.

Randy kicked the tires and pounded on the van. The gas pump

clicked off. He replaced the nozzle and jumped back in. Started up the van and squealed into traffic.

His eyes bored straight ahead, face beet-red. He glanced back at Clarence through the mirror. "You can make this easy, Clarence," Randy yelled, "or make it hard. You decide. Either way, I am delivering you to that nursing home and you don't have a thing to say about it."

Clarence hung his head and stretched to reach his knee with his fingers. "I don't want to go back there."

"What'd you say?"

"Nothing. Nothing at all," he muttered. He stared out the window then closed his eyes.

Memories flashed.

He found himself in the backseat of Sheriff Faeller's 1950 Ford Fairlane patrol car.

Shackled then.

Shackles ...

He jolted awake and blinked. Green lawns beautifully manicured in subdivisions. Church steeples. He closed his eyes again.

"Damn!" Randy slammed on the brakes. "Sorry, Clarence. Sorry to wake you. Traffic is terrible."

Car dealerships—rows and rows of cars lined the concrete.

Hotels, construction, truck stops.

Then fields. Brown grass, trees still bare of leaves that scattered around the corners of farm buildings and houses.

All a blur.

Feeling the van stop, Clarence opened his eyes. He stared at a sign introducing the kingdom of fast food. A statue of a man with red hair and clown costume greeted him with a grand wave. Cars filled the parking lot. Kids bounced in a play area, scooting down a ceiling to floor slide—round and round.

Randy peered into the rearview mirror. "Gonna buy some food." He shifted into park and stared at Clarence in the mirror. "These are your choices: shackles or no shackles. You decide."

Clarence growled and straightened, leaned against the restraints.

"I mean it, Clarence." He pointed to the building. "This is a public place. Little kids. Mommies. Real people. If you aren't gonna behave, you can stay in here, and I'll bring you food." Randy looked out the window. "If you have to use the bathroom, then it's shackles."

Clarence glanced outside, then back at Randy. "I'm not a total jerk."

"Prove it."

Clarence's stomach tightened. "I'll behave."

"I didn't hear you."

Clarence cleared his throat. "I said, I'll behave. I'll do whatever you say." He looked into the mirror. "I give you my word."

Randy stared back, one eyebrow cocked for a full minute. He stared into the restaurant so long, Clarence thought he'd fallen asleep. The driver's door clicked open, then the side door and Randy slowly unlocked each shackle, all without a word. Then stood next to the van. "I think you know the procedure. No—"

"I gave you my word." Clarence stared him down.

Randy nodded, then motioned for Clarence to climb out. "What do you want to eat? Burger, fries, pop? My treat."

Clarence raised his bushy eyebrows.

"No government funds today. I want to buy you lunch."

"Yeah, burger, fries—whatever you said." Clarence shoved out of the van and tested his legs.

A man and woman squeezed past.

A little boy about eight years old, followed by a man, bumped into Clarence. "S'cuze me." High-pitched voice with a lisp. Hair sticking up on top. Focused on a small flat device. So little.

People walked into the building, while others exited, toting bags of food and sodas. No prison jumpsuits. No handcuffs. All free.

He walked up the sidewalk and into the restaurant.

"Got a little limp there, Clarence?"

"Nah, just need to stretch my legs."

Inside, voices echoed off the walls. Children shrieked and laughed as they romped in the play area. Bright colors startled him. A sickening mix of hamburgers, fries, and old grease combined to make his already agitated stomach lurch.

Totally overwhelmed, he spun around. People and colors and smells blurred. He was free. But free to do what? Free to go where?

He found the restroom, rushed into a stall, and the power of that thought overwhelmed him. "Oh God, let me die in here."

Trash littering the floor and missed shots on the toilet made him change his mind.

He finished his business and limped into the restaurant.

Randy waited in a booth close by. The table was spread with a fast food smorgasbord: giant drinks, boxes of fries, wrapped burgers, and single serve pies.

Clarence stood over the table, clenching his fists, stomach churning.

Randy looked up, a fry dangling out of his mouth. He chewed it in. "What? You gonna run away?" He pushed at Clarence's food. "Sit, Clarence. This'll work out. You'll see."

Clarence stood firm.

Randy patted the table.

Clarence sat, coat still buttoned, scarf wound around his neck and stared at the food. He raised his eyes to Randy's. "So this is fast food. Kinda like prison food."

Randy choked, covered his mouth with a napkin, then laughed out loud. "Yeah, I guess it is. I should have gotten you the kids meal. You get a toy with that. Kinda makes the food taste better." He jumped up. "I'll get you one." He raced off.

Clarence picked up a fry and took a bite, watching Randy return with the kid's meal. "Thanks ... for this."

Randy laughed again. "Guess I should have bought you a steak and all the trimmings, huh. Go ahead. Open it."

Clarence read the games on the box then flipped it open. He looked up at Randy. "There's food in here. Like a lunch box." He drew out a brightly-colored cellophane bag. "This the toy?" He held it up. "What is it?"

Randy grinned. "Well, it's ... I don't know. It's a toy."

Clarence set it down and unwrapped the mini-burger. He took a bite. "It does taste better."

"Told you." Randy smiled and studied Clarence's face for a minute. "I get why you acted out back there. This can't be easy. You've done more than your time. Fifty—what—sixty years?"

"Sixty. Every board turned me down for parole. Every one of those bastards."

"You deserve a chance at some life on the outside."

"I don't deserve anything." He lifted the little burger to his mouth but put it down without taking another bite.

"Still carrying the guilt around?" Randy tapped a fry against the container. "You paid your dues, man. And look what you accomplished in prison—getting your law degree and all. Hell, that's a lot more than I've done with my life. You've helped a lot of people."

Clarence's eyes stung with tears he wouldn't let fall. "If you only knew." He picked up his hamburger and bit into it, squeezing mustard, ketchup and onion bits out onto the wrapper. Vision blurred. He fumbled for his napkin and wiped his chin, but not his eyes.

Not here.

Not anywhere.

Not ever.

He hadn't cried yet. All these years. Not once. And he wouldn't start now.

Randy dripped ketchup onto the front of his uniform. It landed right next to the pudding stain on his mountain of a stomach. He chattered on, oblivious.

As Clarence continued to glare, a mass of reddish-blond ringlets rose just above the back of Randy's booth seat.

"So, you can understand why ... " Randy continued.

Clarence leaned closer to Randy but let his line of sight drift to the hair. Then to Randy. Clarence nodded and nibbled on his sandwich.

Slowly the curls shifted higher, shadowing clear smooth skin.

Something stirred in Clarence—something he hadn't felt for so long—something like humor, laughter. Joy.

Randy reached for the pies. "Apple or cherry?" He held them out to Clarence.

Clarence shrugged.

"Okay. I'll take cherry." He shoved the apple pie over to Clarence. "We should have it figured out by then, but ... "

Eyes appeared, shining clear blue and full of mischief. The child hid her face in her arms then peeked with a shy grin.

Clarence shivered. She reminded him of someone. He looked away, out the window.

Someone long ago. Or—

"You're not eating, Clarence. Finish up and we'll be on our way. We still have a long way to go."

Clarence folded the meal into the wrapper and dumped it onto the tray.

Randy glanced up. "Something I said?"

Clarence slid to the edge of the bench and pushed himself up.

Randy blinked. "Uh ... I guess we're ready. Hey, thanks for listening."

Clarence frowned. "What?"

"Thanks for letting me rant. You've been there. You know how it is. You have a perspective on it that most don't." Randy pushed the table away, gathered up his trash and slid out of the booth. "And now you're free."

Clarence scowled at Randy and turned away. Free? No. He was headed for a nursing home. Just another prison.

"Uh, I'll hit the head." Randy stopped. "You'll be here when I come back."

Clarence stepped toward the child's booth.

No child.

He looked up and down the aisle. Searched under the table. Only a tiny mitten remained.

He stretched to pick it up. As he lifted it to his face, a whiff of something so fresh, so real, expanded him into another realm. Another dimension. His feet still planted on earthly soil, but for nanoseconds, his mind and emotions were drawn to another place.

Goosebumps.

Until Randy tapped him on the shoulder. He was buttoning a plaid shirt and carrying a backpack.

"Where's your uniform?"

"Figured I'd change shirts before we got to the nursing home." Randy shrugged. "They don't need to know you came from prison."

Fair enough. Clarence stuffed the mitten into his pocket and dropped the kids meal toy on the table.

Outside, a hawk circled high above, as they walked to the van. It screeched as it hovered, floated down to the next air current, then soared high.

Freedom.

Clarence climbed onto the front passenger seat, the hollow slam of the door adding the final note to the day.

Locked away.

Free for a minute.

Then bound forever.

CHAPTER THREE

Katty Randolph floated into consciousness, hovering between drunken stupor and awareness of something terribly off.

She groaned. Someone had to be holding her head down. Little men with jackhammers pounded inside, even when she told them to stop in no uncertain words. Exhausted, her head fell back onto hard, packed ground.

Something licked her calf. Sandpaper would have felt better. She kicked at it. A startled and indignant snarl sent shivers up her body.

Her eyes wouldn't adjust; the visuals that reached her brain made no sense. Blocks of color bounced off the backs of her eyes. Movement tracked back and forth until she slammed them shut. Her stomach threatened to hurl.

She floated back to stupor. When she tried to open her eyes again, sunlight burned into her eyeballs, making her eyes slam shut.

Something roared, revved up and down. Oh stop!

Her hands flitted from rubbing her throbbing forehead to her ears. Then her watering eyes. Back to her ears.

Waves of dizziness spiked as she lifted her head too fast. Her stomach revolted, and up came too much pizza and too many rounds, the glory of her Bar Queen status tarnished. She moaned and rolled herself into a ball.

A low growl. Her skin crawled. She cracked her eyes open.

Monstrous dog house kingdom, surrounded by a crumpled fence, ruled over by a scarred and dozing dog—one eye open. He appeared more alert each time Katty peeked in his direction.

Shuddering, she pulled at grass and weeds—anything—trying to hide.

The roar in her ears stopped and the silence was broken by a man's deep laughter. "Hey Harriet. It moved. We don't have to bury it. And it's naked!"

The last word pierced her.

She squinted an eye open and peered through her fingers. All she had on were her favorite striped socks.

A sweaty mountain of a man in the next yard grinned. He raised a chain saw high above his head and pulled the cord.

The sound ripped through her head, her body. Every nerve jangled in pain. She inched toward the house, egged on by coarse laughter.

"Look it. Moved again. Nice socks." His laughter now joined by a guttural phlegmy cackle.

The dog king growled along with the laughter. It stood and stretched. Tensed.

Katty gulped.

The snarling dog leaped. Transformed into a huge lion, jaws open, fangs dripping, teeth snapping. It jerked to the end of the log chain, yelping, inches from her feet.

Katty screamed, crouched, scrambled toward the house, but a mud puddle stopped her.

"It speaks." More cackles. "Oh, no. It got its socks muddy." Nasty laughter.

Sobbing, she made a drunken beeline for the back door of the drug house. Her hand on her chest, she reached for the door handle, still crouching, her backside to the audience.

Laughter accompanied her escape. "Aww. Show's over. We could start a new show."

The saw revved, sending a final horror into Katty's soul—through her body—as she fell into the house.

CHAPTER FOUR

The moment Clarence walked through the entrance of Hillcrest Homes, he flipped the emotion switch off. After sixty years in prison, he had that mastered.

He shoved pain and guilt deep, buried beneath the daily grind.

But memory wouldn't stay down.

His dad, Dawes Timmelsen, had never missed a day of the trial and his carpentry business had suffered. His voice broke the day the sheriff and deputies transported Clarence to prison: "Son, no matter what, I love you. Be strong."

Clarence still felt Dad's fingers digging into his shoulders as deputies pried him from his father's arms. His father's face haunted him—pain carved in every line.

That was the last time he had seen his dad.

His first day in prison had assaulted every sense. Musty, rancid odors. Harsh cleansers unable to mask the smells of evil and hatred. Malodorous sewage smells. Hardened eyes staring him down. The sounds of humanity, of a community galaxies apart from where he grew up, had shocked him, but at the same time, complete with its own standards, right or wrong.

All had attacked the newest arrival. Grief and pain became his closest allies.

The nursing home presented its own unique qualities. Years of meals layered with nearly dead floral arrangements rotting in foul water. Harsh cleaning and medicinal smells twisted into his senses, making his fast food lunch, already churning in his stomach, lurch as he followed Randy into the facility.

Old faces blended into no one.

A housekeeper rested on her mop, a slight smile bending her lips, warmth in her eyes.

Clarence looked away.

The pain then.

Pain now.

Always this brick of torment in his belly.

An abandoned walker waited outside a door, tennis balls protecting its feet.

Another reminder—this was the end of the line.

Hydraulic body lifts blocked the hall.

Beds with railings.

Oxygen tanks.

Wheelchairs.

Each time Clarence avoided one visual, he bumped into another. His body temperature boiled.

All logged in his memory to assault him later. All became a constant blur. He was trapped in this next stretch, this last duration of life.

"Hey Clarence," Randy broke in. "This is great. They have a pool table." He patted Clarence's arm. "You gotta get your own stick, man. And look. An ice cream machine. We need to get one of those for the pri—"

Clarence jerked around and glared at him.

A tall shapely woman appearing to be in her fifties walked up behind Randy, waving. "And you are Mr. Timmelsen, I presume."

"Clarence."

"Okay ... Clarence." She stepped beside Randy, and extended a slender hand, fingernails painted bright red. "I'm Miss Henningway, Administrator here at Hillcrest Homes." Her reddish-blond hair was cut in the latest swoop-over-one-eye style, her make-up precisely overdone.

Clarence stared at her hand.

Randy cleared his throat.

When Clarence didn't offer his, Miss Henningway picked at a nonexistent spot on her tight black skirt.

Clarence smirked. "This the way to my room?"

"Well, uh, I was going to give you the tour." She brightened. "The million dollar tour of our humble home."

"Our humble home. This isn't where you live."

"No ... but—"

"Well, show me around. Let's get this over with."

She began an obviously practiced speech in what had to be her best tour bus voice. "Welcome to Hillcrest Homes! I am Miss Henningway—"

"You said that."

"Well, um ... yes, and ... " She trailed off and mumbled under her breath. "Welcome to ... I am Miss ... oh yes!" She placed her hands on her heart. "We are so glad to have you, Mr. Timmelsen."

"Clarence. Just Clarence." He stared, seeing not only her female torso and hefty chest, but in his imagination she became the enemy, cloaked in a demon suit, with horns, tail, and spear, complete with designer glasses. Satan would be proud.

"Uh, yes. Clarence. Come with me, both of you. I'll show you around." She hesitated, squinting. "You're a lawyer, aren't you? I read that in your file, I think." She clapped her hands. "You could be our benefactor, what with your background and influence." She beamed and fluttered her eyes over her glasses. "We could sure use your ... expertise, Mr. uh ... Clarence."

He snorted. "I'm sure you could, especially my influence. I'd be happy to offer it sometime, if I wasn't so busy."

Randy leaned in beside him, hand placed under his arm. "Easy, Cowboy."

Miss Henningway blinked, cleared her throat and slipped a small post-it from her pocket. She scanned it, tucked her arm under Clarence's and began to drag him along. "Okay." She cleared her throat again, poised her feet together and recited, "We are a Christian facility, providing care for all people—all walks of life and abilities. From people who can live on their own, to the elder ... uh—"

"The old and unwanted," Clarence growled and pulled away.

She continued, as if on her own planet. "We provide all forms of care for those patrons and residents who can't take care of themselves." She waved and greeted a man in a wheelchair, as they passed. "People are friendly here."

The man didn't look up or acknowledge her.

She paused then pushed a door wide open. "We have a state-of-the-art kitchen."

Clarence and Randy stepped inside.

Two dietary employees froze. One—her hand raised above her head, gripped a head of cabbage; the other—crouched low, his hands cupped.

Clarence assumed the stance and held out his hands. "Here. Throw it here."

Red-faced, they turned their backs, knives clattering, sending cabbage chunks flying into huge bowls and onto the floor.

Miss Henningway twitched her pursed lips back and forth. Veins in her neck pumped. She backed out of the kitchen and began again. "And this is our beautiful dining room." She practically danced, patting Clarence's arm. "Notice our new flooring." She tapped a foot. "It's smooth and trouble free for wheelchair riders."

"Wheelchair riders?" Clarence rolled his eyes. He skirted around her.

She continued to tap her foot, looking Clarence up and down. "You're tall for your age."

"What?" Clarence stuttered. "Why'd you say that?"

"Well, most men your age have had some loss of height. You are in ama-a-zing shape."

Clarence looked at Randy, then at her. What the hell?

She moved on. "Our living rooms are newly remodeled, also. New sofas, chairs, drapes, carpeting. The works. All the latest home designs." She paused.

"Oh, you want applause?" Clarence obliged with one loud clap.

Miss Henningway frowned. She sucked in a deep breath and blew it out through her teeth. After a short moment, the fake smile reappeared and she turned. "Shall we?" She directed them to a large community room, equipped with tables, chairs and a kitchenette. Residents were gathering in wheelchairs and walkers. A wonderful aroma wafted from the oven.

"We have a baking class once a week. Oh my, the cookies they bake in there." She patted her tummy tires, blushing. "But activities here are not just for women. They're for everyone." She indicated the pool table, leaning on it in a swoon, sliding along the edge toward Clarence.

Only he saw it coming and sidestepped her.

Randy jumped to catch her as Clarence turned away.

"Are you all right?" Randy helped her balance. "You must have tripped with those heels." He cleared his throat. "Or something."

Clarence walked on and passed an old man standing in a doorway.

The man leaned on a walker, chewing on his words. "Another one bites the dust."

Old bastard.

A TV game show host blared behind him, "You have just won a trip to Timbuktu—all expenses paid."

The man raised an eyebrow. His mouth curved at one end.

Clarence glared.

"Harold, don't you have somewhere to be?" said Miss Henningway, stepping between them. "Baking perhaps?"

"Nope, I'm stayin' right here." His eyes never left Clarence's.

Standoff.

Still staring at Harold, Clarence shuffled from one foot to the other, his inner furnace boiled, his fists clenched at his sides. Miss Henningway tugged on his sleeve, dragging him along beside her.

Clarence pulled away.

She motioned to another door. "Here we have the spa, warm and cozy. All new tiles and wallpaper border. A wonderful new jacuzzi, complete with water jets and whirlpools." She swung the door open to reveal a huge walk-in tub, filled to the top with sudsy water, steam curling around an obese woman who sat in the tub scrubbing her red face.

The woman looked up, washcloth in hand, water streaming down her arm. "Eek!" She flopped both arms, sending water cascading over the sides like a stormy sea, splashing onto the tile floor.

A nurse rushed to her with a towel, covered her ample chest, then slammed the door in their faces. But not before giving Miss Henningway a dirty look. "Do you know how to knock?"

Clarence burst out laughing. "Bonus tour."

Miss Henningway stood in place, eyes piercing holes through the door.

Randy coughed. "Mind if we keep this going? I've got to drive all the way back to Chicago tonight."

Miss Henningway puffed out her cheeks, and just as quickly, turned and smiled a last stilted smile. "Well, here we are." Having reached the hall's far end, she marched into a bedroom and swept out her arm, presenting the room as if it were a deluxe suite in a fine hotel, complete with amenities and a view. "You have a window facing ... the parking lot so ... you can see the comings and goings. And you get wonderful sunshine." She paused for effect and pointed to the wall. "Also, your own picture of our Savior, Jesus Christ the Lord."

Clarence almost flipped the emotion switch to full on anger. "Yay. Where has He been the last sixty years and now He's Lord over my room?" Clarence took a step toward the picture.

Randy grabbed his arm and snarled next to his ear. "Back down, Clarence. We can do shackles here, too. You can take the picture down later."

Miss Henningway stared. "Not all believe and—"

"You bet your nursing home I don't believe."

Randy gripped Clarence even harder. "Shackles."

The administrator pursed her lips, her hands pressed together at her mouth.

Randy released Clarence and nodded at Miss Henningway.

"Um ... you have a closet, here." She opened the door to a cupboard, revealing a shelf above and a small clothes bar that would hold one suit and a jacket. Maybe a few shirts.

Clarence glanced down at the shopping bag still in Randy's hand.

"Oh, and the best part. Your bed." She bent down and patted the bright blue coverlet on a hospital-style bed complete with bars.

Finally she opened the only remaining door, revealing a man: pants around his ankles, arms hugging his walker, a grimace on his face.

She gasped. "Mr. Thompson. What are you doing?"

He looked up at her, blinking. "What the hell does it look like I'm doing? I'm taking a crap. Now shut the damn door and leave me in peace."

She complied, holding her nose, eyes watering as she staggered back. "Let's go down the hall to the ... um ... the chapel." She brightened. "Right this way."

Clarence covered his mouth, eyes brimming, and immediately converted his grin to a solemn face. He glanced at Randy.

Randy covered his mouth and clapped one hand on Clarence's shoulder.

Clarence slapped Randy on the back as he wiped his eyes.

"Please." Miss Henningway turned and beckoned to them.

"Follow me." As they reached a set of double doors, her radio went off. She retrieved it and stepped away.

Clarence strolled into the chapel. Whew. Place needed a good airing out. Broken blinds hung in a window and wallpaper border trailed loose.

Miss Henningway glanced at Clarence, bobbed her head up and down several times and replaced the radio on her belt, resuming her air of authority. "I'm sorry about that little interruption. Your room will be put back in order."

Clarence grinned. "You'll kick the son-of-a-bitch out?"

She ignored Clarence and struck a Vanna White pose.

Her thick make-up had taken on an oily appearance. Her hair had turned frizzy, no longer in the smooth swoop. She was no Vanna. And she was fuming.

"A very nice little chapel. We have some fine services here. Priests and ministers come in, each taking turns, giving people of different faiths a chance to hear their doctrine preached." She resumed her air of authority, nodding and patting her chest. "Why, I've preached here on occasion myself."

"That's nice." Clarence scanned the room. Mismatched chairs and small altar. The final decorating touch: a huge body lift in the middle of the room. "I'm sure everybody gets elevated." He pushed the button on the lift. The swing assembly slowly rose as he walked off down the hall.

"Wait. Wait. I have good news," she said.

Clarence turned. "I'm going back to Chicago?"

Randy rushed to the lift, fumbled for the off button and cleared his throat.

Clarence took a deep breath, eyes on Randy. "I was told to be nice." He pointed down the hall. "But kinda tough when there's an old man shitting in my bathroom."

The administrator's face bloomed fiery red, from her neck up to her forehead. Her upper lip twitched to the side, her hands stayed on her hips. The radio went off again and she shook her finger in Clarence's face.

He put his hat on his head, gave the brim a flourish, pulled his gloves on and started back down the hall.

Randy hurried to catch up, still toting the grocery bag. "Wait, Clarence. Come on. She didn't know that guy'd be in there. It's all a misunderstanding."

Clarence nodded and kept on walking. "I agree. A misunderstanding that I'm supposed to be here. Take me back to your famous fast food restaurant on the way to Chicago." His nostrils flared, his breathing accelerated. He chewed the inside of his cheeks as tears dared to fill the corners of his eyes. He stomped past Harold's open door, shaking his head.

Randy caught up. "Clarence, come on. They'll clean your bathroom again." He covered a snicker. "Then you can add your ... uh, you can use it like your own. You'll see."

"They kick me out of prison and dump me here," Clarence growled under his breath. "But it looks like I don't belong here either." He stopped and Randy bumped into him. "Nobody cares whether I live or die. I'm an old man with nobody, nothing." He picked up his pace again. "I need to go to the hills by myself and die."

"You're not going anywhere to die. You have a lot of life to live." Randy caught up to Clarence and edged in closer. "Man, I know this isn't great, but what else have you got?"

Clarence stopped.

In front of him, a TV blared at people in wheelchairs arranged in a semi-circle: snoozing, snoring, some staring with mouths gaping, drool dripping on bibs. One resident rocked from side to side against chair restraints. There was an eerie pause in the racket from the television. No one stirred. One man coughed, spittle hitting the carpet in front of him.

Clarence whispered. "What else have I got?"

CHAPTER FIVE

Katty hiccuped as she lay trembling on the dirty rug, quickly becoming aware of her vulnerability. A sob escaped along with another hiccup as she hugged the tattered rug beneath her. She lifted her head, and her bleary eyes tried to morph her own kitchen into this one. Neither was that great—doors hung off hinges revealing free or stolen glassware. Once-white cupboards became the new dingy cream. Her past bottlenecked into today, making one crappy life.

"Phil, why ... ?" she muttered. Her old boyfriend stood before her, only his body wavered like heat waves. First he was there—then he wasn't. Horror flooded memories every time she spoke or even thought his name. The visual of him hovered just under every present day. She shuddered. A silent cry burst from down deep.

She pushed off the floor and slipped, leaving a trail of muddy sock prints. She looked down and froze.

Naked. That wasn't just a psychotic drug-induced dream. She was "in all her glory" naked. Except for muddy, striped socks.

"Where're my clothes?" Terror crashed in. "I ... I gotta get home. Bea's alone. Oh my god. What time is it?" She rushed to the living room only to be stopped short by grunts and snores. And a stench that smelled of every rotten egg, all the feedlots in Nebraska, and garbage trucks dripping week-old waste.

Sleeping bodies scattered about the room. A couple rolled in blankets on the floor, arms draped over each other. A man sat up against the wall, arms limp by his sides, roach clips and beer bottles scattered beside him.

Vacant sofa. Some party.

She tiptoed around an overstuffed chair where a man sat. He appeared dead until he snorted.

Katty covered her chest, then her privates.

She fled into the hallway, but not before an eye cracked open.

"Ohhh. Gotta go. Gotta find my clothes." Near panic, she tiptoed down the matted carpet and peeked into a bedroom. Three guys—snoring so loud the floor vibrated under her feet. Time on the digital clock was 4:48. Good. Time to sleep it off before Bea ... wait. Light cracked between the tattered shade and window. Oh no.

She slipped into an end bedroom, snagged a pair of jeans three sizes too big and shoved one foot in before falling. She tried again then zipped them. She rummaged in one corner and was rewarded with a T-shirt declaring "Peace in Us."

Good enough.

As she yanked it over her head, she spied her purse on the floor, partly obscured under a man. She bent to retrieve it.

Groans, a punch and a crack came from the living room. She paused, clutching the purse to her chest, still crouched, almost toppling backwards.

Keeping one eye on the hallway, she checked her purse. Empty. Except for dirty Kleenex. Food stamps were gone. Drug money gone.

Another muffled noise, closer. A man stumbled out of the living room. The look in his eyes made her scramble.

She pushed up too fast, choked and threw up onto the man's back.

He never moved.

Kitchen noises.

Every cell in her body screamed run!

Someone rummaged in a drawer. Something dropped onto the floor. A drawer squeaked shut.

Trembling, she peered into the hallway and gasped as a large knife pierced the air, gripped by a thick hand.

Still in her drunken dream world, she cried, "Phil. Don't. I want to have this baby."

Blindly, she stumbled back into the bedroom and frantically scanned the room. A broken window was blocked by an old air conditioner. She stood in the only other escape route.

"I'm gonna find you," a low voice growled. "I'm gonna have what you promised." That voice wasn't Phil's.

A body behind her stirred.

Katty circled to a bleary-eyed woman raised up on an elbow, pointing at her. "That's my shirt ... my... " The woman fell back onto the floor.

Katty tried the closet door as Knife Man entered the bedroom. One second it was Knife Man: eye matted shut, bruised and swollen, blood caked in his beard. The open eye gleamed with a sick evil.

The next second there was Phil. The same terrifying evil lurking in his seductive eyes. Knife in his hand.

They morphed into one. Eyes green on brown. Bruised skin on ruddy. Plaid shirt into bloody sweatshirt.

Knife Man lunged.

They tripped over a body, knife spinning in the air.

Crushed people under their weight.

The knife lodged in someone's back.

Katty scrambled leapfrog style but caught her foot and went sprawling.

Someone grabbed her foot.

She shrieked, wriggled out of the slimy sock and crawled onto the kitchen linoleum.

At the back door she pulled herself up by the doorknob and yanked the door open.

Footsteps pounded behind her.

"Gotta get to Bea."

CHAPTER SIX

Clarence shoved the tray away. His stomach growled, but when he smelled the food, McDonald's threatened to make a reappearance. Damn supper—a cold turkey and cheese sandwich, jello fruit salad, stale potato chips and two cookies. And the ever-present coffee.

He understood the sandwich. No one had known what time he would arrive. According to the digital clock glowing down at him from atop the kitchen pass-through window, it was now 6:18 PM.

Prison food had been better than this.

His legs throbbed, along with his head. His hands shook in his lap. He stretched his fingers against the table surface, but the tremors continued. He was a fit man, having worked out every day, walked every day, more than the younger inmates. But he didn't feel fit now. He felt one footstep away from his funeral.

Randy had driven away less than an hour ago, but it seemed like ages. Randy's last comment: "I'll be back to see you, Clarence. I promise."

Clarence was pretty sure he'd never see Randy again. The trip from Chicago to Osceola was a long one for a man on security guard's pay.

He didn't remember feeling this bad when he was first incarcerated, sixty years ago—longer than most people stayed married. He stared at the dining room floor. Whatsername was right. It was new flooring. It gleamed. One of those new laminated fake floors. Easy to get around on if you used a wheelchair or a walker for your getaway vehicle.

His stomach churned. Worse than butterflies. He belched, and spit gathered in his mouth. He half rose in his chair and frantically scanned the area for a bathroom.

Breathe deep. Think of something else. Distractions. The only thing he could think of right now was how to get out of this place and die. Throwing up was just a side effect of the main event.

His hand flew to his mouth as another threatening belch rumbled up. He sank back down in the chair.

Ahh. Better. It was going away. Just indigestion. That fast food.

Then up it came. McDonald's having its way—all over the table. He belched again, grabbed the extra napkins at the adjoining place setting, shook the utensils free and covered his mouth.

Breathe.

In and out.

He looked at the mess on his tray and almost got sick again. He pushed away and faced the other side of the room.

The table next to him had been long vacated. Dirty plates removed, table scrubbed. The next table over had a lone coffee cup lingering with a crumpled napkin. No chair. Wheelchair driver.

He raised his head.

Table after table, empty.

No wheelchairs.

No walkers.

No staff.

Just him and his tray of ...

A ragged breath bubbled from deep within. A sob stayed just below control. Waiting to roll him over. Waiting to add the capstone to his day.

When he shoved away, his chair legs scraped the floor and bumped the table. Coffee spilled onto the sandwich and seeped under the bottom slice of bread, turning it a dirty shade of brown. That cinched it.

He stood. Blood rushed to his head and he faltered. His hands jerked to the table, bracing for a fall. He found his legs, straightened slowly. Head erect. Breathed deeply.

Okay.

He carefully placed his feet, one at a time, focused with every step.

Whew.

Beside the double doors he paused and read the menu for tomorrow. Tuna casserole. Probably from the same cookbook the prison used. He'd have to make sure he wasn't around for that one.

He looked left and right, down both gray-tiled hallways. Which way? He searched for something familiar—a picture or decoration to jog his memory as to which way back to his room. He should have listened better, or taken a pencil and marked the walls.

Didn't matter. He'd find a place to steal away to—somewhere to get lost—and die. It was either right or left down a doomed hallway. One way or the other. Didn't make any difference.

Funny. A person always knew where he was going in prison.

Here, he had all the choices in the world. He could even shit in someone else's bathroom. He could do anything he wanted, more or less. But he stood crippled with indecision, trapped beside the kitchen door.

He stared down the left hallway and took a step. Almost every door was propped open. TV's blared, each tuned to the same channel. He never missed a word as he wandered down the hall, his hand grasping the continuous railing. Vanna White. Wheel of Fortune. He heard the wheel spinning from one room. Pat Sajak's voice, "One thousand dollars." Next room—applause. The contestant's voice guessing, "P." Pat Sajak's voice, "Three P's," from the next TV. Ping, ping, ping. On down the hall he guessed letters along with the contestants, until he came to the corner.

This wasn't right. He didn't remember a therapy room. The way back was even longer now. He slumped, hands digging into his pockets.

Now TV's shouted, the commercial blared even louder. Motorcycles roared in multi-stereo. Someone yelled, "Woo-hoo!" Howls. "This is why we do this. Freedom. The open road."

Clarence stopped, fists clenched, arms tensed. He had to get out of here, but not tonight. Tomorrow he'd find a way.

The noise pushed him down the hallway until he saw a head peek out farther down.

What was his name? Henry? Harold. Old buzzard. Nosy old bastard. Stained dress shirt untucked over wrinkled outdated dress pants. Dress socks with a hole in one toe.

"Lost aren'tcha." Harold nodded as Clarence passed his doorway.

Clarence glared straight ahead, ignoring the comment.

Deep chuckle. "I did the same thing when I moved here. You'll find your way and the place will get a smaller feel to it."

Clarence chewed on the inside of his cheek, chin jutted out, nostrils flared.

"Okay. Well, talk when you're ready. I'm not goin' anyplace."

Clarence grunted. Neither was he. He made the turn. Yeah. Past the nurses station. One. Two. Four doors on the left, at the end. Whew.

He stepped into his room and checked the bathroom.

Unoccupied.

He inspected the toilet.

Clean.

He walked to the window and stared into darkness, fist on the glass. He pounded softly. Harder still. The window vibrated with each blow. He calmed as his hands reached to grip bars that weren't there. His forehead dropped against the glass, his mind replayed the day, beginning at prison. His insides lurched, his legs went weak.

He turned away.

The grocery bag still sat on top of the chest of drawers, calling him to unpack, to settle in.

He ignored it and stretched out on the bed fully clothed, comforted by his hand resting on the restraining bar.

His hand tightened around it. He stared at the ceiling.

Someone pushed a rattling cart past his doorway. TV voices mixed into indiscernible chatter. A lady called out for a nurse to help her make water. A door slammed.

He closed his eyes.

Beep, beep, beep. An alarm went off somewhere, making him jump.

He closed his eyes again.

First nights.

This first night swam with memories of a first night long ago. He had been terrified. Crippled by grief. Not letting himself cry, he had choked back sobs. Stared at the ceiling and cold concrete walls then. Water-stained, peeling vinyl wallpaper now. Strange bed then. Strange bed now. Unfamiliar sounds. Taunting voices from the next cells, the next rooms.

He rolled to face the wall, gripping the bars with both hands, squeezing his eyes shut.

Whispered threats from the next cell then.

Voices from his own fears, now.

CHAPTER SEVEN

"Bea?" Katty cried. She raced up the trailer house steps. Tripping on weeds growing through the stair treads, she fell hard, slammed her shoulder against the door and landed spread-eagle on the deck.

Rocking back and forth in pain, she held her shoulder. Her toe was bleeding—the foot with no sock. Her mouth spewed what her heart and body felt.

She pulled herself up with the doorknob, only to have it fall off in her hand. She fell back on the deck and stared at the doorknob, then at the door.

Then at the knob.

Chin crumpled. Tears gushed.

"F-n doorknob. F-n day. F-n life."

She heaved the doorknob.

Glass shattered.

She sat up, shoved the glass aside and kicked the door open. It slammed against the wall inside.

She crawled in. "Bea? Beatrice! Where are you?"

Silence.

"Oh, God. Baby Bea?"

Katty struggled to her feet, leaned on the kitchen counter and visually searched the room. The harvest gold kitchen opened to the living room, divided by a dining room of sorts. Only it wasn't used as a dining room. More like a toy room, library, shop, trash bin, storage closet. Reality: kitchen, living room, dining room were all one room—trailer house style.

"Bea?"

Katty slid down the hall against buckled paneling and searched the first bedroom—under and around boxes cluttering the floor. She stumbled, landing on a stack of magazines, creating a small landslide.

No Bea.

Next room. Bea's

Katty barged in. "Bea. I'm home, sweety. Baby Bea. Mommy's here."

Sugar, sugar, sugar.

The bed hadn't been slept in.

She ripped the blankets from the bed, toys from corners, checked under the desk. She slammed the closet door open and swished her hand back and forth among the clothes and toys.

No Bea.

On into the bathroom. Empty. Her heart pumped faster. She tore the shower curtain from the bar above the tub. Shoved at the bottles on the counter, some toppled onto the floor. Nothing. Nothing except a doll's hairbrush on the counter beside the sink. Bea's doll brush.

Katty grabbed it and ran to her bedroom.

"Bea! Where are you? Mommy's here, Baby," she sobbed.

She tore the bed apart, stripped the covers off. Pillows flew. The bedspread slid onto the floor, toppling the bedside lamp with it.

She searched her closet. Slid closet doors back and forth, knocking one off the track.

Finally she heard a hiccup from the corner. She dragged the rocking chair away from the wall and there was her skinny daughter, hair matted against her head. She fit perfectly under the rocker.

"Bea. Why are you hiding?" Katty dragged her out and picked her up.

Bea was trembling, her face wet. A sob escaped her lips. Her brown eyes were swollen and terrified.

"Mommy?" Bea's hoarse voice whispered. "Mommy?"

"You scared me, Bea. I couldn't find you. I looked everywhere and I couldn't find you."

Bea collapsed into Katty's arms. "Mommy. Mommy. Where were you? It got dark and you didn't come back." She sobbed. "You left me alone. Me and Dolly."

Katty crumbled. "I'm so sorry, Bea," she said. "Mommy forgot what time it was and ... I'm sorry, Baby. I'll never do it again. I promise."

#

Morning sun shone through the window curtain. Bea played quietly, brushing Dolly's hair with the hairbrush, softly singing a melody from her heart.

She sat next to Mommy on the bed, wanting to talk to her, but knowing from the way Mommy was stretched out that if she woke her, she'd get yelled at. Or worse. She'd seen Mommy this way before. Sometimes Mommy became that other Mommy.

Bea's tummy rumbled, but she tried to not think about it. She combed Dolly's hair, then her own. Then Dolly's.

Rumble, rumble.

She glanced at sleeping Mommy, then slowly, carefully slipped off the bed and shuffled backwards toward the kitchen, never taking her eyes off Mommy's face. She knew the places on the frayed, carpeted floor that creaked. It became a dance down the dark hall as she lightly hopped and skipped from one safe spot to the next.

She pushed a chair over to the counter, scraping it along the thin linoleum and caught it in a hole. Quickly, she tip-toed to see if the noise woke Mommy.

Whew.

On the counter next to the bread, Bea found her favorite snack—peanut butter. Careful with the knife, she drew it across the bread. She pinched off a corner that was green and threw it away, smothering the rest in more peanut butter. The green didn't look right, but peanut butter made it better.

Bea sang songs to herself and Dolly as she snacked. Sweet little melodies. Softly. Bite the bread. Hum the song. Lick the peanut butter. La-la-la.

Bea looked at Dolly, who had lost interest in the food. Dolly leaned against the cupboard and slowly slid onto the floor. Bea sat her upright and dropped a cracker in Dolly's lap.

"You need to eat your supper, so you can play and grow big and strong," Bea whispered. She patted Dolly on the head and stared at her for a long time. "I promise I won't leave you alone again, Dolly. Ever. Ever."

CHAPTER EIGHT

Head nurse, Carol Neeton stood outside Clarence's door, raised her hand to knock, then withdrew it. Her thumb clicked the ink pen several times. Click, click. She checked the chart again and frowned. Click.

No family listed. No references. Sometimes residents had no surviving family, but ... nobody to even contact?

She skimmed further, shaking her head. Note to self: review Henningway's notes on Clarence. More than once the administrator had conveniently forgotten to chart vital background information. She was administrator; she shouldn't even be charting.

So maybe the man who drove him here was a contact, or even better, a son.

At least Joe had someone. Click, click. Two years since the stroke and he still wasn't responsive. She blew out a breath and blinked. Gotta get there tonight after work—if Henningway didn't rag on her and detain her.

She checked the photo beside Clarence's door. The man was handsome even if he was eighty. Joe was still good looking—stroke or no stroke.

Deep sigh. She replaced the chart in the cart and knocked on the door. "Clarence?"

Silence.

She peeked, then tiptoed into his room. "Clarence? Hi, I'm Carol, Head Nurse. How're you doing? Just checking in ... to see how you're acclimating." Her voice trailed off. "Your nurse told me you've not been out of your room ... at all."

No answer.

She stopped just shy of the bed. Clarence lay facing the wall, gripping the restraining bar. Big man. Long wavy gray hair—Henningway would demand that cut.

Rumpled clothes looked like he hadn't changed since he had been admitted—what two days ago? Black T-shirt, khaki-colored chinos. Still wore socks and joggers.

"Clarence, it's time for dinner." She leaned over his bed but couldn't see his face. She patted his shoulder. "Hamburgers tonight. Brownies for dessert."

No response. Out of habit, she assessed his breathing. Steady, but not deep. Awake.

She cleared her throat. "Clarence, I know you can hear me. You've sequestered yourself in here for two days. If you don't come out, I'll have to request a doctor's order for a feeding tube."

She waited. Shook her head. "And believe me, you don't want that."

Nothing. No response. No movement.

"The next step? Sending you to a psych ward and you don't want that even more."

Barely discernible change in breathing. Slightly faster.

She bent over, speaking close to the back of his head. He hadn't showered or shaved. "Clarence, this has to be the hardest thing you've ever been through, but believe me, it does get better with some effort from you. I have read your blood pressure results myself and I know for sure. You are not dying. You are healthier than me."

"You'd be healthier if you weren't so fat," Clarence said.

Carol grinned.

Before she could think of a comeback, something exploded through the window, pelting them with glass shards.

She uncovered her eyes.

Sitting upright in bed, Clarence stared wide-eyed out the window.

"Holy cow ... what is that?" She pointed at the floor. A huge bloody mass of feathers and talons lay partly obscured by the bed.

Clarence crouched next to it.

She backed away, reaching for her radio. "I'm calling maintenance."

"It's a hawk," said Clarence. He checked the window. "What the hell?" He held his hand against it. "Still alive, I think."

Carol's radio sputtered. "Jim. Jim. You there? We have ... uh," she turned to Clarence. "You said a hawk?"

Clarence nodded.

"We have a hawk in room 204." She glanced at the window. "Oh ... and a broken window. Can you ... can you come right away?"

The radio sputtered. "What? A stalk?"

Carol eyed it. Still not moving. "I said a hawk. You know the bird kind?"

"Hawk?"

"Yup. That's what I said. H-a-w-k. It broke through the window." She leaned over to inspect it. "And it's a big one. Clarence thinks it's still alive."

"Through the window?" Jim's voice cracked over the radio.

She rotated and pointed at the window. "That's what I said ... through the window."

She replaced her radio. "Well, it got you off your butt, Clarence," she said. "Nice bird. Good bird." She leaned over it. "Wow. Big bird."

"Can we keep it?"

"What?" Carol squeaked.

"Can we keep it? In a cage or something." He pushed the bed against the wall to reveal the whole bird. "Rust colored tail. Look at that wingspan."

"It's as big as your bed ... almost. We don't have anything here to ... we need to call the Humane Society ... or a nursing home for birds."

"Its wing is hurt ... bleeding. I don't suppose you'd have any medical supplies here would you?" He turned to face Carol, a glint in his eye, one eyebrow up. "Miss Head Nurse."

Carol scrunched her nose. "Whatever gets you off that bed, Clarence."

She retrieved her radio. "Oh, and Jim? We're gonna need a huge cage. Get all the finches out of the aviary, or something." She crouched to the floor and attached the radio to her belt. That was one huge bird. "Amazing ... something so ... powerful ... so divine."

"In my room. Humph. Coulda killed me if I'd been standing by the window, there."

"But you weren't. You were still on your bed. After two days, Clarence."

He glanced at her, then at the bird. He started to touch the bloody wing, then pulled his hand back. "Why are you here, old bird? What were you thinking, breaking through my window?"

Carol had questions of her own as she watched Clarence stroke the beautiful hawk.

Gasp. "Clarence, your hands. Let me see."

He hid them behind his back. "No. They're fine."

She pulled one forward. "They're burns. What happened?"

He shoved them into his pockets. "It was a long time ago. Never you mind."

Where did this man come from and who was he?

CHAPTER NINE

Bea played on the floor, dressing Dolly and undressing her. She popped her head up every once-in-a-while watching Mommy as she put on her makeup. Mommy fluttered her eyelids. Bea fluttered hers. When Mommy smacked her lips together, Bea smacked hers.

Mommy stood back, held her arms out in a ta-da, fingers holding the mascara wand. She wiped at the corner of each eye, patting at smudges. Sipping from the styrofoam cup, she sighed, looking in the dresser mirror, her hips swaying to music grinding from her phone.

"Aw, hell," she said and added more liner, smudging even more.

She posed her face, first left, then right, then adjusted the clip holding her long dark hair in a swoop.

Mommy leaned close to the mirror and looked directly into Bea's eyes. "What're you looking at?" Mommy's black eyes glared, reflecting back at Bea.

Something in Mommy's eyes flickered, snapped. Stirred fear in Bea. She shivered.

Mommy stepped back and stared at herself for a long time.

Quiet.

"Mommy? Mommy? Are you going out? Mommy?"

Mommy turned and rushed at Bea. "What?"

Nose to nose.

Mommy's eyes had turned dark. "Mommy—"

"Don't Mommy me."

"Your voice sounds funny." Bea's eyes filled with tears. "And your eyes look funny ... your eyes ... you're that other Mommy." Bea scooted back.

"What?" Mommy hesitated. "What?" she said again, her voice sounding more like Mommy's.

Bea hiccuped, swallowed, her chin quivered. She fought it. Held it in until her eyes spilled over, tears streamed down her cheeks. Her mouth clamped tight, her eyes on Mommy's.

Mommy groaned. "I don't have time for this."

Mommy's eyes changed again.

Bea was only four, but she knew her mommy. And right now, pure evil flashed from Mommy's eyes.

Then a flicker of ... Mommy sparked through.

Another change. Evil again.

Back came a twinkle ... of ... Mommy, until Mommy came through. But Bea knew the rage was there, just under the surface.

"Mommy?" Bea whimpered. She swallowed. "Are you going to leave me?"

Mommy gulped. "I'll just be gone for an hour or so." She glanced toward the TV. "I'll set you up with some movies." She smiled, fluttering her eyelids. "And I'll be back before the first movie is over. Okay?" She held out her pinky. "Promise."

Bea stared at Mommy's finger, then up to Mommy's face. What she saw there wasn't comforting, but she decided to play along, hoping against all past experience Mommy wasn't lying.

Again.

Bea hooked her little finger around Mommy's. "Promise." Her eyes searched Mommy's for a sign that this time—this time would be different.

Mommy smiled wide, red lipstick framing her teeth. Her eyes said she really believed she could come home before Bea's bedtime. That whatever she did out there, it wouldn't mean Bea fell asleep alone.

Again.

Bea's eyes pleaded that just this once, Mommy could do it. That she could come home when she said and make Bea feel safe.

"Mommy?" Bea gulped. "Mommy, could you stay home?"

"You don't think I'd put all this makeup on just for you, do you?"

Bea blinked.

Mommy reached for her drink and downed it, licking a last drop off her lips. She walked to the TV and shuffled through DVDs until she found one and set it up, starting the TV.

"There. Now there's only one movie in and you just watch your old mom." She shook her finger. "She'll ... I'll be home before this movie is over. You'll see." She posed herself in the full-length mirror. "Uh-huh. Now, don't I look smashing."

Bea just stood there. Mommy looked beautiful against the backdrop of cartoons already flashing from the TV. But she was going away again. Bea was scared to answer. She wanted Mommy to stay home, but Mommy never did. It didn't matter what Bea said, Mommy would still leave.

Mommy swooped down and breathed on Bea. "Don't I look pretty?"

Her mouth had that evil smell again.

Bea backed away.

"Don't I?"

"Yes, Mommy. You look pretty."

"That's what I thought."

Mommy blew a kiss and slammed the door on her way out.

The movie blared. The beginning exploded with color and excitement.

But Bea stared at the door.

All alone.

She crawled once again under the rocking chair, dragging her pillow and blanket along with her.

CHAPTER TEN

The next morning, Clarence tapped on the chicken wire enclosure of the aviary in the entrance of Hillcrest Homes. "They had to remodel the finches' house for you, didn't they?"

The hawk dominated the cage. Massive. Its tail feathers caught on the wire floor, curling. Even though its wings were tucked, they still commanded the space. Beady eyes stared at Clarence. Talons gripped a branch too big for finches. "I'm sure those silly birds don't mind loaning it to you for a while."

Miss Henningway walked up to the temporary birdcage positioned beside the aviary. Red, yellow, brown and green finches fluttered around a lone blue and white speckled parakeet. The tiny birds pecked at the larger bird. Their wings flapped against its head and body.

She clucked at them. "Poor little birdies. Sweet things." She studied the aviary, then the birdcage. "Did that big old mean bird take your pretty cage?" Cluck, cluck.

The hawk quaked and suddenly spread its wings, rocking the aviary.

Clarence jumped back. "Your wing! It's ... it's—"

"Eek!" Miss Henningway stumbled.

Clarence rushed to keep her upright. She might be the enemy, but he couldn't let her fall.

She swooned against him. Her eyeglasses magnified fluttering eyes. She clutched at his arms.

He shoved her upright and pushed her away.

"Humph. You are rude ... " She clamped her bright red lips shut and stomped away.

"I know how you feel, old boy," Clarence said. Every possible escape route had been patched. Not that a hawk could squeeze through any, but the finches had tried a few. "That's what you get for breaking into my room."

Old Harold Dexter shuffled into view. "Talking to birds now I see. Next it'll be the dog in the dining room."

"There's a dog in the dining room?"

"Naw. Just wanted to see if you were listening."

Clarence growled. He waited for Harold to mosey on down the hall. "Looks like your wing is healing already. Pretty fast. You ought to be outa here in … I oughta be out of here … in … "

The bird stared.

Clarence stared back. He looked behind him, then back to the hawk. "Me, too." He clicked on the wire with his nail. "Cohorts in crime." Tap, tap. "They'll throw you out, just like the prison threw me out."

Tap, tap, tap. A nurse in the nurses station was busy charting or whatever. Another walked away from him, down the hall. She disappeared into a room. "How are you this morning, Mrs. Albertson?" A very loud voice. The door closed.

That hall was empty. He slowly rotated to another. Quiet. A body lift stood at the end of the hall. The exit was far away. He slipped past the wheelchair rows, all facing the TV.

The woman in the nurses station hadn't moved from the desk.

His eyes focused on the exit and he started shuffling toward it.

Just before the exit, a door opened and a big black woman entered the hallway. She had to weigh three hundred pounds. "Sho your family'll be here Saturday. It's yo birthday fo pete's sake."

He stepped closer.

Her hand was on the door jamb, her eyes never left Clarence's face. Someone answered from inside the room, but he couldn't hear what was said. The black woman answered. "They be here this year fo sure. It ain't everyday a person turns ninety. Punch yo call light if you needs me."

Closer. He glanced at the exit. Shuffle. Shuffle.

The woman leaned against the wall, her arms folded across her ample chest. Her hair was tied in those dread things and gathered in a big bun at the back of her head, only some stuck out behind. Her bright blue uniform had little yellow ducks all over it; on that big of a uniform, that was a lot of ducks. She fiddled with a stethoscope hanging around her neck as he walked closer. Her eyes focused on him.

"Hey, Mr. Timmelsen. How's it goin'?"

"Name's Clarence. I'm just taking the tour. Getting some exercise." He raised one knee, then the other. "I'm used to a specialized gym workout."

"Uh-huh. You get all settled in didyanow?"

"Sure." He reached the end of the hallway—right next to the exit door. Was she ever going to get back to work? He could almost smell the spring air.

Her radio went off. "Well, Mr. Clarence, have yoself a good day and let us know if we can be of hep to you." She checked the radio and moseyed on down the hall. Just as Clarence was going to push the door open, she turned. "Goin' to get some air?"

"Uh. Just looking outside." He faced the door and pointed against the glass. "You have a nice little garden."

Her radio beeped again. "We sho do. Gotta run. Mrs. Hatly is persistent today."

She turned the corner and Clarence pushed the door open, slipping out into the sunshine. He stood tucked next to the exit, in the space between the door and a window, leaning against the building. He paused there for a minute and breathed in the fresh air. The birds chattered and squirrels chased each other around tree trunks.

As soon as the door closed, he hustled to the closest tree. Then to another. He hid behind the sign proclaiming Hillcrest Homes. Across the street and into the park.

F-r-e-e-d-o-m.

An hour later, Clarence stood on the sidewalk outside a grocery store. He peeped in, shuffling side-to-side, trying to spy between flyers taped to the inside of the glass. He leaned back and checked out the exterior: white paint peeled from old red bricks, a frayed awning flapped in the wind over the entry door. A sign with faded letters swayed slightly askew overhead—The Olde Towne Market.

He cupped his eyes with his hands and peered inside again, leaning against the glass. Lights on. The radio blared the newest canned music from an outside speaker. Country twang.

A slender woman wearing a white shirt, too-tight jeans and a green-and-white-striped necktie clomped toward the front door. Clarence caught the word Manager on her name tag but couldn't read her name. She stuck a single cigarette in her shirt pocket, her hand on the door.

Oh-oh. She glanced his way. He spun around to avoid being seen.

Wait. No one was onto him here. He was a customer, just like that guy inside the store, pushing a cart full of baby food and diapers.

Clarence stepped close to the glass again, eyed the ads taped haphazardly to the glass and pretended to scan them carefully. "Oh, look. Here's an ad for puppies. Six weeks old, had their shots," he read. "Aww, cute little things." Someone bumped into him. He nodded at a pretty young woman heading up the sidewalk toward the store entrance, and he tapped the glass. She smiled at him. "I should have my shots," he muttered. He pointed to the phone number fringe at the bottom. "I need to get one of those." He tilted his head. "402-572-1224. Gotta call or they'll be gone."

The woman glanced at him and entered the store, letting the door close behind her.

He stretched to read another ad higher up, letting his eyes fall to the manager inside. Now she stood pointing toward him, jaws jabberwalking to another white-shirted employee—a tall young male. He tied a green apron low on his hips.

Clarence rotated a quarter turn, toward the cars in the parking lot, jingling coins in his pocket. He turned toward the store.

Out of the corner of his eye, he spied the manager and employee walking toward the back of the store. They stopped, pointed to a leaning display, then pointed to the front, the back, and another aisle. Standing face to face in disagreement. The manager tucked her cigarette over her ear, reached out and shook the display, knocking several cans to the floor.

Now.

He put on the smile, eyes twinkling. He opened the door and located the puppy ad. "I need one of those." He tore one strip off. "402-572-1224. I'll call this number as soon as I get back home." He strutted to a cash register.

"Hello, Sir. What'd you say?" A tubby girl, sixteen or so, stood next to the cash register. She cocked her head at him, revealing an obnoxious red stripe running throughout her mouse brown hair.

He didn't answer.

Louder. "Uh ... how're ya doin' today? Lookin' for some puppies?" She yanked at the plastic shopping bags on a stand, separating them, pulling the end one open. Her fake gold name tag said MINDY ASHTON.

Clarence stopped and watched everything she did. "I see you're really busy today. Got your bags all ready, do you? Ready for that rush?" He smirked and pushed his fist into the air with the old one-two. "Where're you from anyway? Nebraska? Shelby? Chicaaaa-go?"

"Sir, I'm from here." She pointed to the floor. "Osceola, Nebraska. This is where it's at, Dude." She grinned, braces gleaming, and crossed her dark eyes above her glasses. Red pockmarks scarred her light skin. Doughnut rolls circled her middle.

"Dude?" He cleared his throat. "Why in my day—"

"In your day, you didn't have pop, TV, cell phones, or internet." The tall, gangly employee had returned, carrying a roll of trash bags. JOHN POTTER, according to his name tag. He glanced toward Mindy and smacked his forehead. "Oh, yeah. You had internet. But back then, it was called Pony Express."

Grrr. "Where're you from? The devil?" Clarence stomped past the registers and found himself face-to-face with the manager, arms across her chest, one pierced eyebrow raised.

"Sir." She greeted him and tapped her foot. "Or should I call you, Osceola?"

"I'm not from here."

She grinned. "Okay. So where are you from?" She tapped his chest. "You're new in these here parts, right?"

He looked down at her finger touching his shirt, at her name tag—TANDY LARKIN—then up to her face. "Did you know that your clerk up there, whatshername, is doing nothing? Absolutely nothing?" He looked back at Mindy and pointed. "See? She's just hangin' out."

Mindy grinned at him and waved, twining a lock of her hair.

"If she was busier, she lose some of that baby fat. She's never going to find a boyfriend with all that hanging on her."

Mindy's face fell, smile disappeared.

John stepped in front of her, pushed his black-rimmed glasses up on his pointy nose and slicked back his dark shaggy hair. Hands on his hips.

"Oh. Oh, I get it. She does have a boyfriend. It's that loser. The one from the devil." Back to the manager. "Where's he from?"

John adjusted his apron and boomed out. "Omaha."

Clarence swung back to John. "Oh. Omaha. That explains it." He sauntered past Tandy.

"Sir, what's your name? I don't believe the customer's always right with you around. That was just plain mean. We try to be nice—"

"Nice." He planted his feet in the middle of the aisle. "If you were nice, you'd get me outa that place up there on the hill." He shook his head. "It's nasty up there. The place stinks. The people stink. They shit in any bathroom they want."

John crept up beside Clarence. "Oh, so you're from ... up there." He pointed, a mock villainous expression on his face. "Then it's a good fit, huh. Nasty, stinky place for a nasty, stinky man. High five, Osceola!" He held his hand well above Clarence's head. "No, wait. You can't reach." He looked way up at his hand, on the end of his long skinny arm, then down at Clarence.

"John, get to work." Tandy eyed Clarence. "And as for you Mr. Osceola, you'd better get your little tooshie up front and apologize to Mindy."

Mindy smiled and picked up a bulging trash bag, spun it around and fastened it. "That's all right. Sticks and stones will break my bones, but words will never hurt me." She carried the trash bag past them, bumping it against her leg with each step.

Clarence stepped in behind Mindy and swaggered in her footsteps.

"Osceola, stop! That's enough." John held his hand out traffic-cop-style in front of Clarence.

Mindy sighed. "It's really okay. He reminds me of Grandpa—sorta. Grandpa was mean, too."

Tandy started toward the back of the store. "Okay, kids. I have work to do." She retrieved the cigarette from her ear. "I hope that in my absence you can all behave yourselves, get your work done, and be nice." She slowed and turned toward Clarence and waved the cigarette in his face. "Extra nice."

A buzzer went off at the check stand. They all twirled to see who had set it off.

Clarence made a bee-line for the back room but got wedged between the manager and a shelf of cereal boxes.

"Let me go," he puffed. "I have to find some ... sardines and crackers." He tried again. "I need to use the bathroom."

Glass crashed up front. Tandy immediately forgot Clarence and ran in the direction of the noise.

"Oh, no. I hope it's not pickles again."

"Bring the broom."

"Grab the mop and paper towels."

"Mop emergency in aisle ... by the check stands," It sounded like John's voice over the loudspeaker. "Whew. Pickles."

Clarence edged to the back room and bolted for the door. "Saved by the buzzer," he whispered. He looked over his shoulder. "And pickles." Quietly he opened the back door, but the wind caught it and slammed it against the building. He glimpsed a hawk rising with the wind current—just like the one that had broken through his window. The sunshine blinded him right at the spot the bird flew into. He stepped outside, shielding his eyes. The bird circled the building as he shut the door.

"Where're you going, beautiful bird? What are you circling?"

Clarence rotated with the hawk, following its lead. Around and around he followed the bird in a rhythmic dance—the bird in the air, Clarence on the ground. The hawk rose, glided, dove, then soared again on the wind current. Show-off. A bandage appeared partly torn off one wing.

He squinted into the sun. They let it loose already? Maybe it wasn't hurt as bad as they thought. Or maybe that demon lady, Henningway, claimed the aviary back for those little fake birds.

Silence.

The hawk hovered, wings hugging the flow of air. Then the powerful bird lifted, banked, and dove right for Clarence.

He ducked and lost his balance.

As he flailed, the bird screeched, piercing his eardrums, sending shivers up his spine.

He tumbled on the concrete, to his hands and knees, and the bird flew behind him. "Are you hunting me?" He tried to track it, but the sun blinded him. "I helped you," he shouted. "If I had a gun I'd shoot you right now, I would, you old buzzard. I'd shoot you dead."

Clarence grappled for a handhold. He staggered to his feet, and leaned against the building, catching his breath. He brushed his jeans off and examined the palms of his hands. Old, tough ropy scars lined them, traveling up the inside of one arm. One little finger curved inward, like a claw.

Smoke swirled, transporting him back in time—back to when he was a small boy. His mother had just died of polio and he had blindly run away into the cold night. Firelight drew him just over the next ridge from their house where a seasoned hobo had been warming beans over a fire. The old man had shown him how to warm his hands, but before the man could stop him, Clarence stuck his hands into the flames. He was so cold, he kept reaching out and touching the fire, terribly burning the palms of his hands. Grief-numbed, he had hardly felt the pain.

Smoke cleared.

Clarence stumbled backward along the wall of the grocery store. His foot kicked a pile of old dirty pipes, and he bent to pick one up. He shook the pipe at the hawk. "You coulda gotten me killed, old bird."

The hawk circled and screeched, dove at Clarence, and pulled up, just missing him again.

Clarence's hand pounded his chest as he gasped for breath.

CHAPTER ELEVEN

Bea's little fingers braided Dolly's hair over and over. Braided, then combed out. Braided, then combed. The doll's hair broke off easily from age, but also from being brushed again and again. Braided again and again. Ever since Mommy had taught Bea to braid.

She smoothed her own hair. Then Dolly's. Then hers again.

Comfy in her car seat, Bea hummed and swayed her head with the melody. The car was quiet and warm, with a window partway open. Licking her thumb, she washed Dolly's dirty face, just as Mommy did her own. One doll eye stuck open, the other eye blinked. Bea held up the doll to admire and smiled. Then she hugged Dolly, sighed, and settled in to wait for Mommy.

Almost asleep—

Screech!

Bea jumped and looked at Dolly, then at the store front. No Mommy. She closed her eyes again and relaxed.

Screech!

This time she jumped out of her car seat. She checked the entry door of the store.

No Mommy.

She dropped Dolly to the floor, bending to peek under the seat, the floor, around her car seat.

Screech!

Goosebumps rose on her arms and she shivered, rubbing them. She picked up Dolly and hugged her tight as she looked out the car windows, left and right.

Stop.

There.

She pressed her face against the window, eyes wide. An old man. And a bird. A big bird. The bird flapped its wings, flew higher, then dove for the man.

Mommy opened the car door and tossed a sack onto the seat. Glass clinked in the bag. "F-n store. F-n people. F-n headache." She rubbed her temples. "But. But, big score. We can eat for weeks. Months."

Screech!

"What the ... what's that sound?" Mommy turned behind her, hands covered her ears. "God that hurts." She gasped. "That bird is going to kill him." She turned to look at Bea. "Wha?"

Bea lifted her eyebrows and shoulders.

"Stay here, Bea." Mommy slammed the door and started running.

#

Katty dashed to the old man who stood pounding his chest, gasping. The hawk flew off, flapping its huge wings.

The man turned away as she rushed toward him. "I'm all right. Leave an old man alone."

"That's exactly why I won't leave you alone. Because you're old."

He rushed her, armed with a pipe, and glared. "Yeah, I'm old, but I'm not dead."

"I didn't say you were, old man." She bent to brush his pants off, blocking herself from the pipe.

He slapped her hand away. "Stop. I'm okay."

"Old fool. Old man. Where's your family, old man?"

"I don't have any family," he yelled. "Just me. Nobody else."

"Why? You chase 'em off, didsha?"

He clenched his fists. "None of your damn business." He looked behind her. "You're drunk. You can't even take care of the family you have." He pointed toward her Nova station wagon.

She swung around. Bea was crawling out the open car door. Katty yelled. "Bea. Get the f- back in the car seat." She charged back toward the car. "You know better than that. Get. Back. In. There."

Bea stopped short of stepping onto the concrete. She whimpered, her eyes focused behind Katty.

"Baby, I know I kept you waiting a long time, but I'm sick. And I broke a jar of pickles in the store and made a mess." She smelled her hands. "Shtinky."

Bea wrinkled her nose.

Katty picked her up tossed her into the car seat. "Stay there. We don't have far to go. Just sit still."

Katty dragged herself into the car, slammed the door and turned over the engine, then glanced at the old man. The bird still circled above the parking lot. "Stupid old man. He's gonna get hurt by a stupid bird." Gunning the car, she backed out only to slam on the brakes as another car swerved into the parking space beside her. "Damn! Why don't people look where they're going?"

She reached behind her. "You okay baby?" She pushed Bea back onto her car seat, then gunned the car again, only this time—

Scream.

Thud.

"Oh, God. Oh God. I hit something." Katty gripped the steering wheel. "Or someone. Oh God. What'd I do?"

She shifted into park, slowly opened the car door and stepped outside. One foot in front of the other. Until she reached the back of the car.

"Oh no."

A woman pushed herself off the concrete, brushed herself off and picked up her purse. "You hit me! I thought you saw me. What were you thinking?"

Katty leaned over to help pick up the woman's groceries, and the world started spinning. She reached out to steady herself on the car.

"You are drunk. You shouldn't even be driving. And you have a child with you." She grabbed a can of peaches from Katty. "Of all the nerve. You should be arrested."

"Oh no. Please Ma'am. I just got over the ... flu ... and I had to come out to get my baby some milk. It's not what you think."

"Liar. You're just lucky I'm not hurt. By the looks of you, I'd never get a dime out of you anyway." She shoved Katty away and limped to her car.

"Ma'am, everything okay?"

Katty spun around.

Oh oh.

A young officer, black haired and skinny, tipped his hat to Katty. "I was driving by when the department got a call from the store here. Are you all right?"

Katty slowly put her hand on the bumper of her car. Deep breath. Hopefully the pickle stink covered up her breath. "We're fine. Just a little shaken up." She pointed to the woman walking away. "She said she's fine, too. This parking lot is dangherous."

He walked to the side of the car. "This your daughter? She isn't buckled in."

Katty jumped. "Oh! Did she get out again? She is getting good at that."

He smiled down at Bea. "Hey there, Little Houdini. Cute." Hand on his pistol, he returned to Katty. "I don't think I know you ... uh, I'm new in ... "

Her lips curved into a seductive smile. "Thesh parts?"

The officer nodded. "Yeah. Um, I didn't catch your name."

"That's because I didn't throw it at you." She grinned and shrugged her shoulders. Good line. "Why do I feel like we're in a movie?"

He smiled and hesitated. "I just need to see your driver's license before I let you get back to your daughter." He nodded at Katty and waited.

Katty stopped breathing. "Uh, yeah. Sure." She didn't move.

"Is there a problem, Ma'am?"

"No. No. I'll just shcoot by you to get my purse." One step at a time. "It's right here."

She sat in the driver's seat and rummaged in her purse. "Yeah ... " She opened the glove box and dug around. Oh oh. "It's here somewhere." She attempted a laugh then staunched it. Back to her purse. "It's here ... " She panicked. She flashed a smile. "It must be in my other purse. I'm so sorry."

He shoved his hat off his forehead and reached inside his jacket. Ticket pad out. Pen poised. "I'm going to have to give you a warning. Driving without a license." He scribbled then tore off a sheet. "Here you go. You need to be sure you have your license with you at all times."

Katty folded the paper and stuffed it in her jeans pocket. "Yes. I'll go right home and get that purse." She snapped her fingers at Bea. "Bea, don't let me forget to do that."

He pointed at Bea. "You might have to tie and buckle her in the car seat."

Deep slow breath. She attempted a laugh. "Thanks, uh, Officer for stopping. Nice to know you'll be around ... uh ... you're around when I need you ... when we have problems." Katty fluttered her eyelids. She stood slowly, opened Bea's passenger door and climbed in. "Let me buckle you in again, Sweetie. I don't know how you get out."

She leaned into the car, her face inches from Bea's. "Now let's pretend these straps aren't all twisted and," she dug under the liner, "all caught and I'm buckling you in, okay, Sweetie?"

Bea nodded; they played the game well. "Okay Mommy. I'll sit still while you buckle me in again."

Katty smiled and rubbed noses with Bea as she made a clicking sound with her teeth and tongue. "There. You're all safe again." She ruffled Bea's hair. "Now don't unbuckle yourself again, ya hear?"

Katty stood slowly, gaze following the young officer to his squad car. Her stomach churned. Her head was pounding.

Breathe.

#

Bea gripped the sides of her seat and stretched to see the old man.

As Mommy slowly backed the car out, something happened. Bea stared at the old man's eyes; he stared into hers. She didn't understand but knew she couldn't look anywhere else but his blue, blue eyes.

CHAPTER TWELVE

Carol glanced at the chart. More med changes? What was Miss Henningway thinking? Residents were already nodding off in their mashed potatoes.

She searched the dining hall again. Each empty chair should have a definite reason for being vacant. Mrs. Samuelson was still at physical therapy. Andy had checked out to spend time with family. Mr. Butress's empty chair hadn't found a replacement resident.

Carol rotated.

Clarence's chair was empty. Bib draped over the back, table set for lunch. Water in the glass. Coffee cooling in the cup.

"Where is that man?" she muttered. Her inner alarm went off. AWOL. She wasn't sure if she'd rather have him depressed in his bed or ... missing.

She replaced the chart in her med cart and spun slowly. Scanned again. Maybe he'd sat in the wrong chair. Eyes on each resident.

Mrs. Samuelson tottered in, slowly placing her walker a step ahead and walking into it. Each step careful and measured. Determination on Mrs. Samuelson's face—never to fall again. She stepped over and over until she reached her table and lowered herself down.

Staff hurried to serve her, leaning into her good ear, yelling, "It's baked chicken breasts, mashed potatoes with gravy, corn and cole slaw today, Mrs. Samuelson." The aide shook out her bib and attached it around her neck. "Then for dessert, we have apple crisp."

"Oh, that all sounds good, dear." Mrs. Samuelson fussed with her bib and patted her tummy. "I'm hungry today."

Carol continued around the dining room.

Mrs. Getty's head nodded into her food. Carol gently lifted it and squeezed her shoulders, wiping cole slaw off her nose with her bib.

She kept scanning the room.

Harold's eyes caught hers, and he smiled. His attire looked out of place among the flannel shirts and sweat pants the men usually wore: open suit jacket—the lapel sporting an American flag pin, dress shirt and snagged dress pants. "He's gone, I bet." Always the detective on the job.

Carol grinned. "You read minds, don't you, Harold."

He grinned. "Naw, just goin' on past experience."

She nodded and adjusted his bib and napkin. "Sorry you have to wear this, but—"

"Regulations," he finished her sentence. "It's okay. Somedays I don't spill a drop. Others?" He rolled his eyes and lifted the bib to reveal several spots of pink yogurt from breakfast, smudged on his shirt pocket. "I missed."

"Uh-huh. I know. Me too." She opened her white nurses jacket and licked a finger, sampling an imaginary spot on her shirt. "Yup—mmmm. Me, too. I had chocolate yogurt. What flavor's yours?"

He laughed. "Strawberry."

She patted his bib. "I'd better go check his room. See you later." She passed him, backed up beside him again and rubbed his shoulder. "You're a good man, Harold."

He bowed his head, then lifted his eyes to Carol's and whispered. "You're a good woman and nurse, Carol. You listen to our words ... but you listen to our hearts."

She hugged him. "I only hear what God gives me, but thanks." She straightened and extended her imaginary sword. "Now, onward. On to be the vigilante, the detective." She glanced at him. "The warrior, to search out this nursing home kingdom for Sir Clarence."

He burst out laughing, cupping his bib to his mouth. He coughed and swallowed. Cleared his throat and sputtered.

"You okay, Harold?" She knelt beside him. "Sorry. Didn't mean to make you choke. That's kinda frowned upon here. I don't want to have to chart you up."

"Naw. You made me laugh. That's always good for spitting food." He wiped his mouth. "I'm fine. Hope you find your missing kid."

"Yup." Carol nodded as she stepped away. "Me too." She waved as she headed down the hall, past residents wheeling and walking back to their rooms.

The nurse's station was first on her list. "April, have you seen Clarence?"

The aide looked up from charting on the handheld computer, squinting, glasses slipping down her nose. She rubbed her temples. "What?"

"Ha. You'll catch on to that monster machine. If I can do it, you can." Carol drummed on the desk beside her. "Clarence. Have you seen him?"

"I got him another plate of eggs this morning. He seemed extra hungry for some reason. But that's the last time I remember seeing him."

"Okay. Could you help search the place? Then let me know what you find and we'll put it out on the radios. Just a hunch."

"K." She rose, pocketed her computer and followed Carol.

Carol took one direction. April went the opposite.

Carol surveyed the common living room right outside the nurse's station. Several wheelchairs were already in place. Only one little lady intently watched TV—the only one sitting in a straight back chair. She glanced up and reached out her hand as Carol passed her.

"You'll find him."

Carol stopped in her tracks. "Who, Mrs. Hatly?"

"Why Clarence, of course." She smiled sweetly. Chin-length, gray hair curled around a pink ribbon. A flowered dress and matching sweater hid bony flesh. Skinny sup-hose-clad legs dangled from the chair. "He seems to be a nice man. When I first moved in here, I wanted to run away, too." She patted the arm of the chair. "But something kept me from doing just that."

Carol hugged Mrs. Hatly's thin shoulders and kept on maneuvering and squeezing between each chair and wheelchair, making a note to herself: spend more time with Mrs. Hatly. Such wisdom tucked in there. She always felt good after talking to her.

Last chair.

No Clarence.

Down another hall.

She opened the laundry room door and walked in, pushing hanging sheets aside. Washers and driers chugging away in some kind of Indian drum cadence made her want to dance along. She pushed aside one last damp sheet to see Rosita, one of the newest employees, folding towels at a large table.

Rosita's face was flushed. Sweat beaded on her upper lip and dripped from her forehead, her dark hair wet in ringlets.

"Do you always hang sheets to dry?" Carol asked, still grasping a sheet.

"Sí. The dryers don't keep up."

"It's hot in here." Carol fanned her jacket out and in, shaking her head. "Is it always this hot?"

Rosita wiped at her forehead with a tissue. "Sí. And this is spring." She nodded toward the open window, a last snow bank right outside. "Snow air cooled."

Carol could feel the breeze where she stood. "Don't catch cold, Rosita."

"I sweat so much, no germ could live in here." She patted her chest. "And I pray."

Carol stopped short, her hand on the table. "What?"

Rosita stopped folding. "I pray." She eyed Carol and added the towel to the pile.

Carol stared.

Wow. "Me, too."

Rosita smiled. "Now, what'd you come into my little office for, Miss Head Nurse Carol?"

Back on task. "I ... oh, I can't find Clarence. You know, the new guy from Chicago? Have you seen him?"

"Naw. The lady reses sometime come in to help fold, but a man has never come in."

"Yeah. Okay." Carol laughed and stepped through the open doorway and paused. "Thanks, Rosita." She started to close the door, but opened it again. "Keep on doing that praying stuff, okay?"

"Sí, Miss Director, Ma'am."

Carol paused outside the closed door and made another note to herself: go fold clothes with Rosita on breaks. She could rub against that stuff all day.

She knocked on Clarence's open door. "Clarence, it's me, Carol." She shook her head. Nobody home. The bed was empty. The bathroom was empty. She poked into the closet. His jacket hung on the hook, and his flap hat sat on the shelf.

She punched the button on the radio. "Hello all. Keep an eye out for Clarence. He isn't in his room or bathroom and his jacket and hat are still here. Check all halls, gardens, conference rooms—all rooms. Chapel. Report back ASAP. I do not want to call the Sheriff on a resident, again. We all know what happened last time."

Various voices chattered from the speaker.

"Right on."

"Okay. On it."

CHAPTER THIRTEEN

Bea kicked the back of Mommy's seat. The old man had looked at her, like grandpas did on TV. Bea squirmed to keep him in sight as Mommy steered the car into the street.

"Bea! Quit kicking!" Mommy tore open a pack of cigarettes and tossed the wrapper toward the floor on the passenger side, only to have the clear wrapper stick to her fingers like tape. Bea had loved playing with tape until she got in trouble. She hadn't meant to use the whole roll on her favorite book, but it was in pieces and needed fixing. Mean Mommy had come out then.

Mommy shook her hand hard, again and again, but the wrapper wouldn't let go.

Bea giggled, but stopped when Mommy glared at her in the rearview mirror. Mommy flicked harder and the wrapper floated away. She tapped the end of the pack, popped a cigarette out and reached for the lighter but hit the radio instead. Music blared louder than the siren did when the dogs howled at lunchtime:

"Though Satan should buffet, though trials should come,
Let this blest assurance control,
That Christ has regarded my helpless estate,
And hath shed His own blood for my soul.
It is well, with my soul,
It is well, it is well with my —"

"F-n radio! Damn it! Shut-up!" Mommy pounded every button until the music stopped. Quiet. Now the wipers were on—back and forth, back and forth.

Bea's head followed—back and forth, back and forth.

Mommy was funny today, but Bea knew she couldn't laugh. Something was happening. Mean Mommy again.

She lit the cigarette and sucked in on it, her cheeks pulled in, eyes closed. Head dropped back against the headrest as she slowed for the red light. She held her breath then blew the smoke out.

Cars screeched to a halt on both sides of their station wagon. Horns honked. But their car floated through the intersection.

Mommy opened her eyes but drifted away into her own world— her world of smoky cigarettes.

Traffic swerved.

Someone honked in the car behind.

"Mommy?" Bea whispered.

Mommy squinted one eye open and shivered. She sat up and held the cigarette between her pointer finger and middle finger, letting it stick up like a beam from a little flashlight.

Bea mimicked Mommy, holding an imaginary cigarette in her fingers.

More horns honked.

The cigarette smoke curled up to the ceiling of the car, swirling along every crevice and opening. When it drifted into the back seat, she coughed and coughed. "Mommy?"

"Oh, sorry. I'll open my window." She pushed the window button, but it didn't work. "Damn." She pounded on it, but it didn't open. She cracked her door. The smoke floated toward the opening. "That better, Bea?"

The car zigzagged.

Bea grabbed the arms of her car seat. "Mommy, why do you smoke? It stinks. It makes my eyes burn. Don't your eyes burn, too?"

Mommy slammed on the brakes, flipped around in her seat, face to face with Bea. Something moved in Mommy's eyes.

Another horn blared.

Bea pressed back into her car seat, hugging Dolly.

"I smoke ... because I like it." Her voice became louder with each word. "Okay? That's all you need to know." She turned to the front and pounded the steering wheel. The car lurched forward.

"Mommy?"

The car swerved into a parking lot, just missing a delivery van.

"Mommy?" Bea coughed. "Could you buckle me in?"

"Not now!" Mommy snickered. "I've never strapped you in and I don't need to start now! I never had a car seat when I was your age." Mommy kicked the car door open wider, pushed out, and slammed the door behind her.

Bea blinked. Her chin quivered as she wound her finger in Dolly's hair.

Mommy paced back and forth, puffing on the cigarette. She glanced at Bea, shook her head, then quickly looked away. Glanced again and stomped her foot. She sucked on the cigarette. Her eyes squinted through the smoke. Then she stood still, looking away, and flicked cigarette ashes to the pavement. One more suck on the cigarette and she dropped it to the concrete and ground it with her boot. She put her hand on the car door handle but didn't open the door.

Bea hugged Dolly tighter. "Mommy?" she said. A tear slid down her cheek.

Finally the car door clicked and Mommy climbed in. Fresh air rushed in until she shut the door.

She looked down at the steering wheel. "I need them. Cigarettes. I need them, okay?" She stopped. "I have to do it." She stuck her jaw out, nostrils flaring. "I'm not proud of it. Not any more. I used to think it was cool." The clear wrapper crackled as she squeezed the cigarette pack. "But now, I don't. I hate it." She threw the pack against the passenger door window. "I hate it."

Mommy stared at Bea in the rearview mirror, then looked away. "I can't stop, Baby Bea. I'm ... addicted to it. Do you know what that means?"

Bea shook her head, hiding behind Dolly.

"It means I have to have it. I can't go a minute without thinking about it."

Silence.

Mommy stared at Bea in the rearview mirror and started to cry. Tears ran down Bea's cheeks, too.

Mommy picked up the cigarette pack, crinkled it and popped another cigarette out. She looked back at Bea. "I get sick when I try not to smoke. I can't help it."

Bea's stared at the cigarette in Mommy's hand. "Mommy—"

"I know. That's icky, but it's true." She stopped. "I don't know why I am telling you all this, but I am. I'm sorry Mommy smokes, Baby Bea. I'm sorry I can't stop. It's like a demon inside of me, chasing me. Picking at me. Telling me to have another cigarette. Getting me all sick and … mean." She sputtered. "Making me cough." She turned and stared at Bea. "Making you cough." She rustled on the front seat, then held a kleenex to her mouth and coughed.

Bea stared again at the cigarette, then at her mommy, then at the smoke still filling the car.

She jumped down onto the floor, right behind Mommy. "Don't get sick. I love you, Mommy. Don't get sick. Please just throw them away. Throw them out the window. Flush them down the toilet. I saw you do that once. You flushed them and some pills down the toilet. Do it, Mommy. Do it again."

Mommy whipped around in her seat and faced Bea, nose to nose, her eyes wide. "You saw me do that? Pills too?" Her face turned red and the car engine roared. "Well, you can just get sick then. Just get sick for all I care. You deserve it for spying on me."

Bea hugged Dolly tight against her chest. She scrambled onto her car seat and squeezed her eyes shut, kissing Dolly's head. She whispered, "Dolly, I won't ever smoke. I won't make you smell that smoke. I won't ever do that to you. I love you Dolly." A tear slid down her cheek and dripped onto Dolly's head.

Mommy stared into the rearview mirror and choked, breaking into a rattly cough. Giving Bea a mean look, she grabbed the cigarette and lit up, sucked on it, then swerved the car out onto the street. A lone tear streamed down her cheek. She sucked on the cigarette again then opened the window—this time it worked—and threw the cigarette out. She grabbed the pack of cigarettes and threw them, too.

She yanked open the glove box and dug around, the car weaving into the other lane.

A car headed right at them. It blared its horn, and Mommy drove the car back on her own side, the car rocking back and forth. "There!" Mommy yelled. She grabbed one more pack of cigarettes and threw it out the window.

Mommy caught Bea's eyes in the rearview mirror. "No more," she yelled. "Okay?" Then she lowered her voice. "No more cigarettes, Baby Bea." Sobs broke from her throat and her eyes filled with tears. The car swerved back and forth.

Bea held on tight to her car seat and coughed again, eyes scrunched closed.

CHAPTER FOURTEEN

Clarence picked a path around debris in the alley behind the grocery store, sidestepping the occasional dog pile, puddle and tire rut. Arms extended on either side, he felt like a tightrope walker—minus the pole. He stopped to rest every once in a while. Felt like he'd been gone all day. Missed lunch. His stomach rumbled. Maybe supper, too.

He stooped to pick up an object that drew his attention from among the weeds. Key? No. Junk. He tossed it down and took another step. He tripped when he spied something and leaned over for what turned out to be a gum wrapper. Wrigley's. He threw it to the wind.

Something else sparkled—a bright something. He balanced, only to find another candy wrapper.

Half burned trash and papers littered the alley and lot. Rusty pipes, bent this way and that. Overgrown weeds and brush.

Another shiny object gleamed through the refuse. He groaned as he bent to pick it up, turning it over in his hand. A dime store ring. Cheap plastic thing. The finish had rubbed off and the rhinestone was loose. He flung it away and gasped as a scene from his past unfolded before him.

A much younger Clarence squatted easily and sifted through the tall grass to fish out the gleaming diamond ring, dazzling and blinding as it reflected the sun's rays. He knelt on the hard gravel and stared at the beauty of the facets, turned it this way and that, admiring the cut, the brilliance, the colors emanating from deep within.

Stunning.

"And I will not marry you in a hundred million years," Sally wailed. "Not ever. Ever."

Clarence glanced at her, and stared as the young woman slowly morphed into a tree standing in the distance, his mind still in the past, his body stuck in the present.

Deep rattly breath.

A train whistle startled him.

He trembled as mind and body reconnected, searching in the weeds, parting the grass, combing through the debris. Where had it gone? He cut his finger on a rusty can. Damn. That nurse Carol would make him get a tetanus shot. Or take some kind of antibiotics. Or both. He sucked on the cut.

A white van drove up the hill. Large green letters on the side read Hillcrest Home, "Home of God's Most Beloved."

Cringing, he ducked behind the corner of the grocery store then peered out. He hated that slogan. If he were God's Beloved, he certainly wouldn't be living at Hillcrest.

He'd be back in prison.

Or dead.

The van turned into the parking lot, then circled back out. Jim the maintenance man was driving, and Bill his assistant hung out the passenger window, squirming in his seat, craning his neck, his ball hat cockeyed on his head.

"Buzzards," Clarence muttered. "Flying around looking for dead stuff." He ducked behind the brick wall, scanning the alley, feeling more alive than he had in years. He could barely make out the silhouette of a hawk in the tree against the darkening sky. "Ha, old bird. Trying to sneak up on me, huh. You thought you had me."

Clarence studied the bird as it cocked its head, studying him. Stare-down. Man against bird. Bird against man. Neither giving in. Both stubborn. Both toughened against life.

Clarence held up a fist. "What have you got in you, old bird? What are you made of?" He stopped to listen and dropped his fist against his leg. "You are made of feathers and that's all. Feathers. You hear me, old bird? Just feathers and bones."

Screech!

Clarence jumped and covered his ears. The bird pushed out of the tree, wings flapping, beating the wind, rising higher. Powerful.

Damn, that wingspread had to be over four feet.

Something tiny dropped out of the sky. Clarence ducked, covering his head with his arms. It bounced off his shoulder and pinged off a rock, into the rubble below.

He sighted in on the landing place, crawled to it, and picked up the dime store ring.

"Argh." He sat in the dirt and held it up. The cheap metal and rhinestone barely reflected the remaining sunlight. "This again."

He searched the sky for the hawk.

Gone.

CHAPTER FIFTEEN

Carol peeked through the front window of the grocery store, shuffled to her right, then left, scoping out the front end. Clarence wasn't in sight. Calling the Sheriff was the last thing she wanted to do.

Hand on door pull. Smile on face.

Ding. The door alarm announced her entrance.

A young clerk—Carol recognized Mindy—peeked from around the end of a shelf. "Hi. Can I help you find anything?"

"Well, it's not an anything I need to find. It's an anyone. Like in a person."

Mindy rounded the end cap and stood at the register, straightening her green apron. "Yeah? Who, anyone?" She grinned.

Carol dug into her jacket pocket and pulled out the admissions picture. She held it for Mindy to see. "His name is Clarence ... "

Mindy grabbed the picture. "Oh, I know Clarence." She tapped the picture. "He was just here today. He's ... uh ... well, let's put it this way—"

"He's rude, mean, loud, and insulting." A tall, male employee walked up beside Mindy. "And that's just the beginning. He's—"

Mindy poked him. "That's enough, John. I think she gets the idea, don't you, Ma'am."

Carol grimaced. "Sounds like you've met Clarence, all right. Can you tell me when, where? What'd he do that was so bad?"

John glanced at Mindy.

Oh-oh. This can't be good.

"Well ... he was here a little while ago."

"What time?"

He checked his watch. "An hour ago? You know, give or take."

"Did he say where he was headed?"

"Wait a minute. Is he in trouble? I mean, like in danger? Because, well, I did see him head out back," Mindy said, her hands in her apron pocket. "He was being, well—"

"Mean. He was being mean." John interrupted her.

Mindy squirmed and retied her apron. "Yes. I said that Clarence is so much like my old grandpa. Clarence is nicer looking, but Grampa was always outa sorts."

"Your grandpa was mean, Mindy." John touched her shoulder. "You've told me about stuff he did. Burning your little doll. And other stuff."

Mindy nodded. "Yeah. He was mean." She rubbed her arm and seemed distracted for a minute. "And Clarence ... well, I felt like I used to feel when Grandpa was around."

Carol sighed. "I'm so sorry he hurt you. I wish I knew more about his past. He has no family—no wife, no kids. He grew up around here, but as far as I know, he moved away soon after he grew up." She checked the aisle. "I shouldn't have told you that, but if you know more about him, maybe you can understand him. Maybe you can help us find him. He moved back here because he had nowhere else to go. He couldn't live on his own, but no one would take him in."

"Sounds just like Grandpa, but we took him in."

"So, he lived with you?" Carol shook her head. "Must have been tough."

Mindy sighed and rearranged the newspapers. "Yeah. But he's gone now." She bowed her head. "I only hope—"

"Do you think you could show me where you saw Clarence heading? It might be a place to start." She checked her watch. "He's getting past med time. He already missed lunch. And supper."

"Sure. I need to tell my boss, though."

"That's fine." Carol said. "I'll wait."

Poor girl. First her grandpa and now Clarence.

Mindy returned a few minutes later. "It was right after he left the store. I opened the door to bring a bag of trash out," she pointed to the dumpster, "and that's when I saw him again."

"What was he doing?"

"Well, at first I thought he was hiding, or looked like it. But when

I opened the dumpster, I looked up and saw him bending down over here someplace. I almost said something to him, but my boss hollered at me to come help her. It's truck day today, so there's lots to do. Groceries to put away and stuff."

"I understand." Carol stepped to the spot. "He was maybe about here?"

"Yeah."

Carol bent over, looking onto the ground. Maybe he had dropped something and bent down to retrieve it. She brushed her hand over the tall weeds, trying to see the ground.

Mindy closed the dumpster lid. "Why doesn't he have any family? Even Grandpa had us. We weren't much. At least he didn't think so, but we helped him when he needed it. Fed him. Took care of him and stuff. A place to sleep." Mindy shook her head. "That's tough. And lonely."

Carol straightened and searched the girl's face. "Yes, Mindy. Lonely, it is."

Joe in a nursing home thirty miles away. Joe staring at her with vacant eyes. Only once in the last two years had he greeted her with a flicker of recognition. Lonely it is.

The back door opened and John pushed a cart loaded with trash outside.

Carol cocked her head. "Are you okay?"

Mindy nodded. "Yeah, it's just that, well, I feel bad. Grandpa had us. Clarence has nobody." She shifted her weight. "And, well, we like kinda talked back to him."

John flipped the dumpster lid open and tossed in trash bags. "No, Mindy. You didn't talk back to him." He slammed the lid shut. "I did. He was saying stuff about you and he can't do that. Not on my watch."

Carol half smiled.

Mindy blushed.

John stretched taller.

"That's okay, John." Carol said. "Sometimes I find I get along better with him when I stand up to him. But I'm still getting to know him. He just got here." She shrugged. "I've already told you way too much for that privacy act." She pointed along the brick building that led to the alley. "Did he go down that way?"

"I hope not. That's not safe." Mindy pointed down the alley. "He might have gone over there. Maybe."

An older woman wearing a long green-and-white striped necktie appeared at the store's back door. "Mindy? John?" she called. "You still work here?" Her head turned toward Carol. "Oh, I'm sorry. I thought you left." She approached the threesome. "Are you getting what you need?"

Carol nodded. "Well, it's a start. I appreciate your help, Mindy." She shook her hand, then John's. "And yours, John." She glanced at the older woman—obviously the manager—and back to the kids. "Please, with your boss's permission, if you see him or hear anything, could you call me at this number?" She handed Mindy her business card.

"Sure."

"Thanks, you two. Have a good night." She shook hands with the manager. "They're good kids. Thanks for giving me their time."

"Sure. Hope you find him. Let us know if we can do anything else."

Carol turned to go, but not before she caught sight of a huge bird perched in the tree above them. Was that? Couldn't be the same hawk. "Do you see that?"

John rotated his head, looking at all the branches. "Where? Oh, the hawk? He lives here."

"Like he's your neighborhood hawk?" Carol chuckled. "They must be all over. We had one break into the home, through a window." Her eyes opened wide. "Clarence's window, as a matter of fact."

John folded his arms across his chest. "Really."

"I wish he could tell us what he sees day in and day out." Carol cooed to the bird. "Wait, wrong bird. What sound does a hawk make?"

As if in answer, the hawk lifted off the tree branch and swooped down toward them, screeching.

Carol covered her ears and ducked. Huge. Loud.

The others hid behind the dumpster.

"That's what they sound like," John said.

"I'll know next time." Carol adjusted her jacket. "I swear it heard me ask."

The manager brushed dirt from her shirt and re-clipped her tie as the bird flew back to the branch in the tree. "I'm calling the Sheriff's Office or a wildlife association to come pick him up. He's dangerous."

"Please don't," John piped up. "I'm out here every day, doing the trash, running the compactor. He's never done that before and believe me, I've teased him so he should have." He grinned. He held up his hands. "Really. I feel something from him."

The manager cut in. "Fe-e-el something?"

John's head dropped to his chest. "I know it's weird. Sounds creepy. But I think he serves a purpose. I don't know how to say it, but really he has never done that before. Please give him another chance."

"If he does it again, he's gone. We can't have him dive bombing customers. We won't destroy him, but the guys can catch him and take him into the country somewhere, where we'll all be safe. Us and him."

John nodded his head and kicked at the gravel. "Fair enough."

"Nature boy." Mindy squeezed John's hand.

"I don't know, John. What purpose could a bird have? But, hear me bird." Mrs. Larkin spoke loudly and distinctly. "I'm putting you on notice. You dive at anybody again, and you're a gonner." She pointed at the hawk. "Ya hear?"

The hawk stared down at them.

John half chuckled, half breathed out. "See what I mean? He's got some ... purpose."

"Then tell us where Clarence is, Mr. Hawk." Carol waved as she walked to her car. "Please."

CHAPTER SIXTEEN

Clarence hid behind a tree right off the nursing home parking lot, hugging his arms. Chilly this evening.

Miss Henningway slammed her car door—hard.

Hurry up and leave Administrator Lady. The bathroom beckoned.

On with her sunglasses.

Clarence checked the level of the sun and doubted she'd need them past the parking lot exit. She didn't look happy ... but then she never looked happy unless she was bragging about nursing home award she had achieved.

Oh, and when she came onto him. Flirt. No, there were other words for women like her. It'd been less than a week and she had: brought him coffee, made herself his tablemate in the dining room, offered to help him get ready for bed. What the hell? He'd been sixty years without a woman and he sure as hell didn't want to jump back in the game with her. Something stinketh in Hillcrest Homes and it was only a matter of time before the stink erupted.

She drove away. Finally.

Having a room on the parking lot side of the old people's home had its advantages: it was easy to escape, easy to keep an eye on the coming and going of the enemy, and a cinch to get to the bathroom.

He picked up the pipes and watched the side entrance door and windows. No one coming or going. He needed a spotter inside. He made a run for it as fast as his old legs could carry him. Dropped a pipe. Not going back. He crouched beside the tan brick building.

Almost home.

The windows in this wing opened into resident rooms, his

included. He shoved the pipes under a bush, reached the door, pushed the automatic door opener and peeked in. One hallway—clear. He couldn't see down the other. TVs blared. Someone dropped a bedpan. The sound echoed over background voices and TV chatter.

He slipped inside and tiptoed straight to his room. Nice and handy.

He hustled to the bathroom but froze when he felt a hand on his shoulder. He swung around face-to-face with the dark-skinned woman, huge in stature and girth, grinning at him. Lots of big teeth. Dreads sticking out from the back of her head.

He pointed. "Uh, I gotta go in here. It's been too long."

She never stopped grinning. "Uh-huh. It has been too long. You go somewhere, Clarence? Did you have a date? How'd you git your shirt so dirty?" She brushed at it.

"You are mean. I gotta go." He slipped into the bathroom and slammed the door against the visual of her. "She better think twice about pushing me around."

"What you say, Clarence?" She cracked the door open. "Sorry, couldn't hear."

All he could see was teeth.

"What'd you say again?"

He grabbed the doorknob and slammed the door, shutting her name tag lanyard in the door jamb. He could read her name as he relieved himself. Lisha. He chuckled. A visual of her hanging by a cord to his bathroom door made him burst out in laughter. He opened the door.

"Oh, you think that's funny, Mr. Clarence?" She tucked her lanyard under her white uniform jacket covering the little yellow duckies, cupped his shoulder, and steered him in front of her—eye to eye.

Black eyes. An inch from his blue ones. Freckles. And large pores on her nose.

"Yeah. I thought that was funny. Didn't you?" He laughed his best fake laugh, then stopped and sneered his best fake smile.

She scowled. "You are in so much trouble Mr. Clarence. We might get to chain you to your chair. Or at least to your bed. Maybe torture you with, I donno, drops of water or sumthin."

Clarence raised his eyebrows. "Oh, yeah?" He squinted. "Iss on."
Her right eyebrow quivered. She slowly released his shoulder.
"You missed din-ner. I 'spose you're spectin' dessert? Are you all
washed up?" She headed down the hall, laughing.

Ha. Ha.

He walked to his window and stared at the trees waving in the
wind. Even the leaves seemed to taunt him. He sighed and shook his
head, hands slipped into his pockets, and muttered, "Bastard judge.
Had this all figured out, huh?" He jingled his coins then patted his
back pockets. What the f-? He patted his shirt pockets. "Where is ...
my f-n wallet?"

"Clarence." A female voice spoke behind him. "How did you get
back in here and where did you go and why did you put me through
all this and ... and ... ? You are in so much trouble."

He turned to face Carol, red-faced, huffing and puffing.

Clarence started in. "You need to lose weight," he snapped.
"You're out of shape and breathless. You can't even walk down the
hall without overexerting yourself."

Carol stomped her foot. "Stop. Shame on you, Clarence. Shame
on you for putting me through ... no, for putting all of us through
this. You've been gone all day! We were worried sick!"

He swallowed. "You were just worried because you would have
to call the Sheriff. You were just worried about your record with the
home office. Your point system or whatever it is." He grimaced as
he patted his back pocket. "You weren't worried about me. Just your
job."

Carol stopped. "Yes, I was worried about all that. Of course.
It's my job to be on top of all that. That's what I do." She took a
step toward him. "But I was also worried about you, Clarence." She
poked his chest and backed him to the window. "Because I care
about you. I care about each and every resident. So when you pull a
stunt like you did today, I worry. Are you all right? Did you get hurt?
Did you fall?"

Silence.

There was so much in those brown eyes of hers. "That's not my
job, Clarence. That's my heart."

He stared. "You still need to lose weight. All of you do. You eat
too much here. And where the hell is ... " On second thought, she

didn't need to know about his wallet. He'd find it—without her or anybody else's help.

"Where's what?"

"Never you mind."

Carol's chest rose and fell. She squinted and her chin quivered. She left the room.

Clarence turned to the window, hands in his pockets, as a tear started down his cheek. He quickly wiped it away.

"So you're back. You're in so much trouble." Yet another voice from the open door.

Clarence turned and slammed the door in Harold's face, but not before he heard Harold say, "Hey, you're crying. I'm sorry. You okay?"

He leaned against the door and choked back the tears.

CHAPTER SEVENTEEN

Bea sat at the kitchen table, stirring her cereal as she chewed, singing softly, swinging her legs in time.

Slam! Mommy dropped the washer lid.

Bea jumped.

"He'd better call." Mommy checked the clock then turned the washer dial. Water rushed into the machine. "Bea! Can you stop that singing already?" Mommy's voice got louder, along with the clicking of her long black polished nails on the metal lid. She turned and glared at Bea. "Really. Can't you stop?"

Bea sucked in a breath and choked on a piece of cereal, eyes wide, the spoon frozen in the air, dripping milk onto the table and floor. Her face turned hot as she coughed up cereal chunks. The spoon clattered to the floor.

"Bea! You're dripping milk all over." Mommy said her name in a hard, angry voice and rushed to the table. "You're making a mess. Why can't you eat right, like everybody else?" She slammed her hand onto the table beside Bea's bowl.

Everything jumped, including Bea.

"Look, you spilled on your shirt. Now you'll have to change."

Mommy grabbed the spoon and threw it into the sink. "Get yourself cleaned up. Now!" She pointed toward the bathroom. "And brush your teeth."

Bea cleared her throat. Her lower lip quivered, and she felt hot tears in her eyes. "I'm still hungry."

"I'm still hungry," Mommy mimicked in a high, scary voice. She grabbed the cereal bowl, spilling more milk on Bea's shirt.

Bea scooted off the chair and ran down the hall. When she shut the bathroom door, she made sure the latch was silent. She let go of the knob, one turn at a time, until it stopped, then stepped onto the stool in front of the sink.

As she looked into the mirror, the tears flowed down her cheeks. No sound. Not a sob. Just tears streaming from her eyes, dripping onto the counter, into the sink.

The pretty brown eyes in the mirror watched the hurt and pain drip down. The little girl in the mirror calmed her, helped the tears stop. Told her to be strong.

Bea sighed a deep ragged breath, changed into a clean T-shirt and picked up her toothbrush and toothpaste. The water from the faucet stirred a song, each drop played a note. While she squirted toothpaste onto the brush, and screwed the cap on straight, a quiet melody stirred in her heart and she began to hum as she brushed her teeth.

"Do I hear water running?" Mommy's loud voice broke in. Loud raps on the door echoed into the bathroom, into Bea's song.

Bea turned the water off.

"You know better than to let the water run." Mommy pounded on the door again. Bea jumped and dropped her toothbrush. It bounced down her shirt, trailing toothpaste all the way down.

Bea took one look and let out a wail.

The door burst open. Mommy stepped into the room. Her face didn't look like Mommy. Dark glinted in her eyes, her forehead scrunched, lips stretched over her teeth.

This was somebody else.

Bea cried harder and harder as Mommy crept closer.

Mommy leaned over her. She shook her head and crouched low, face to face with Bea.

Bea stepped back. Almost falling off the stool, she gripped the sink.

Mommy grabbed Bea's wrist and slapped her hard on the cheek.

Bea shrieked and tried to pull away.

Mommy's face changed. Her eyes turned soft. She sucked in a deep breath and shook all over.

She held onto Bea. "I'm sorry Baby," Mommy said. Her voice sounded softer, sad. "I'm sorry. I don't know what got into me. I ... I'm sorry." She started to cry.

Bea struggled, but Mommy held on, saying over and over and over, "I'm sorry. I'm so sorry. Baby, I would never hurt you." Her eyes fluttered up. "I ... oh." Cupping Bea's burning cheek with her hand, she buried her head against Bea's chest and cried again.

Bea's cheek stung as Mommy stroked it. She slowly circled Mommy's neck with her arms and smelled Mommy's hair. Her own sobs spilled out, and she crumpled onto the floor in Mommy's arms.

CHAPTER EIGHTEEN

Clarence found his jacket and stretched one arm into a sleeve. Then stopped.

He couldn't wear this. They would know.

He shrugged it off and hung it back in his closet. Anyway, it covered up those pipes. His hat had to stay, too.

Slowly he closed the squeaky closet door. The morning had dragged between breakfast, bingo and baking—or, cookie sample time.

He checked his watch. Meds, check. Lunch, done. He should have till supper.

He glanced at his bed. Pillows curved to simulate his body. He tucked in the bedspread to make the "legs" bend right. Jingled coins in his pocket.

Out of habit, he patted his back pocket. Grrr. Where was that wallet? It had ... money yes, but also his only picture of her in this world.

He walked to the window looking out on his escape route. His fingers lightly skimmed over the pipes he'd hung there. Nice wind chime. Deep sigh. Sixty years in a cell produced crazy habits.

Clarence moved to the open door and listened for movement, then stepped into the hallway. Prison Break 101: one skill he hadn't learned as an inmate in that other prison.

He lifted his head. Stuck out his chest.

No. Head down. Hands in pockets. Sour look on face—well that part wasn't hard. Shuffle feet.

"Hi, Clarence." A cheerful voice stopped him.

He looked up. The dietician.

"Uh ... hi." Head back down. Shuffle. Shuffle. Hand out of pocket to wipe his cheek. That'd get her. Deep sigh.

Shuffle on past.

"Hey, Clarence. You gonna come into the activity room? Baking pies this afternoon."

"Naw. Gonna move around a bit, then take a nap." That'd fit perfectly with the bed arrangement—all those plumped up pillows. He should have been a criminal. No wait. He was one. He had studied with the best of them.

Besides, he had never baked in his life. Even cooked for that matter. Mess call. Line up. March to the mess room. Stand in line to pick up food tray. Place tray on table. Stand behind chair until released. Sit. Eat. That was it for his cooking experience.

He reached the end of the hallway. He looked out the window. Sad, sad.

About face.

Shuffle. Shuffle. Shuffle.

"Excuse me, please. Can you help me?" Mrs. Hatly held her hand out to him from her doorway.

Oh my. Her hair was disheveled, glasses askew.

Clarence quickly looked away.

Naked. Her hands shook as they gripped the walker.

He looked to his escape route—and back to Mrs. Hatly. Eyes cast down.

"Mrs. Hatly, you must be cold. Let me get your robe and," he searched her room, "warm you up."

A pink and white robe lay rumpled on the floor beside her bed. He snapped it up, gently wrapping it around her. He buttoned the top button and searched her face.

She looked up at him, and apparently something clicked.

No more confusion there.

"Was I?" She checked herself. "Was I ... " She grimaced and looked away.

"As a jailbird." He nodded. "But it's okay. Nobody saw."

A tiny tear slipped from under her glasses and dripped to her robe. "I was a teacher. High school physics. I had a mind."

Clarence reached to wipe her cheek, then caught himself and shoved his hand in his pocket.

"I do that sometimes." She shook her head. "I get confused and don't know where I am." She closed her eyes, her head bent low. "And ... well ... you know."

"It's okay, Mrs. Hatly. I didn't see a thing. I'm just glad you're back."

"You're a liar and a gentleman." She peered up at him over her glasses and offered a sweet smile.

He chuckled. "Well, you got the first part right." He looked behind him. "Hey, I'd better let you go. I'm on a mission."

"I know," she whispered. "Be safe."

Clarence stopped. He cocked his head. Then leaned forward and gave her a light peck on her cheek.

She gasped. Her fingers caressed the spot.

Clarence stumbled and backed away. "I'm sorry. I didn't mean to do that." He pushed his hands at her. "Sorry." He bumped into the doorway then rushed down the hall, peeking behind him.

She watched him from her door.

Smiling.

He made his way to the exit door. His hand rested on the door handle.

Looked both ways. Back to Mrs. Hatly, who stood where he left her, her hand still on her cheek, pink robe making her bloom, still faintly smiling.

Exit. Easy.

Oops. Carol.

Back inside.

Shuffle to other doorway. Head down.

Coast clear.

Open door.

Jailbreak.

CHAPTER NINETEEN

Bea bounced onto the sofa, picked up Dolly and hugged her tight. "You're such a good dolly," she whispered, kissing her. She smoothed the doll's hair, then began to undress it, carefully unbuttoned the tiny jacket and removed it, sleeve by sleeve. She unsnapped the onesie and checked the doll's diaper and groaned. "Oh, gross. You're poopy. Now I'll have to clean you a-l-l-l up."

Bea hesitated and looked into the doll's eyes. "That's okay, Dolly. It's okay. You can't help it." She snuggled the doll's face. Kiss. Kiss. Kiss. "You're just a baby. I'll take care of you."

"No new messages. Damn him." Mommy pounded the counter. "Why doesn't he call?" She smiled a little smile.

Bea hid her face in doll clothes.

"Whatcha doing, Baby Bea?" Mommy asked. She played with some papers on the counter and patted her shirt pocket. She walked to Bea and leaned over her.

Bea peeked up into Mommy's face.

Mommy was back. Real Mommy.

She turned her face away. "I'm playing," Bea said. She held Dolly up for Mommy to see. "Dolly's got dirty pants and I have to change her." She gathered up clothes and play wipes, then looked away. Her other hand brushed her sore cheek.

Mommy sat on the edge of the sofa. "Baby, I'm sorry about earlier." She wiped her eyes. "That wasn't me. That's not the way I treat you. I'm struggling with not smoking. It's really hard."

Bea looked up at Mommy's face.

"Okay. Drugs too. I really want a cigarette. Booze. Drugs.

Anything. Bad." Mommy rubbed her arm. "I've got to do this. For you. I've got to do it for you."

Bea took a deep breath. "No you don't, Mommy."

Mommy stiffened beside Bea. "What?"

"You don't do it for me, Mommy. Do it for," Bea pointed at Mommy's chest, "you, Mommy." She patted Dolly's back.

Mommy grasped Bea's finger with her own. She drew their hands to her mouth and kissed Bea's fingers. Then rubbed her face against Bea's hand.

"How did I get so lucky to have you for my little girl?" She stretched her hands wide. "If all the little girls in this big world were lined up, I'd always choose you."

Bea searched Mommy's face and then held out her arms.

Mommy pulled Bea onto her lap and tucked Bea's head under her chin. She always fit just right.

A deep breath filled Bea's chest, and she blew it out.

"I'm so sorry for the way I treated you Bea. Please forgive me."

"I forgive you, Mommy."

"Please say a little prayer for me to get over the cig ... all of it. It's harder than I ever knew. I think about them, dream about them. When I'm in the grocery store, I walk by them five times." She shook.

"I do pray for you Mommy. And I'll help you. When you want a cigarette, come to me and we can play dolls. Or read a book. We could go to the park." Her chest burst as ideas came to mind.

Mommy laughed. "Oh I get it. When I need a cigarette, you'll help me by letting me do something you want to do, right?"

Bea covered her mouth.

"Sounds good to me."

Bea gasped in a giggle. "Mean it, Mommy?"

"Well, for you. An-n-nd, for me, too. It'll be fun, if we make it fun." She tipped her head to the side. "Sounds like what my dad used to say, sort of. He always said that life was what you made of it. If you made it shi ... well, crappy, then it'd be crappy. But if you chose to make it good, then—"

Bea piped up. "Then it'll be good."

CHAPTER TWENTY

Clarence stumbled along the alley behind Hillcrest. He glanced behind him. Scanned the row of trees as best he could. They grew close together, almost hiding the houses on the other side.

Good cover. No one was tailing him, so far as he could tell. Good to get outside again. He suffocated in that place.

He scanned the sky. No wind. It was chilly, but the sun beamed through the tangle of branches and warmed his head and back. A good spring afternoon.

He checked his perimeters and straightened, on alert. With sixty years of being incarcerated, moving in and out of solitary, of frequent pat-downs and spread-eagle searches, and threats from other inmates, he had never relaxed. Never trusted. He barely breathed without permission.

Now, he breathed deeply of the fresh clean air. No stale nursing home air for him.

Birds twittered brightly. They called back and forth, answering each other.

Clarence listened to the different songs. "Even the birds have friends." He stumbled, arms outstretched.

"You'd walk better if you watched where you are going."

Clarence froze. He slowly u-turned in search of the voice, to see Harold sitting in his wheelchair, partially hidden by a tree. His beady eyes stared through the branches, the sun glinting off the always-present flag pin on his lapel.

"Weren't you ever a Boy Scout? They always taught you to walk without making a sound."

Clarence stomped toward Harold. "What are you doing out here? Did they send you to spy on me?" He gripped Harold's sleeve, wobbling the wheelchair. "Come on, did they?"

Harold grabbed hold. "No! I knew you'd be out here. I saw you the last time you ran away. You're not pulling anything over on me, Clarence." He grunted. "And honestly, you're not fooling anybody else, either. I've been following people all my life and you aren't the slickest escapee I've ever tracked."

Clarence squinted, then spit on the ground in front of Harold. "I don't care. You can't hurt me. You're in a wheelchair. By the time you get inside to tattle on me, I'm long gone."

"Oh yea, right. You'll get as far as the grocery store again, then get tired and turn around and come home. Or you'll get hungry and need supper. You ain't pullin' the wool over my eyes, buddy."

"Buddy." Clarence clinched his fists. "You call me buddy? Why, I ought to—"

"Ought to what, Clarence?" Harold's head jerked up. "Come on, buddy. Buddy, Buddy, Buddy. Lay it on me. You'll do what?" He straightened in his wheelchair, arms braced on the wheels.

"You shouldn't have come out here. You shouldn't have followed me." Clarence kicked the wheelchair, knocking it onto one wheel. "How're you gonna get back inside, huh?" He kicked it again, toppling it into a tree.

Harold struggled to regain balance. He pushed against the tree. "You don't scare me, Clarence." He righted the wheelchair, steadied it. "You can't do anything more to me than what's already been done."

"Oh, yeah? You're the one stuck out here. Did you bring your girlfriend with you? What's her name?" Clarence made a play of searching the trees. "I don't see her."

Harold coughed, his hand on his chest. "You're mean." He coughed again. "You must be really unhappy inside to be that cruel," he sputtered.

Clarence turned his back on Harold and mimicked him in a high, sing-songy voice. "You must be so unhappy to be that cruel." He growled as he kicked stones onto the road ahead of him. "Yeah, I'm mean. Been called that and worse all my life. Mean. Bad. Ugly. Murd—" He turned back to Harold and kicked rocks at him, one narrowly missing his head. "All my life, people hated me, kicked me when I was down." His eyes swam. "But I decided one day that no one would ever hurt me again. No one, you hear?"

He turned, fists at his side and stomped through the trees, then across the street into the park behind the community building. Litter from picnics long past gathered into mini mountains: gum and candy bar wrappers, dried leaves, cigarette butts. He kicked them all into the air. A wind current whipped the trash into a funnel twisting and slapping into Clarence. He covered his eyes until it died down. Damn leaves. Damn trash. Damn life!

From tree to tree he walked and hid, walked and hid, until he crossed the railroad tracks, finding his way out of the park.

Across the highway.

Then up the hill to the store.

He turned and searched his winding path. No one followed. The glint of the sun on a wheelchair was barely visible through the trees.

#

"Miss Carol? I need you in Clarence's room right away." Lisha's voice sounded agitated even over Carol's radio. "You're not gonna believe this."

"On my way." Carol dropped the chart onto the desk. What now? Those days he didn't come out of his room were easier than this. At least they knew where ...

Lisha met her in the hall, carrying ... pipes? An armload of old plumbing—different lengths and sizes. And a trail of rust and dirt.

"Lisha, what are you doing? Where'd you find those?" Carol caught one as it fell. "You been dumpster diving again?"

"No, silly. Guess."

"Pft. How would I know?"

Lisha's head bobbed up and down as she chopped the air with a pipe. "In the bottom of Clarence's closet. Along with the picture of Jesus. And he made his bed to look like he's in it."

Carol pushed the door into Clarence's room and Lisha followed.

Lisha pointed a pipe at the window. "What's wrong wit this man?"

Hanging from the top of the window were pipes and rods—all

kinds and sizes—rusted ones, shiny and polished ones, skinny ones. Connected with old shoelaces and cord.

Carol walked to the window and touched one. "Well, I'll be. Did he make wind chimes?"

Lisha tapped one, knocking it into another. "Thas not wind chimes, fer sure. Sounds like sh—" Lisha tapped one with her fingernail. "Nuthin."

"Maybe he doesn't want another hawk breaking in." Carol grasped a pipe in each hand as she faced the window. "Feels like I'm in a prison cell."

"Or ... I'm tryin here ... sun reflectors? What are they? Sun catchers?"

Carol turned to Lisha, exasperated. "With lead pipes?"

CHAPTER TWENTY-ONE

"My Dolly is so beautiful," Bea sang softly. She tickled Dolly's neck, kissed her on the forehead and picked up the brush, singing as she brushed the doll's hair. A car honked and she jumped, looked out at the street flying by, then back at her doll.

Her legs swung up and down with each stroke of the brush. Up and down went the brush. Up and down went her legs, like that dancer on the TV show. Singing as she brushed. Singing as she kicked. Up and down. Up and down. She could dance like that girl.

Mommy cussed and stomped on the brakes. Bea gripped the car seat and Dolly flew to the floor. The car started moving again as Bea jumped down and picked up the doll. She scrambled into her car seat, watching Mommy in the rearview mirror.

"Can't you see, you damn jerk?" Mommy slammed on the brakes again. Bea slid forward in her seat, dropping Dolly again.

Mommy's cell phone rang. "Grrr. Not now." She grabbed her purse and dug in it, eyes on her purse. "Where did all these cars come from?"

The car zigzagged.

Mommy cussed.

She found the phone. "Whatdya want? Oh, hi. How are you?" Her voice changed. This voice was sweet, like honey on Bea's peanut butter. Mommy slammed on the brakes. "I'm fine. It's so good to hear your voice."

A car honked, and Mommy turned the steering wheel fast.

Bea scooted herself back as the car jerked, sending her flat against the seat. For a split second, she glanced out the car window as the street whizzed by.

The old man. He saw her.

She saw his blue eyes. Something stirred inside. She leaned in her car seat as they passed, straining to keep him in sight.

"Well, let me see. I think so. Sure." Mommy looked back. "Bea, sit back."

Bea scooted back, then lifted off her seat and faced the rear of the car.

The man turned his head. He stopped walking and watched as they drove past.

"Bea Baby, you need to sit down or I'll have to buckle you in." Mommy always said that, but never buckled her in. "I mean it." To the phone. "I'm sure we can work out some sort of babysitter."

Bea looked behind her at the rearview mirror and saw a mean look on Mommy's face. With the way Mommy had been lately, she knew she'd better turn around. She sat down, holding Dolly by the hair.

The brush slid down to the floor.

"Ohhh," Bea said. She looked at Mommy's face in the mirror.

Mommy chattered into the phone.

Bea peeked down at the floor, then back up at Mommy. Mommy's face was set forward, eyes on the street ahead.

"What do you want to do?"

Floor.

Mommy.

Floor.

"Okay, that sounds fun. Party on!" She looked at the rearview mirror. "Hold on to your cookies, Bea." said Mommy.

The car swerved to the left, throwing her and Dolly right. The brush slid and bumped across the floor of the car and stopped against the other door.

She hung her head, staring at the brush. Back to Mommy. Down to the brush.

She slipped out of her seat, making each movement like a kitty on attack. Eyes on target. Feet stretched toward the floor. Stop. Toes touched the floor. Stop. Sliding shoes along the floor. Stop. Hold. Mommy glanced back and smiled, still on the phone.

Bea smiled back, straining to hold her place.

Hold it.

Hold it.

Mommy's eyes focused on the road ahead. "Well, I miss you, too."

Move. Scramble to the brush. Back to her seat. Climb up, knee in the seat. Slowly turn around and sit down.

Mommy glanced in the mirror. "We're almost to the park, Baby." She cocked her head to the side. "You okay? You're usually singing."

Bea nodded her head, hair bouncing with each bump. Eyes wide, looking ahead through the windshield.

Mommy's eyes fastened on the street again. "Okay. Well, I gotta go. See ya then." She threw the phone onto the passenger seat.

Whew.

"You're sure being quiet this afternoon." Mommy stretched to see all of Bea. "You sure you're okay? Is Dolly okay?"

Bea nodded her head, kicked her feet with each nod and held up Dolly so Mommy could see her. She smiled a sweet smile, then looked down at her dolly. Her hand gripped the doll's hair. Her fingers wrapped around the brush. She blew out a breath, glanced out the window and began brushing the doll's hair again.

Quick glance to Mommy in the mirror. Back down to the doll. Out the window again.

She remembered the old man's eyes as she smoothed Dolly's hair. Blue eyes. And long, wavy gray hair.

"My Dolly is so beautiful," she sang again, swinging her feet, kicking the back of the driver's seat. "My Dolly is so sweet."

Mommy chimed in. "My Bea is so beautiful. She is so sweet. But quit kicking my seat."

Bea laughed and sang along until Mommy's phone rang again.

CHAPTER TWENTY-TWO

Clarence climbed up the hill into the grocery store parking lot. He shouldn't be here. They'd turn him in one of these times.

But not this afternoon ... he hoped.

He peeked between the tattered fliers taped to the inside then checked the side parking lot to see who was working. Mindy's ancient Chevy sat there sporting a pink stripe across the door. The beat up Toyota pickup was John's.

Smiling, Clarence crossed his arms across his chest. After all, what was the worst they could do? Send him back to prison? Not a problem.

He pulled on the door handle and peeked in.

"Boom! Boom!"

Clarence jumped back out. The door closed in his face. He searched the interior of the store through the glass. John stood peeking around the nearest aisle end cap, grinning, brandishing an invisible gun.

Clarence shook his head. Jerk! The kid should be in a mental hospital. He turned to walk away, but Mindy pushed the other door open from the inside.

"Don't let John get to you, Clarence. He's a bug. He's harmless. He doesn't even hurt small children. So he won't hurt you." She stuck out her tongue at John. "I'll make sure of that." She held out her hand. "Come on in. Boss Lady isn't even here, so you're safe."

Clarence hesitated then entered the store. "I'm not afraid of him. I'm afraid of what I will do to him, given half a chance."

John guffawed and walked from behind the shelves. "Oh you

would hurt me?" He posed, fists up, feet in a fighter's stance, beckoning with one finger. "Bring it on, Dude."

Clarence busted out laughing. "Okay—Dude." Fists up, he pranced back and forth. His mind blinked to a few sparring lessons in prison. "I may be eighty, but I can handle you. I've done a little fighting in my day." He threw a right jab into John's face but missed.

"Ha! You can't reach me. You're too short." He started to punch Clarence, but Mindy stepped between them and pushed John away.

John stretched his long arms around her and punched at Clarence, grazing Clarence's cheek.

"Stop. You have to respect your elders, John."

"Yeah, John. Respect your elders." Clarence punched John hard in the shoulder. "I haven't lost my touch. I used to win some trophies in my day."

Another memory blinked in—the trophy of a black eye.

"Ouch! Respect? For the way he talks to you? Why are you being so nice to him, anyways?" John took another swing, his jaw jutted. "He's been nothing but mean to you and you know it."

Mindy ducked John's right hook. "I know, but it says we're supposed to turn the other cheek, if I remember right." She looked at Clarence. "Doesn't it?"

Clarence turned his other cheek.

John reached around Mindy and slugged Clarence in the jaw.

Clarence staggered back. "Ow." He held his cheek then lunged at John but hit Mindy instead.

Mindy stumbled, blinking.

"Mindy, you okay?" John grabbed her shoulders and peered into her eyes.

She stuttered—stunned for a minute. "Uh ... yeah. I'm fine. I have brothers, remember?" She faced Clarence, rubbing her cheek. "You hit me!"

"Look at him." John shielded Mindy with his body, leaving plenty of her visible on either side of him, and pointed at Clarence. "He doesn't respect you. Besides, if you turn the other cheek with him he'll spit on that one too. Don't open yourself up to him. He'll just bite you in the butt."

Clarence stopped and cleared his throat, fists still in the air. "First of all, I would never bite a woman in the butt. It's just not sanitary."

Mindy opened her eyes wide, took one look at John and burst out laughing.

"And secondly, I've been sued more times than I can count and I always win. Put that in your pipe or bong or whatever you use, and smoke it."

"Your what?" John said.

Mindy stopped and turned to Clarence. "Wait a minute. What did you do in your life? I mean, what was your job?"

Clarence looked at her, then at John. "Never mind. None of your damn business. You wouldn't care anyway." He shifted his weight and noticed the display of candy bars behind John. "Toss me one of those candy bars and I'll be on my way exploring this inspiring burg of a town. I won't bother you two again."

John reached in, pulled out a large candy bar and flung it at Clarence. "Might as well get him for all he's got. Ring it up, Mindy."

"John, you have no respect. You need—"

"It's okay, Mindy. I'm used to that kind of treatment." Clarence shoved his hand in his pocket. "Doesn't bother me anymore, if it ever did. He's just like one of the peons that I used to put in prison."

Mindy raised her eyebrows.

John took a step toward Clarence.

"John. Down. Settle."

John didn't seem to hear. He pushed toward Clarence, bumping into Mindy. Hands in fists, eyes squinting, lips pursed.

"Not again." Clarence rubbed his cheek.

"John you can't do that, he's elderly." She looked over at Clarence. "Sorry Clarence, but you ... are. Kinda."

Clarence smirked at John, threw two dollars onto the check stand and pushed out the door. "Thank you for your hospitality, Mindy, John. It's been a real interesting experience. Have a terrible day. Both of you."

Footsteps thudded behind Clarence. He turned in time to see Mindy rush John.

John reached out to punch Clarence but hit her instead.

"Ow. Ow." She shoved him back. "Again?"

"Mindy! Why did you do that?" His voice cracked. "Are you okay?"

"I'm fine." She rubbed her cheek.

Clarence popped his head back in. "Good thing your girlfriend is hefty. She can keep you in line better."

"You Muther @#$%^*%!" John came at him, hands raised, Mindy right behind him. "I oughta punch your lights out, old man. Show you what a real man is made of."

Clarence stood outside the door, hands against the glass, one finger beckoning, then walked away. He tore open the candy bar and threw the wrapper onto the concrete.

John pounded on the door. His cussing filtered through the glass.

Clarence smiled, relishing what he'd stirred up. Mmmm. Candy bar—good. Battle with John—score.

He rubbed his jaw as he walked up the hill. Kid has a mean punch.

A demolition zone ahead, surrounded by yellow barricade tape, drew him.

He shoved the last bit of candy in his mouth, brushing his hands together.

The yellow tape stopped him and he scanned the site. The insides of adjoining walls were visible; old wallpaper peeled from crumbling plaster. There were holes in the walls where demolition equipment had cut in. Downstairs, the walls still displayed a variety of wallpaper and paint in blues, greens, browns and roses, each telling layers of history. A pile of dirt remained in the middle. No floor, just dirt. The far wall was totally gone, revealing bricks from the adjacent building.

Clarence scanned the whole site—walls, bricks, dirt. What used to be here? He jingled coins in his pockets. His fingers caught on the tiny dime-store ring in his pocket, and his heart stopped. He staggered a step back from the tape, gasping and coughing. His other hand pounded his chest.

"The bank. Oh my God. The First National Bank of Osceola." He gasped again and sucked in a deep breath, hand on his chest.

The building grew before him out of the debris to stand in its former grandeur. New rose-brown bricks. The entrance opened on the diagonal of the front corner with a beautiful overhead portico, columns and entrance lights. Windows beside the entrance framed the loan department. He remembered it well. He and Dad always made appointments there, to ask or beg for a loan to keep the wood-working business going. It was a big bank, had three teller windows. Rich striped wallpaper covered the walls, creating a backdrop for the modern lighting.

He remembered the woodwork especially. He and his dad had handcrafted it all. Measured, sawed, pieced, hammered, sanded. When they were done, it was more than functional. It was beautiful. His dad had fabricated corner pieces and trim, making useful and beautiful additions, all because it was his passion to give more.

That was Dad.

Clarence pictured his dad leaning over a section of board, sanding back and forth. He would stop to examine it with his fingers, testing to see if it was glass-smooth, as Dad used to say. He'd blow the sawdust away then begin again. He never tired of making a piece as beautiful as he possibly could. Dad had fit the pieces together in this bank—a giant jigsaw puzzle of offices, paneling, teller booths. Stained each piece to perfection, rubbed the finish to a smooth glossy sheen.

He toyed with the coins in his pockets, fingers coming to rest on the tiny ring, exploring it. He withdrew it from his pocket and flipped it over and over. Cheap little thing. Probably some little girl's heartthrob gave it to her as a grade school promise. The band had tarnished. The rhinestone was loose, ready to fall out.

He let it drop to the ground without thinking and reverted again, back in time, to that moment when another ring had fallen to the ground.

He looked up at the bank building to see Sally, his fiancé, screaming at him from the top step. Her lips moved, her forehead appeared damp, her face beet red. Anger revealed her true character, hidden under surface beauty. Natural curls circled her head, mocking him as she shook, stomping her foot on the step.

The words trailed across time, once again. "You slime. I never want to see you again. I can kiss who I want to kiss. You were never good enough for me." And the bomb that blew the depths of his heart. "I never loved you anyway."

Clarence remembered looking down at the ground as he did now, only back then, the beautiful diamond had sparkled in betrayal, mocking him.

He bent down, picked up the dime-store ring and examined it in the bright sunlight.

He glanced around to see if anyone watched him.

No one.

But who had witnessed the scene on that day long ago?

The whole town.

He looked over the building in his memory, shaking his head. What had been a monument to his dad's fine workmanship was now Clarence's empty tomb of tortured pain.

Until he remembered one more thing.

He had started to turn away from the bank that day, but not before he glimpsed a different young woman—her sympathetic eyes gazing at him from a back window. He still felt the tug on his heart.

He had tossed the diamond up in the air and caught it, to the tune of Sally still screaming obscenities and stomping her foot. The farther he walked away, the lighter he felt.

Oh Annie ...

CHAPTER TWENTY-THREE

Carol closed the chart. "I wish I had family to call." She glanced around the conference table at the staff members taking notes on her shift report. "Someone who cares—"

"I wish I had someone to call, too. I'd give 'em a piece of my mind." Lisha built up steam and let it power her words. "That Clarence is a pain in the a—"

"Enough, Lisha." Carol slapped her hand on the table. "We don't talk like that here. You took an oath when you completed the classes. No foul language. And more than that, you agreed to care for these residents, to honor them, and to support them."

"I didn't agree to get bossed around and cussed out to my face." Her jowls bounced as she shook her face back and forth. "I didn't agree to that." She folded her arms across her ample chest. "What's it say in the Bi-i-i-ble? Do unto others as they do to you."

Carol laughed out loud. "That is not what it says and you know it. You are twisting the Word of God. He'll getcha for that."

"Whatever. That man is mean to the core. He has no respect for anybody or anything. I'll be nice to him to save my job, but that's it. Otherwise, iss on."

Miss Henningway burst into the room, a photo in her hand. She shoved it in front of Carol. "This has to go. Today!"

Carol took the picture from her. "Clarence? Clarence has to go?"

"All right!" Lisha nodded.

Miss Henningway shook her head and grabbed the picture back. "No! His hair. His hair has to go." She straightened. "Today."

"But—"

"It looks awful. It's greasy. He probably has head lice. It has to go." The color on her neck and face changed from fake tan to red blush; her earrings quivered from some indiscernible vibration. "So inform his nurse that she must send him to the barber—today."

"Well, he needs to be consulted—"

"No! It has to be done! Today!" She tapped her shoes together and left the room, the picture floating to the table. Her heels thudded down the carpeted hall.

Carol picked it up.

"He's not gonna like—"

"He's gonna be so pissed. Glad you're his nurse, Lisha."

Carol hesitated. She examined the picture. "All right." Carol stared at her notes, shaking her head and biting her lips. "I just want you all to know," she said, choosing her words carefully. She scanned each face at the conference table, checking the open door. "When you are under my watch, you will be respectful, helpful, loving, and honorable to each and every resident. Is that clear?"

Quiet.

"Is that clear?" Carol repeated louder, her head bobbing forward with each word.

Staff eyed each other. Heads nodded.

Carol met eyes with Lisha, who was not budging an inch.

Carol's voice softened but rose in authority and firmness. "Is that clear?"

Lisha stared back.

Carol held her ground. Didn't move a muscle. Never broke eye contact.

Lisha squirmed. "Okay. I give. But only because of you. He is a mean man. I've had too many of those kind in my life. Lording over me and crushing what I want, who I am." A breath caught in her throat and she glanced around the table. "I'll do it for you. Because I respect you, Miss Carol." Her eyes diverted to the door Miss Henningway had exited through and back to Carol. "Only for you." She leaned back.

Carol still held her ground, but she gave Lisha a nod. "Thank you. I appreciate that you respect me. I also challenge you to give others respect no matter what you get in return. Maybe you can't do that right away. But day by day, I want you to become that kind of person, because you are that kind of woman."

Lisha sighed and mimicked. "Day by day."

Carol patted her notes and charts. "Are we all good?" She paused. "The elderly have been through so much and given so much. We can learn from their wisdom. They still have a lot to give and it's up to us to make their last years blessed."

"All Clarence gives out is—"

"Lisha."

Lisha stopped and bowed her head.

"Okay. Let's get at it. Does everyone understand Mrs. Gelt's new treatment and how to ambulate her?"

Heads nodded, including Lisha's.

Carol rose and pushed in her chair. "Any questions? Revisions?" Carol headed for the door.

Behind her, Lisha's voice: "Well, maybe."

Carol stopped at the door and looked over her shoulder. "Yes?"

Lisha stood. All heads turned toward her. She cleared her throat. "You're a nice lady, Miss Carol, don't get me wrong, or nuthin'. But, uh, you haven't had a hard life like some of us here. You jes don't understand how hard it is."

Carol pursed her lips and stared back. Just last night she had held Joe's hand and prayed for God to take him. So he wouldn't suffer anymore, but also that she would be free from this burden. "You have no idea, do you?" she snapped. "You only think about yourself and your life. You don't stop to think ... "

Silence.

She scanned the room before her. Each one looked down, fidgeted, held her breath, pretended to read her notes.

Carol turned and left the room.

CHAPTER TWENTY-FOUR

Clarence half waved at the little girl, as the car sped past.

She stretched around to see him.

She remembered him. He shoved his hands into his pockets, jingled his change and kicked at rocks in the street.

He'd remember her anywhere. He glanced behind him at the car. A picture flashed into his mind of the kid in McDonald's on that terrible day.

Jingle. Jingle.

Heedless of cracks in the concrete, he plodded along the sidewalk, squeezing each fingertip and the thumb of the tiny glove in his pocket, memorizing the itchiness of the wool.

Until he bumped into a rebar stake driven into the ground.

He backed away and pivoted to get his bearings. Rubbed his jaw. Ow. That John had a strong right punch.

What building once stood here?

He couldn't think. It'd been too long.

He pointed next door. "That used to be ... and next to that was ... "

He counted back down the street and shook his head. Dress shop—Mrs. Gordon. New facade, new windows, but still the same old building. He just ... couldn't remember the next one. Shaking his head, he stepped along. Each building held stories from his past, just with the last sixty years layered in.

One brick building stirred memories of the day Dad bought Clarence his own gun. A real gun. That was the day he put all the toy guns away. Blanky, the train set that played "They'll be Comin'

Round the Mountain," and dump trucks were all stored away. The only toys he'd kept out were a teddy bear his mother made and the toy carpenter set.

He rotated toward a newer building, the hardware store, where Dad sent him on a regular basis. He stepped to the glass and cupped his hands around his eyes, peering inside.

A haze parted, and he was inside the old hardware store, as a boy. He reached into the nail bins lined up against the counter and gathered the cold nails in his hand—cold, even in summer. They clinked, as one by one, they slid from his hand into the bin.

Tools appeared in rows along one wall. Hammers, screwdrivers, lathes, saws, levels. He slid his hand over the new wood in the handles and saws. The smell of new wood, new tools, always made his skin tingle. He ran his finger along a saw blade. His father reprimanded him, telling him he would cut himself. He always cut his fingers. Always.

Deep sigh.

The past began to clear. Inside the building a man stood scowling. The man's mouth moved. He pointed to a woman sitting at a desk.

Clarence couldn't pull away from his memories, every screw, each piece of hardware. He was only aware of himself and his dad, moseying through the old hardware store, examining everything.

"Oh, I miss those days," he whispered and gulped. "I miss my dad. Wish I could see him again."

"Hey mister."

Clarence jumped away from the window. "What the—"

"Mister, move along. You can't just stand out here, spying through my windows. You're loitering. You're supposed to come in and spend your money. If you're not gonna do that, then buzz off." The man waved him on.

"Says who? Who do you think you are?" Clarence squinted at the man. Tan skin—he was a player—either on a golf course or on a boat. Short blond hair and by the looks of him, it should be gray.

"I'm Pete Malovitch, that's who. And this is my business. My building." Pete's hands circled his hips, chin jutted out. "Quit peeking in people's windows, old man."

Clarence looked into the store, seeing the actual inside this time. A desk and a counter. Signs on the wall advertised insurance deals. Books lined shelves along one wall. A young woman smiled from behind the desk, earpiece wrapping itself around her jaw. She moved her lips, tapped on a computer, and waved at him, all at the same time.

Clarence started to wave then caught himself, his hand dangled at his side. Anybody working with this guy was of the devil.

He shook his head, let it fall to his chest and shuffled on.

Pete. Pete Malovitch, selling gambling, er insurance policies where that wonderful hardware store used to stand.

Criminal.

CHAPTER TWENTY-FIVE

Bea held out her hand to Mommy and jumped out of the car. Mommy grabbed her and twirled her around and around. Bea squealed and giggled as trees spun in circles, sun sparkled through branches, leaves danced.

When Mommy released her, Bea walked away in dizzy drunken footsteps, still giggling, arms outstretched. She stopped and turned to Mommy. "Mommy, Dolly wants to come with. She loves the slide."

"No, Bea. Dolly has to stay in the car. When you get tired, you always shove her off on me. Got it?"

Bea stopped and looked into Mommy's face. "Are you okay, Mommy? Do we need to talk? Play dolls?"

Mommy looked angry. "Why do you think we're at the park? I am slipping. I want a puff. Just one puff of a cigarette." She clasped her hands together behind Bea's head and pulled her close, then whispered, "Or something else."

Bea's heart lurched, but she let herself be pulled in.

Mommy began to tickle, making her giggle. Every time she tickled in her tummy, her armpits, Bea tried to hold back, until she laughed out loud.

"Mommy, stop."

Mommy didn't stop but kept on tickling, pinching Bea.

"Ow, Mommy, stop. You're hurting me."

Scary mommy was back.

"Mommy. That hurts." Bea tried to push Mommy away, but Mommy was strong and Bea was not. "Help me Mommy."

Mommy didn't stop. Bea pushed at Mommy's hands, her fingers.

She pinched at Mommy to make her quit, but couldn't find a hold. She fell to the grass and kicked for all a four year old was worth.

Bea cried. "Mommy. Mommy."

Big hands grabbed Bea from the ground and snatched her away. Bea looked up into the old man's blue eyes and threw her arms around his neck, sobbing. She huddled into his chest. The gray whiskers on his face scratched her tender skin, but she didn't care.

He spoke softly. "Hey. Hey. You're holding on so tight, I can hardly breathe. It's okay now, Little One. You can relax. I won't let her hurt you." He pulled her arms from around his shoulders. "See, she's walking away. It's okay. She's not hurting you anymore."

Bea's shoulders shook with each hiccup, as she watched Mommy. "Mommy." The man set her down. She escaped from his arms and ran, crying.

Mommy fell to the ground, sobbing, just as Bea reached her.

"Bea Baby. I need help. I can't do this alone anymore. I hurt you." She uncovered her eyes and searched Bea's arms, her legs. She pointed. "See? I hurt you. I scratched you. Oh, God, you're even bleeding." She erupted into sobs. Her hands covered her eyes.

"Mommy. It's okay. I'm okay. It doesn't hurt anymore. See?" She wiped at the blood, but only succeeded in rubbing it around and making a mess on her shirt. Her lower lip quivered.

Gentle hands lifted her again.

The blue-eyed old man sat on a park bench and snuggled Bea onto his lap. He wasn't scary at all. He snuggled Bea, her head tucked under his chin.

He smoothed her hair with his fingers. "Shhh, Little One. Shhh. It's okay now. It's okay."

Bea relaxed, catching a whiff of something like Mommy's perfume, only cleaner, like outside smelled sometimes. His whiskers caught her hair. His warmth made her feel better, drowsy.

Mommy pushed herself off the ground, brushing leaves and dirt from her jeans. "I'm an awful Mom. I hurt my own child." She looked up into the man's eyes. "I need help. I can't do this alone."

Bea put her hands on either side of the man's scratchy cheeks and turned his face toward hers. "Mommy doesn't smoke anymore. She threw her cigarettes out the window yesterday. She is a good Mommy, isn't she? She loves me." Bea burst into tears. "She's a good mommy, isn't she?" The last words broke into a wail.

The man patted her head and rocked side to side. "Yes. She is a good mommy because she threw her cigarettes away. She just needs some ... someone to help her through the rough spots. That's all." He rubbed Bea's cheek with his thumb. "She's a good mommy, Little One."

Bea nodded and slumped against his chest, patting his arm. She coughed and closed her eyes, curving into him.

#

Clarence continued to comb through the little girl's fine curly hair, kissing the top of her head. He closed his eyes. His arms were full, his heart full. Was this what it was like to have his own ... ?

As she relaxed against him, he focused on the young woman. "Um ... do you ... do you have anyone around here to help you?"

The young woman opened her eyes. "Who me? I don't need help. I'm fine." She glared at him, stumbled, reached out her hand to steady herself against the bench.

"You're full of shit and you know it." Clarence hesitated as he stroked the child's hair. "You hurt your daughter. She is precious. And you can't pull the wool over my eyes. I have dealt with every kind of evil there is." He covered Bea's free ear. "What if I hadn't come along when I did. Would you have stopped?"

She arched her back, her eyes snapped. "Yes. I wouldn't hurt my own child."

Clarence smoothed the girl's hair from his stubble, pushed her sleeve up revealing bloody scratches and gave the woman a stern eye until she turned away.

The little girl watched her mother walk away, but stiffened when she pivoted back to them.

Tears filled the woman's mascara-smudged eyes. "Oh, God. Oh, God." She slumped onto the bench beside Clarence. "I don't have anybody. No one. It's just her and me." She hugged herself. "I don't know what to do." She shivered. "Sometimes I become someone else. I go from me to ... that other mommy and she is mean. She is ... violent." She gasped. "I'm afraid of her too."

Clarence didn't soften his tone, just his volume. "Will you let me help you?" He looked down at the child. "And her?" He hugged the little girl into his chest. "Before you hurt her permanently?"

The woman started. Her eyes squinted. "Who are you and why would you want to help us?"

Why indeed? "I asked you a question first. Will you let me help you and her? I can find people to help."

"Why? What's in it for you? What are you going to get out of it?" She jerked her head close to his. "Are you a cop? Who put you up to this? Huh?"

Clarence didn't flinch, but gazed into her eyes, then looked down at the child. "Nobody puts me up to anything. I was a lawyer in my day and a damn good one."

The woman lurched upright, as if someone had pulled on her marionette strings. "A lawyer? We don't need a lawyer. I can't pay a lawyer." She jumped up and grabbed at the girl's arm. "Come on Bea. Let's go home."

Bea. Her name was Bea.

Bea clung to Clarence's neck. Tears stung his eyes as he embraced her even harder.

The woman stopped and searched Bea's face. "Bea, I'm your Mommy. We have to go. There are things—"

"No Mommy. He can help us. He can. I know he can." She locked her fingers behind Clarence's neck.

"But ... " The woman stomped away, hands clenched, head down. She kicked at rocks on the pathway then slumped.

Clarence patted the bench beside him.

She walked back to them, stared into Clarence's eyes for a moment. She held out her hand. "I'm Katty."

"Clarence." He shook hers.

Bea relaxed.

"What if ... if I—"

Clarence shook his head. "One step at a time. We'll take this one day at a time."

A glint of hope registered in Katty's eyes. Fear, too.

He knew the feeling.

Katty crouched in front of them. "Honey. Baby Bea." She glanced away, fidgeting with Bea's shoelaces. Clearing her throat, she directed her gaze to Bea. "I haven't been a very nice Mommy today."

She swallowed, shivered. "Not a nice Mommy for a long time." She retied Bea's shoelaces. A tear dropped onto one. "Bea, Mommy did some things that if we let this man help us, I could go to jail." She glanced up at Clarence. "I should go to jail. It's more than the cigarettes, Baby Bea. Much more."

For the first time, he sensed purpose for his life.

A reason to live.

CHAPTER TWENTY-SIX

Mindy leaned over, slid the metal trash container out of the check-out stand and gathered the corners of the trash bag. She shook the trash together and pulled the bag out of the can. It stuck. She yanked again. She pulled harder just as a hand slipped around her chubby waist.

"What are you doing, Mindy?" John's voice was so deep.

She jumped. Her head bumped up and met with a bony chin. Hard. "Ouch. Dude."

The bag tore and spilled smelly contents all over the floor. Moldy, runny tomatoes. Black bananas. Cigarette butts. Wet store ads.

"Oh man. Look what you made me do now." She reached up to smack John's cheek, just as he grabbed her hand and kissed the back of it.

"Not here."

"You say that no matter where we are. Can we anywhere?"

Mindy laughed and hugged his waist. "You are so funny." She pointed to the security cameras. "She can see us, you know. We're gonna hear about this." She pulled a new trash bag out of the box. "Look at this mess. Stinky stinky."

"I'll help. I made you do it."

She pointed at the camera again and raised her voice. "Did you hear that? Darn right, he made me do it."

A voice blared over the intercom. "Devil made ya do it! I saw it all!"

Mindy poked John. "See?"

"Grrr!" He bent to hold the bag while Mindy tossed the garbage in.

"Hey, look," she said. "A wallet. How did it get in there?" She wiped her hands on her apron, retrieved it from the mess and opened it up. "Huh. No credit cards." She looked at John. "Who doesn't have credit cards today? No driver's license. Here's an ID ... kinda strange. And ... no mo-ney." She picked through it and straightened. "Wait. Under this flap. Lots of mo-ney. Whoever owns this is rich."

John leaned over her shoulder and counted as she flitted through it. "One million, two million—"

"Stop." She slapped it closed. "But there is a lot in there." She looked up at John, eyes wide, braces flashing. "If you hadn't tried to kiss me, and I hadn't of jumped and torn the bag, we wouldn't have found this wallet in the trash. Amazing."

"Yeah, so, can we try it again?" He moved closer, his lips puckered. "The kiss thing, I mean. See what else happens."

Mindy laughed and shoved him out of the way. "I've gotta get this to Boss Lady." She glanced at the camera. "I mean, Mrs. Larkin. Sorry. I'll be coming right there to give this to you." She waved the wallet at the camera.

The entrance door buzzed, and in walked Clarence.

"Hi Clarence. Back again? You're looking chipper. It's been a great day outside, isn't it?"

"How would you know?"

Mindy smiled. "Well, I drove to work with my window down. That's how I know. It's beautiful out."

"What would you know about beautiful? You are fat and have braces and pimples."

Just like Grandpa. Mean.

John stepped in front of her, fists up. "You ready to get beat up again?"

"It's okay, John. Sticks and stones, remember? Although that was extremely harsh." She slipped in front of John and took a deep breath. "What can we help you with, Clarence? Another candy bar? The food probably isn't that great at Hillcrest, is it?"

Clarence stood still for a long time and stared at Mindy, rubbing his jaw.

Oh-oh. "I ... is something wrong, Clarence?"

His blue eyes were set deep. For being old, his skin didn't look very wrinkled.

"Why are you so nice to me?" He combed his fingers through his hair. "When I am so mean to you."

Oh that. "You're trying to be nice right now, aren't you? It's just as easy to be nice to people as it is to be mean."

Clarence kept staring at her. "That's the stupidest thing I've ever heard. And I've heard every remark and every excuse."

"Oh, have you, Clarence." Mrs. Larkin walked up behind him. "Does the nursing home know where you are? Or should I let them know?"

He shook his head. "No, you shouldn't let them know, because they know where I am. So there. And yes, I've heard it all."

"Well, then, I bet you've heard this one, too. Go home. Go back to the nursing home and stay there. You cause trouble and hurt feelings here." Hands on her hips. "Go home."

"Mrs. Larkin, um, he wanted to buy a candy bar. Didn't you, Clarence?" Mindy walked to the candy end cap. "What kind? Baby Ruth? Snickers? We've got 'em all."

Clarence walked up beside her and checked out the assortment. He picked one up. "What's this one?"

"Twix."

"That's the one on TV. On the commercials." He dropped it back into the box. "I don't want it. I used to really like ... I don't see it. What kind do you like, Fatty?"

Her reflection in the metal sign spoke the truth and she hugged her middle. "Well, I like 'em all, but I really like Baby Ruth, Gramps."

He glared at her. "Don't you call me that."

John piped up. "Then don't call her ... uh ..."

"Fatty?" He turned from John to Mindy. "I can call you Fatty, can't I?"

Mindy leaned into Clarence's face. "Sure. If I can call you Gramps, Gramps."

Clarence's face turned red. His nostrils flared.

"Caught at your own tricks, huh Clarence." John stuffed his hands in his apron pockets and rocked on his heels.

"You'd better be nice to these kids, Clarence." Mrs. Larkin pointed to Mindy and John and held out her hand. "The wallet, please."

Mindy dropped it into her hand.

Clarence leaned toward Mrs. Larkin and tried to swipe it.

She turned away and opened it, exposing the money. She flipped through it and checked the ID and frowned. She looked at the document, then at Clarence.

Quiet.

"I guess this is yours." She thumbed through the money. "No one here touched your cash. No one stole from you. And you have your wallet back. I want it said about us at Olde Towne Store that we are honest and upstanding. You owe John and Mindy a big thank you for finding this. You hear me?"

He held out his hand and she slapped the wallet onto his palm.

"Don't you ever insult Mindy and John, again. They are the good kids."

Mindy wanted to burst. Nobody had ever said that about her before. Not Dad. Never Gramps. And never Mrs. Larkin. Everybody always called her white trash.

"Well, if they are the good ones, I gotta see the bad ones."

Mrs. Larkin's head popped up. "I ought to call the cops on you. As a matter of fact, I—"

Mindy rested a hand on Mrs. Larkin's arm. "Please don't. He's just an angry old man. Just like my Grandpa."

Clarence was already out the door, but his last words found their way inside. "You bet, I'm angry. I got my wallet back, but my whole life's been stolen from me."

CHAPTER TWENTY-SEVEN

Still parked near the playground, Katty pounded the steering wheel and pressed her fingers to her eyes. "Oh God. Oh God. Oh God!" Hands clammy, she cringed, gasping. "He knows. Someone knows."

"Mommy?"

"Not now, Bea." She shivered.

"You cold, Mommy?"

"Bea!"

Kick. Kick.

"Bea. Stop kicking the back of my seat!" She whipped around, swinging her hand toward Bea.

Bea's eyes widened. Her sweet demeanor changed into a terrified, vulnerable child. She ducked.

For the first time, Katty saw the change before she hit. She stared at Bea, terrified herself. Horrified of who she had become. Scared of what she might do.

Time slowed. Light specks floated and sparked between Katty and Bea—flowed back and forth. Mesmerizing.

The terror softened on Bea's face.

Bea seemed transfixed too. The light specks became elongated and wrapped around her. She held her hands out, and whatever it was, touched her hands in such a real way that Bea's hands moved—clapped. The expression on Bea's face was not fear but awe.

"Patty-cake." Bea kicked. Her hands moved again. "Patty-cake, Mommy. Patty-cake." She giggled and kicked. Her eyes followed the light flashes.

Katty wiped her wet cheeks and stared into Bea's brown eyes as Bea stared back.

Bea jumped when her hands moved again. One shot way up above her head and jerked back. It jerked again. Bea laughed. "High-five." She kicked Katty's seat.

Spellbound, Katty ignored the kicking. She held her breath as Bea laughed again, so melodic, like a wren on a spring morning.

The light disappeared as quickly as it had appeared. Katty searched the interior of the car but everything appeared normal. Whatever it had been, it was gone.

Deep sigh.

Was it a flashback from drugs?

Bea looked at Katty and started to say something but closed her mouth.

"What, Bea?"

"What was that, Mommy?"

Not a flashback. Bea saw it too. Bea played with it. "I don't know, Honey, but I feel so good right now. So peaceful." A tear rolled down her cheek, her fist at her chest. "Somehow, everything's gonna be okay. I don't know how or when, but I just know."

CHAPTER TWENTY-EIGHT

Carol kicked at a piece of rock strayed from the rose bed in front of Hillcrest as Sheriff Dennison radioed the dispatcher. She had hated calling the police about Clarence's disappearance, but now he'd missed supper too. She couldn't let him think he could leave any time without checking out. If she let him get away with it once, he'd do it again and again.

She crossed her arms across her chest and paced, glancing at the sun slicing lower in the sky. The birds had begun evening twitterings and lullabies.

Clarence had no family to call.

No one to reinforce the dangers.

No one to back her up.

No one to care whether he lived or died.

Sheriff Dennison replaced the radio and faced her. He raked his fingers through his already tousled sandy hair. No pot belly on him.

But those dark eyelashes.

"Well, they spotted him at the grocery store down on Central Street. He was fine—ornery, but fine. Not involved in the hit-and-run."

Relieved, she shrugged. "He seems like he doesn't care, but there is something deeper about him. I haven't quite figured him out yet."

"You care too much. He's just an old man that doesn't want to be here. They're all that way at first, right?"

Carol nodded. "Some." She nodded again and bit her lips. "Most."

"Hey, don't take it so hard. I'm sure he's all right. The grocery store manager said he was, anyway." Sheriff Dennison chuckled. "In fact, she said he was pretty stalwart, I think was the word. Or, maybe she said stubborn. I'm not sure."

Carol smiled. "Okay. Well, keep in touch. I'm sure he'll come back. I hate calling you, but with him, his physical status is so good, he could go to the next county and back. Or ... not back."

He nodded. "Maybe he will. More power to him."

Carol raised an eyebrow. "You, sir, don't have to answer to the state or the home office about why one of your residents has run away."

He shrugged. "Tell them he's a community mediator between the nursing home and the town." He grinned. "Besides, it happens from time to time. And I'm sure you're not the only facility to go through this." He raised his eyebrows. "Right?"

Carol nodded and turned to go inside. She looked over her shoulder. "Thanks, Denny. Thanks for caring."

He saluted. "Sure thing, Carol. Sure thing." His radio started squawking. "Hey." He picked it up. "You took great care of Mom. And you probably will of me, too." He grinned. "That's scary. Gotta go." He spoke into the radio, "Dennison here. Still at the grocery store? Okay. Thanks."

Carol slowly nodded and took her time walking up the sidewalk.

"Hey Carol. How's your husband doing? I mean, has he gotten to come home yet?"

Facing the building, she shook her head.

"Is he any better?"

"No. He still can't talk. Sometimes I think he knows me."

Silence.

Footsteps scattered gravel behind her. Denny walked in front of her and spoke softly. "We could go for ice cream sometime. You and me. It wouldn't hurt anything." He shrugged. "Just friends."

Carol looked deep into his green eyes framed with those lashes. She hadn't forgotten staring longingly into them many years ago. Before Joe.

Deep sigh.

And a smile.

"Thanks, Denny." She studied the sidewalk, hands in her jacket pockets. Then back into those eyes. "Really. Thanks."

"But ... no."

"You know I can't." Breathe. "Won't."

He nodded. "I know. I had to ask. You're a godly woman that any man would be proud to be married to." He nodded again. "And I know that deep down your husband still knows that."

Carol held her breath. Joe was just fifty years old. They'd had twenty wonderful years together before the stroke took him down. "I hope so."

They gazed at each other for a full moment.

The radio sputtered. "Sheriff—checking in. These stories don't quite check out. Might need to talk to you."

Denny smiled. "Gotta go." He bowed low, hand on his heart.

Carol giggled and curtsied. "I do too. I really hope no one's looking out the windows right now."

"Ahh, the gossip begins."

Carol smiled as he jogged back to the squad car.

She started up the walk again, but stopped outside the entrance and turned to look toward town. Sigh. "Where are you, Clarence?" She hoped he came back before she had to let the home office know he was gone.

Shading her eyes, she grimaced. On the other hand, she'd lied to the home office before on the residents' behalf. Why stop now?

She glanced at the trees, the rose garden, the view of the town. Beautiful. Peaceful. She could live here. Somebody cooks for you. Somebody bathes you, cleans for you. Rosita does your laundry. No responsibility at all.

She sighed. No, when the time came she'd probably resist living here, too.

She pushed the automatic door button and the door swung open. She walked through, her arms outstretched. Her subjects awaited. Like a queen, she entered her domain.

CHAPTER TWENTY-NINE

Phil Daynton sat across from the most beautiful young woman he had ever beheld. He'd seen plenty, but few ever gave him the time of day. Those long legs reminded him of ... yup. Everything except the blond hair smacked of Katty.

"So how about some dinner." He checked his phone. "It's about eight-ish. We have all night-ish, Trishanna." He caressed her bare arm.

The angel behind her stiffened, rising to full height.

Forces from inside him mesmerized the girl. Forces of desire, layered with wickedness, goaded on by demons. They swirled around her eyes, obscuring her vision. Flowed into her sweet ears filtering out everything but Phil's voice and the pounding music.

He could tell she wanted to. Goosebumps rose on her tanned supple skin.

She wanted him.

What a great idea to stop at the cathedral.

He'd driven by it everyday for a year or more. He'd stopped at the traffic light on the corner of Church and Religion, or better yet, Seduction and Deception. Whatever it was.

And everyday, he'd driven on past, on his way to wherever the next job lured him. Most led him to very unsavory locations. So unlike the cathedral.

The only time he'd ever noticed the huge church building was to admire the architecture. Huge spires. Massive glass reflecting the humanity zooming past. Expansive lot—painted lines mapped out parking for the unsuspecting victims.

Until today.

A demonic GPS beam had tracked this charming little soul as she sat unsuspectingly at her desk in the church, answering the phone and making copies of Sunday sermons.

It'd be such a kick to tarnish this Sunday School—

"I should get home." She shivered and pulled her sweater around her shoulders.

His discerning fingertips massaged the goosebumps. Where she let him touch her at least.

His insides twitched and writhed. He knew the nature of the demonic presence. He knew what they wanted. He had known since the age of six.

Since then, he had followed every demand except one. He meant to make good on that one too. He just had to find her.

He pulled Trishanna's fingers to his lips. Just one more drink and she'd yield.

A waitress stepped to their table with the next round. Timing was everything.

He paid an obnoxious tip. Always best to invest in future possibilities.

She winked and swayed away.

He tipped his whiskey glass to tap her wine goblet. The anticipated ting was interrupted when a hand grabbed the goblet and threw it against the wall.

"Mom!"

"What are you doing here, young lady?"

The woman appeared barely older than Trishanna. Same short skirt revealed long shapely legs. Slender arms. Long, flowing blond hair. Beautifully made up face. Same revealing neckline.

Whew. Might be worth his effort to play both sides of this relationship.

Mom upended the table.

The whiskey. "That was vintage—"

"Don't you ever come near my daughter again!" Mom yanked up Trishanna and marched her out the door.

The bartender chuckled.

Phil shot him a glance that would have melted a tire factory. Waves of evil followed that glance and toppled the blender, splashing the contents onto the bartender.

The waitress laughed. She sauntered over and righted the table. "Too bad. The girl looked like a fresh catch." She lined a row of shots in front of him.

He didn't stop to respond, but tipped each one. The burn fueled the rage.

He slammed the last one down.

He knew a fresher catch than that bitch.

CHAPTER THIRTY

The next morning, Clarence stood hiding behind the office door, waiting for his chance. The office lady was on break. No one could see him, or so he hoped. Buttons on his dark shirt scraped against the door. Damn! He sucked in his stomach and held his breath.

Silence.

With the morning he'd had already, he wasn't sure he'd ever come back. Miss Henningway had knocked loudly on his door, waking him, and announced he was getting a haircut today—his greasy, long hair was gone. She had rounded up Lisha and two maintenance men to hold him down. He had hollered about his rights as a resident, a citizen of the United States. And he was a lawyer—he could sue their asses. He cussed until they were done and were sweeping up his hair. Even *his* ears burned. Damn them all to hell!

He pushed aside thoughts of digging for his file. Another time. He had to get out of here—one way or another. He raked his fingers through the inch-long hair and peered through the gap between the door and doorjamb.

The branches of an overgrown plant across the hall almost covered the main entrance door. A pedestal stood beside the plant, topped by an already spent floral arrangement.

The automatic door opened, making Clarence jump. A motorized wheelchair occupied by an elderly gentleman wearing huge dark glasses drove in, turning down the left hallway. The door paused open long enough for him to hear a car door slam, an engine rev, and tires crunch on concrete as a car left the parking lot. Light reflections traveled across the walls until the door closed.

He blew out a breath. Why was he so nervous? Back at prison, he'd snuck into the kitchen for more chicken for Dirk. That guy never got enough to eat and with Clarence's special privileges, he had helped him out a couple times. This was a cinch in comparison.

Voices chattered past his hiding place. Footsteps clomped on the carpet. "We need to call the police."

"I know, but you heard Carol."

"Maybe we should just do it ourselves. Call the Sheriff's office. You and me. Call it in."

"No. You can. I'm not doing it. I'm already in enough trouble as it is."

"Wait a minute. I thought you were just agreeing with me that we should call. Weren't you?"

Quiet.

"Well?"

"I don't know. It seems kind of mean, don't you think? He's so old and stuff. He doesn't ever hurt anybody." Slurp on a straw. "If I lived here, I'd run away too."

"You are so talking out of both sides of your mouth ... " The conversation trailed off as the door closed behind them.

Clarence peeked out.

Gone.

He peered into the reception area. Empty. The only movement was the plant—leaves fanning up and down in the breeze from the closing door.

Now or never.

He edged from behind the door into the hall and bumped into Mrs. Hatly.

Her face lit up. "Clarence." She clapped her hands. "Just who I wanted to see." She stopped. "You got a haircut."

He cringed, raking his fingers through his hair. "Yeah. They had to hold me down to cut it."

She nodded. "I heard you. It ... you look nice." She cocked her head. "And you have a bruise on your cheek." She lightly touched his jaw. "What happened?"

"Oh ... I misjudged a doorway." He wasn't about to tell her John had beaten him up. He held a finger to his lips. "Shhh. I've got to go out. Don't tell, okay?"

She giggled and nodded. "Okay." She put her finger to her lips too. "Shhh."

Loud voices approached.

"Did you check her chart?"

"No."

"It gives explicit instructions on how the doctor wants the treatment done."

Lisha and another aide marched into the reception area, holding hand-held computers side-by-side. Lisha pointed to hers. The aide nodded. They were on a mission.

"Oh." Lisha looked from Clarence to Mrs. Hatly. Back to Clarence. "What are you two up to? Going for coffee in the dining room? Gonna go to baking?" She grinned. Those big teeth. "Good to see you here, Clarence."

He tried not to smirk. "Good to see you, too."

"No. That's not what I meant. I meant—"

The other aide grabbed her arm. "Better not. 'Member what Carol told us."

Clarence looked from Lisha to the other aide. "What'd Carol tell you?"

Mrs. Hatly stepped up and lightly put her hand on his arm.

Lisha sighed and stepped away. "Oh she tells us a lot of things, huh. And I am being nice to you today, Clarence. I made the choice." She widened her grin. "Always a kind word to you." She nodded to Mrs. Hatly. "And you too, Mrs. Hatly."

Mrs. Hatly giggled, hand still on Clarence's arm.

A buzzer went off somewhere down the hall.

Lisha checked her watch. "It's almost time for that treatment. Let's go." She saluted them. "See ya around." She looked back. "Oh, and nice haircut, Clarence."

He growled and hung his head. He leaned into the hallway with Mrs. Hatly to watch both aides disappear into a room down the hall. He turned toward her and paused, their hands still clasped.

"Ohhh. Your hands." She gently turned them over. "Oh, my. How did you ... what happened?"

"Burned 'em. I was just a kid." He squeezed hers and gently removed his hands from her grasp. "Gotta go."

Her brown eyes twinkled, as if she enjoyed being part of the conspiracy to undermine the regime.

Clarence tipped a nonexistent hat and walked to the door, waving.

Her gnarled and swollen fingers fluttered. "Bye, Clarence. Bye-bye."

He pushed the door, letting automation open it the rest of the way. Stepping through, he paused to look behind him. He put his finger to his mouth, winked, and walked down the sidewalk to the parking area.

He surveyed the building, noting each window, each shadow. Checked for security, or to be exact, Lisha.

Made it. Made it out again.

He breathed deeply, patting his chest. It had been too long.

Still, he scanned the rows of windows again.

There. Harold. Shaking his finger.

Clarence shook his backside at Harold and gave the old prison salute, sticking his tongue out for good measure. "You old buzzard. Don't you tell." He wagged his finger with each word. "Don't. You. Tell."

Harold gave Clarence two thumbs up.

Mrs. Hatly appeared behind Harold and tried to give thumbs up too, only hers turned sideways. Thumbing for a ride.

A half smile crossed his lips.

The sun was shining. The birds chirped.

What a day.

#

Miss Henningway hid behind the designer drapes in her plush office as she watched Clarence walk down the sidewalk. He skipped like a giddy kid going to the movies.

She'd make sure he slowed down. He was rude. And spurned her advances. She'd find a way into his bank accounts. She qualified for the job: experience and the right education—Deception 101.

She opened his file. Flipped a few pages until she found his former address. Bet he'd had a killer house, him being a lawyer.

She typed the address into a Google search and hit enter.

Pictures began to load. She checked the address. The right address. Somebody sure made a typo.

She typed in the address again. Pictures of a prison loaded on the desktop of her monitor.

#

Ahhh, downtown. He turned and looked behind him. He didn't remember walking through the park, past the grocery store or the flower shop.

He trudged on down the sidewalk.

A door slammed behind him. Footsteps. He nodded at a passerby. Voices greeted voices. One seemed familiar ... he turned to see. Pete Malovitch, the insurance man, selling gambling policies.

"That old man ought to have a permanent residence in the cemetery."

Clarence stiffened. He plodded on, his hands balled into fists, as a door opened and shut behind him and the voices faded.

He stopped in front of another building, but not before he looked behind him, making sure Pete wasn't watching.

No Pete. He slipped to the window and peered inside.

Shocked, he jumped inside a restaurant—back sixty years. And not just any restaurant, but The Dinnerbell, the most popular place in town. People traveled from miles around to taste the roast beef dinner and apple pie Mrs. Darcy prepared. Cooking for nine brothers and sisters had been her cooking school.

Clarence sat at a table by the windows. He had no idea what he wanted to eat, much less what the menu said. He couldn't take his eyes off Annie, that beautiful reddish-blond haired girl, who had watched with such sympathy from the bank when Sally had flung back the diamond ring.

She scanned the menu across from him then handed it to the waitress. "I'll have the hot beef sandwich." She reached for her glass and brought it to her lips.

"And for you, Clarence?" The waitress poised her pencil above the pad.

"What?" He fumbled with the menu and closed it. "I'll have your special, whatever it is."

"Sure thing, Clarence. Coming right up. Beef Stew for Two?"

Annie raised both eyebrows, a sweet, teasing smile on her lips. Her shoulder length hair curled around her neck and ringlets escaped her barrettes. Her brown eyes and smile made the sun shine in his heart.

And to think she was the judge's daughter.

"Uhhh, no. J-Just a cheeseburger."

"Okay. Comes with chips. Is that okay?"

"Uhhh, yeah. Chips." He continued to feast on Annie's every feature that was above her neck.

She blushed, cleared her throat and sipped her water again.

Clarence watched her—everything about her. Her smile. Her eyes. Her hair haloed about her head. Her teeth. Her—

"You're staring at me."

He slowly nodded, then leaned forward and clasped his hands together, elbows on the table. He reached across to her and held out his hand.

"It's okay," Clarence whispered.

She searched the restaurant, her eyes wide, and slid her hand toward his. Their fingertips barely touched.

He whispered again. "No one's watching."

She placed her hand in his.

He closed his fingers around hers.

A slow smile spread across her face, and he relished the warmth.

The waitress brought their meal and they ate one-handed. When their dirty dishes were cleared away, they still held hands. Dessert came and went. The waitress dropped off the check and Clarence paid it.

Still they clasped hands.

"I have to go, Clarence."

"I know."

Moments later. "I really need to go."

Annie looked down at their hands ... and winced. "What did you do to your hands?" She opened them and gently fingered broad, ropey scars. "What happened?"

He shrugged. "It happened when I was a kid. It's nothing."

She shook her head. "Nothing? Those are burns, are they not?"

He nodded. "Yeah. When I was little ... it was the night Mom died." He sat still then sucked in a breath. "I was ... I ran away and found myself by an old hobo's fire."

She gasped.

"Oh, he didn't do it. It was me. It was cold out, and I stuck my hands in the flame. I couldn't even feel it. He yelled at me to pull them out. I 'spose I was hurting so bad missing Mom, I didn't care."

Annie stared at his face, then his hands. She pulled them to her lips and closed her eyes.

And prayed.

Clarence could still feel his hands in hers, her lips on his fingers, this many years later. Goosebumps skittered across his arms; chills made him tremble, just as he had back then. He leaned against the window, hand against his chest. His eyes filled with tears.

He examined both hands, still scarred. They had softened some with age and time, but were still disfigured.

Only then did he see reality inside the store. Boards piled along one wall, stacks of old flooring. An electric table saw commanded the center of the room, whining as a man pushed wood toward the blade. Sawdust covered the floor around the man's feet. The smell of fresh sawed wood wafted through the open screen door. Next to the saw was a worktable littered with scraps of crumpled sandpaper and a half-finished cradle. Boards of different shapes and sizes were propped against it. Cans of varnish and stain lined open shelving.

A deep breath escaped his chest. He wiped at his eyes.

The whine of the saw paused, and the man waved.

Clarence half-waved and pretended to turn away.

The man dipped his head, gesturing for Clarence to come inside. When Clarence didn't budge, the man walked to the door and opened it. "Come on in."

Clarence backed away, hands held up in protest. "No. I have places to go."

The man laughed and reached for Clarence's hand, dragging him inside. "Me, too. But what is more important than playing in sawdust?" He wiped his hand on a rag and then held it out in greeting. "I'm Michael. This is my woodworking shop. And you are ... "

Clarence stared at Michael's rough, outstretched hand—a long fresh wound running up his right arm, then at his own scarred hands.

He shifted his gaze to the interior of the store, taking it all in.

"Your name, sir?"

Clarence rubbed his hand on his shirt and offered it. "Uh, Clarence. My name's Clarence."

"Welcome, Clarence. Good to meet you." Michael spread his arm wide. He was unusually tall and muscular, dark tight curls covered his head and trailed down the nape of his neck. "Welcome to my humble," he kicked aside wood scraps on the floor, "wood shop. Are you a woodworker?"

"I ... uh ... used to be. Long time ago." His eyes followed Michael's arm around the shop, then back to his dusty face. "Way before you were born. Way."

Michael chuckled. "I bet some of it's still the same. I used to only use old tools. No electricity." He pointed to a wall display. "But I gave up when I couldn't meet customer deadlines."

Clarence found himself across the room, gazing at the antique tools. He reached up to touch the old wood and metal, and immediately transported back to his dad's workshop. As he touched each smooth surface, every blade, he saw his dad using it, working with it. Clarence caressed them one by one, shuffling along the wall.

He stopped, turned and half smiled, letting his head drop to his chest. "I ... I'm sorry. I don't know where I went just now."

"You know where you went, Clarence. Where?"

Clarence turned to the wall of tools for another feast, wiped his eyes, then faced Michael. "I guess ... I went to my dad's workshop. He owned all these tools, or ones like them, and I worked with him every minute I could." He tipped his head. "Or should I say, I hindered him as he worked?" He swallowed. "I'd forgotten how much I loved working with wood, but ... working with him."

"Don't be embarrassed, Clarence. I have the same memories of my dad." He patted the table saw. "Only with power tools instead of those." He motioned toward the wall. "I can't imagine getting to create usable furniture or even a house with those."

"Yeah. It's sure different now." Clarence, hands in his pockets, wandered to the workbench where Michael stood. "May I?"

"You bet. Help yourself." Michael continued to sand the wood, holding pieces and fitting them together. He lined them up, forming the rest of the cradle.

Clarence watched him then picked up a piece that had already been sanded and rubbed his fingers across the edges. "There is nothing like that smooth edge. Nothing like it."

Michael tossed him a piece of sandpaper, his eyebrows raised.

Clarence stared at the paper before he grasped it in his hand. He scraped his nail along it, letting his fingertips feel the rough surface. Slowly he picked up a piece of wood from the table, and watched Michael rub the paper along the edge of the wood. He sanded for just a few seconds then abruptly dropped the wood, along with the sandpaper, and started to leave.

"Clarence. You don't have to go." Michael stopped sanding and walked around the table. "I enjoy having someone to talk to, to share time with. Kinda like old times with our dads. Please stay."

Clarence stopped mid stride, breathing faster, then pushed his hand at Michael and walked out.

Michael followed him to the door. "Come back, Clarence. Sometime."

CHAPTER THIRTY-ONE

That old buzzard was loose again.

Pete Malovitch thumped his finger against the window frame in his insurance office. The day had only just begun, but he had to put on his doctor's hat and fill out bogus claims. Dad had taught him well; the extra income came in handy when he needed to shut up his wife and kids.

Was that bastard ever actually inside Hillcrest? Pete was willing to bet he didn't even go to the bathroom there anymore. How could he, when he was always downtown?

He watched the old man swagger down the street. He clicked his fingernail on the metal frame repeatedly ... and paused.

Something swirled in his head. Memories. Pictures mixed with voices. Images of his dad reading the newspaper at the kitchen table.

His little boy eyes had watched Dad's thick fingers rub the newsprint until ink blackened his thumb and fingertips. The weakened paper crumpled even more when Dad cussed. His little boy's ears and heart had blistered with the profanity.

"Tess, look what's in the obits. Old man Timmelsen died."

Pete's mom rushed to the table, grabbing her purse and jacket, ready for work. "What? That old—"

"Who's old man Timmelsen, Dad?" Pete peered over the table.

"He's just about the biggest ... "

He only heard tidbits of the rest, because his mother cupped her hands over his ears. But he could guess what came next. It always did. Never failed. His dad read the newspaper and cussed his way through until the weather. He cussed that too—only not as bad.

Pete loved to watch him read the comics. His belly shook so. Dad even read some to him. Real father-son time.

Pete whistled through his teeth as he continued to spy on Clarence. "I wonder ... "

He rushed to his desk, turned the computer monitor toward him and typed in Dawes Timmelsen. He glanced to the window. What was the son's name?

Dawes had done a bunch of work for Dad: repairs on buildings, bookcases, cabinets. He had been a master at furniture. He could make anything. Dad had told him to make false backs or bottoms in the bookcases. Perfect for hiding incriminating evidence, only he told Dawes it was for keeping food safe for orphans and widows in case of disaster. Still had them. Still used them.

He clicked enter. Dawes Timmelsen. As he scrolled down, he read aloud, "died Tuesday of complications." So how old was the article? "June 6, 1989."

He stopped scanning mid-page, where it read, "Timmelsen will be remembered for crafting some of the most well-known buildings in Osceola, Nebraska and appreciated for remodeling and erecting most people's homes and barns. After the fire of 1895, when all but two buildings were destroyed, Timmelsen reconstructed many, often for a nominal fee, making him number one in the hearts of the community." Pete nodded. Timmelsen had built this very building, too.

Outside a truck roared past, but inside, silence.

Pete read on. Time stopped and switched directions. He reached the article's final words: "Mr. Dawes Timmelsen was the father of Clarence Timmelsen, who was incarcerated for ... "

The son went to prison? For killing his wife?

"Woah." Pete rolled his chair away from the desk, hands in the air.

He jumped up and rushed to the window, sliding left and right. "Where is he?" He pounded the window, accompanied by his father's choice words. "That's what we have living here amongst our wives and children?" Not that he honestly cared, but he'd heard the phrase his whole life. Adding the word 'amongst' gave his fury real Biblical clarity. Clout.

He tapped the glass again.

"Sarah?" He raced to his secretary's adjoining office. "Sarah!"

Sarah stood at her desk, brushing crumbs from her short red skirt. Her black blouse gapped at the buttons and if she turned just right, which she did frequently, her black lace bra showed. She rushed to the door. Tall and beautiful, her spiked hair added three inches to her height. "Pete. What's wrong?"

"See if we have anything in our archives about Dawes Timmelsen—Clarence Timmelsen, too. Both of them." He marched to the wall of files and ran his finger down the labels. "T. T, where're the Ts?"

"Let me." Sarah shoved him to the side, lingering next to him, and pulled open a drawer marked inactive. Her polished fingernails clicked down each file until she pulled one out. "Dawes Timmelsen." She pulled another. "Clarence." She served them with a wink. "Anything else?"

Pete blew out a breath. "No. Not for now. But hold that thought."

He rushed to his office and slammed the door behind him. Tossing the files on his already cluttered desk, he filled his coffee cup and sat, sloshing it.

He muttered as he read, pulled at a tissue and soaked up the spilled liquid.

An hour later, Sarah knocked on the door and opened it. "You still reading those old files?" She shook her head. "Hey, I'm going out to grab a bite to eat. Want me to get you anything?"

Pete shook his head. "No, but when you get back, cancel this afternoon. We have work to do."

She wrinkled her nose and sighed. "Okay. But, no overtime tonight. My son—"

"I know. He has a game. This won't take long." Pete looked up at her. "I promise."

She opened her mouth, then clamped it shut, eyebrows arched. "Oh, and you have someone," she looked behind her, "that is insistent on seeing you. Now."

A woman, with her hand extended, pushed past Sarah. "I'm Miss Henningway, the administrator at Hillcrest Homes. I'm here to see you about insurance."

Pete glanced at the file open in front of him on Clarence Timmelsen. Hillcrest Homes, huh.

He closed the file and waved her to a chair. "Come on in. No problem. We have a clear afternoon."

Hours later, Miss Henningway left and Pete couldn't believe his good luck. She had literally opened a door—two doors—for Pete to strut through. She had presented, in her subtle but sly way, a business venture he could not refuse. And she had provided a way into the very guts of Hillcrest—a backdoor way of getting back at Timmelsen.

Pete fingered a newspaper photo of young Clarence Timmelsen. Lucky day. Lucky chance meeting with Miss Henningway. It seemed they both had it in for Mr. Clarence Timmelsen.

CHAPTER THIRTY-TWO

Clarence stumbled along the worn path behind the old library. He pictured people, mainly kids, cutting through, from the back alley to the front door of the library—from individual homes, into streets, onto the path, converging at the library.

Paint peeled off the old sign and the lettering had faded, but the words were still readable: Public Library ~ Hours: 10-5 p.m., Monday through Friday. 1-5 p.m., Saturday. Open to the public. "Books are the answer to questions," by Mabel Linger.

Ha. That old librarian.

He and Dad had put that sign up.

Leaves swirled around his feet. They skittered off the sidewalk and gathered in bunches in midair, obscuring the sign. When they cleared, he emerged, a young boy dressed in denim overalls over a plaid shirt, hands deep in his pockets, brain deep in thought.

At home, seated at their table, Dad pored over library plans. Clarence perched close by and leaned over his shoulder, firing out question after question. What is that room? Where do we check out books? And the most important one: where are the bathrooms?

The building took shape, while he and Dad climbed up and down ladders, nailed the window trim in place, painted the boards, waved at passersby, and whistled as they carried boxes of donated books. He remembered every step of the creation. He even remembered his dad painting the words and times on the new wooden sign.

The building materialized before Clarence's eyes. Original wood, new paint, brick laid in an impressive diamond pattern at the top, window glass sparkling, reflecting Clarence and Dad. A shiny brass doorknob beckoned.

Dad sat back on his heels, inspecting the paint job on the sign. "Did I spell it all right, son? Is it straight and even?"

Clarence leaned against his dad. Then he stood, scanning the sign with the building as background. "It's all good, Dad."

Leaves scattered again.

Cars gathered in the parking lot.

Clarence walked up the sidewalk, pulled the door open—no more brass doorknob—and stuck his head inside. Chairs, curving around a central speaker at a podium, were almost filled. Mostly older women, but some men of various ages were in attendance. The woman at the podium looked up and smiled at him.

"Come on in and join us. There are some chairs available yet." She motioned for him to be seated.

He nodded and slipped onto a chair in the back row next to a young man, maybe in his thirties. They exchanged a nod and turned their attention to the front.

"As I was saying—"

Clarence's mind strayed again to the building dedication, when Annie, his future wife, had given the welcome. As a clean-cut young man in a long-sleeved plaid shirt, typical of his age group and working class, he rubbed his palms down the sides of his new jeans and hid his hat under the chair.

Annie cleared her throat and began. "I'd like to welcome you all to the Polk County Library Dedication. The building is now complete, well constructed by Mr. Dawes Timmelsen and his crew." She continued, "I'm sure the whole community will gain enjoyment and education in this building throughout the coming years. Please ... "

Clarence didn't hear much else. Annie's brown eyes were so beautiful, framed with dark lashes and her mouth was sweet as it moved around her words. Tendrils escaped a formal bun at the back of her head. Thankfully all he could see above the podium was her neck, pure and white above her blouse; otherwise, his mind might have wandered where it ought not to go.

"It's time for refreshments. Son, would you like a cup of punch?"

Clarence didn't respond.

"Son?" Dawes shook Clarence by the shoulder. He shook harder and spoke directly in Clarence's ear. "Son."

Clarence jumped and kicked over the chair in front of him,

causing a domino effect with folding chairs in front of it, clattering and crashing to the floor. He tried to catch them too late; he shook his head at the pile in front of him.

"Son, where were you? Why didn't you answer me?"

Clarence picked up a chair and righted it. Then another and another.

"Help me Dad. Hurry," Clarence whispered, eyes pleading for help.

Dawes looked at Clarence, then at Annie. A big grin spread across his face.

Clarence's face burned hot.

"Well, well, well, Son. I suspect there is a story to tell here." He continued to pass looks between Clarence and Annie.

Clarence righted the last chair and stood facing his father. "What, sir? What was that you said just now?" He wiped his face with his hands and stood straight. Firing squad stance.

His father brushed off Clarence's shirt. "Nothing. I just finally figured things out."

"Things?"

"Yes, things. I just figured out the rest of the story." He looked at the podium where Annie stood visiting with local dignitaries. He nodded his head to the front. "That, or rather, she is the rest of the story."

Clarence's eyes followed his father's direction. He punched his hands in his pockets, jingling change, his neck heating up all over again. "Sir?"

Dawes clapped his son on the shoulder and laughed. "It's okay, Clarence. I'm sure this will all play out soon enough." He paused. "You want some punch? You might want to offer Miss Annie some while you're at it." A gentle teasing smile curved the corners of his mouth as he slapped Clarence on the back. "And while you're at it, get me some too. I'm a little thirsty."

Clarence half smiled at his dad, then peeked up front, meeting Annie's eyes.

Dawes doubled over in laughter. "So," he gasped, "it's mutual. That's the best kind."

Clarence hurried to the refreshment table and knocked over a stack of glass cups, breaking two and catching four. He set the rescued cups on the table, brushed up the crumbs of broken glass into his scar-protected hands. He carried them out the door and down the sidewalk, his father's laughter in the background.

He walked the mile to their house and shop and muttered to himself the whole way. He'd never felt so stupid. Or so embarrassed.

Annie was so pretty.

She'd never talk to him again.

He'd have to pay for those glass cups. Dad was going to either kill him or tease him to death, one or the other. Or both.

Once he arrived at the shop, he dumped the glass into the trash barrel, brushed the shards off and wiped his hands on the slop cloth. "Ow! You might know it. I knock over chairs, break glasses, and cut myself in all of this. This is not a good day. I wished I drank because I'd be headed there right now."

He stomped to the house, changed clothes and whistled for his dad's horse, Leather. "Come on, boy. We're going for a ride and I hope you are up to a wild one. Because that's what I need to blow off this afternoon."

They galloped away to the hills behind the house and didn't come back until sundown.

By that time, Clarence had simmered down a bit. He'd worn himself and the horse out.

Talking a mile a minute, he pulled the saddle off, hung it and brushed down the horse. "She is the prettiest thing I've ever seen. She's like ... like the brightest star in heaven. She's prettier than the prettiest flower on this earth. Leather, you hearing me? She is so smart, because they don't ask just anybody to lead a dedication celebration."

Someone cleared their throat.

Clarence spun around and knocked over the grain bucket Leather was eating from.

His father grinned and picked up the bucket and scraped the grain back into it.

"It's okay Son. I was the same way the first time I laid eyes on your mother. And I said all those things you were saying just now, to my horse. And I've kicked over some things and almost died of embarrassment just like I think you must have today. Your mom still loved me and even married me, after I had the stickers removed from my back side."

Clarence looked at his dad. "Stickers? What did you do, Dad?"

Dawes hung his head then looked his son in the eye. "I ... was showing off for her, swinging by a rope into the river and instead of landing in the water, I landed in a patch of stickers."

Clarence groaned. "Oh Dad."

"Uh-huh. I know. It was real bad, I'll admit. And she was the one that helped Doc pull them out." This time Dad blushed. "Yeah. Way to meet each other. She was Doc's assistant for a time. You think I was embarrassed? Damn right, I was. My bare bottom upside while your mom held a light over me, so Doc could see better. You bet I was embarrassed. I cried into my pillow that night."

Clarence gasped, wide eyed, then busted out in laughter so hard he fell against the fence.

Dad grabbed Clarence and pounded his back.

Clarence wiped his eyes and laughed again at the visual. "I never knew, Dad. Is that why she was always snapping your behind with a towel?"

His dad wiped his eyes. "Well, that's another way to see it." He looked out over the hills behind the place. "You remember more than I thought. I miss your mom so much. It feels like forever since she passed." He rubbed Clarence's neck. "I wish you could have known her better. She loved you so, the little time she had with you. Planned for you. Sewed little ... things for you. She just beamed when she held you. And when you sang in that Christmas program at church, she cried."

He shook his head. "My, my. I didn't mean to go over all that. But it feels good to talk about her."

"Dad ... um ... you think Annie is a good match for me?" Clarence picked at the cut on his hand. "Is she the one?"

"Son, only you will know that. Only you and her and ... um ...." He pointed to the sky. "Him."

Dad never spoke of God.

They stood together and watched the evening sky change from blues, to pinks, purples, oranges, yellows and rich dark blues. Silently they walked to the house.

"Sir?"

Clarence jumped. "Wha? What did you say, Dad?"

He looked into the face of the young man sitting beside him.

"Dad? Sorry, sir. Are you okay?"

Clarence stared at him then glanced around.

The woman still stood at the podium in front, now smiling and writing in a book while someone waited to chat with her. A refreshment table was set up complete with a coffee urn, cups, sugar cubes and creamer. People gathered around a small plate of cookies, dropping crumbs onto the table and floor as they munched and chatted.

The man addressed him. "Would you like something to drink? They have coffee and maybe punch."

Clarence nodded. "I'm sorry, I was remembering this library back when it was first built, and I guess I was more there than here."

"So-o-o, coffee or punch?"

"Coffee sounds good."

"I'll be right back."

Clarence searched the faces of those standing around the room. Could anyone here be a descendant of people he once knew? Like Annie's family? A niece? Clarence thought back. A sister? A sister had worked at the hardware store. Annie had been so proud of her because she was a woman before her time. Annie had talked about her with respect and admiration, even written stories about her. Annie had been a wonderful writer—so full of promise.

Annie's dad was another story. Jackass.

"Here you go, sir. Here's your coffee. I assumed you wanted black—no sugar or cream?"

"Black is fine. Thank you."

"So-o-o, you said you knew this building back when it was built?"

"Don't I know you from someplace? Do you work at the nursing home?"

"No. You just stopped in at my shop."

"Oh, sure." Clarence tapped his temple. "I don't remember your name."

"Michael." He reached over and held out his hand. "And you are ... Clarence?"

"Right." Clarence grasped Michael's hand. Michael's jacket sleeve slid up on his arm, revealing a wound, deep and long, obviously still healing by the fiery red color.

Clarence pointed. "That's quite a scar." Something clicked. "I remember you. Your scar." He glanced at his own.

Michael pulled his sleeve down. "Yeah. So you knew this building back then."

"Yup. My dad built it."

"Did he? Who was your dad?"

"Dawes Timmelsen. He was a carpenter, builder, fixer upper, father, banker, farmer. Well, you get the idea. Jack of all trades. He could fix anything, but being a carpenter was his golden job. He created beautiful buildings in this town."

Michael bent to sip from his styrofoam cup. "Did you work with him?"

"As much as he'd let me. I learned a lot from that man."

Michael leaned nearer. His eyes were a deep blue, bluer than Clarence's. His skin was as smooth as a baby's. "And he learned a lot from you, too."

Clarence raised his head and looked right into Michael's eyes for a few seconds. "What on earth do you mean by that? He learned from me, too?" Another second. "And how would you know anything about him—or me?"

"Just what I've heard from you … and … seeing his work." Michael averted his eyes. "He seems like the kind of man that was humble, kind, teachable." He looked at Clarence. "Am I right?"

"Well, yeah. Sure." Clarence gazed out the window. "He was upstanding. A kind man to everybody." Clarence met Michael's eyes again. "But how could he have learned anything from me? I was … I was—"

Michael leaned into Clarence. "You were a young man hit hard by circumstances, by life, and your dad watched you go through some of the same things he had gone through. Only worse."

Clarence flinched and spilled coffee onto his pants. He pulled the hot fabric away from his skin.

Michael scrambled for napkins. He rushed to Clarence, sat and blotted at the stain.

Clarence pushed his hands away. "No. No. It's … I'm just clumsy." He sat back and stared at Michael, his voice soft. "How'd you know all that?"

CHAPTER THIRTY-THREE

Bea happily swung her feet back and forth and munched on chicken strips, one in each hand. She traded one for a French fry, singing, "French fry first. Chicken bite next. French fry first—"

"Bea! Shush. You're driving me crazy." Mommy sipped her drink. "Just eat your lunch."

Bea hummed the same melody, switching the fries and chicken bites back and forth. She glanced at the front window of the Tasty View Dive Inn and spied the old man walking outside. She kicked her feet faster and watched the entrance door.

No old man.

Back at the window, she stretched her neck and saw his back as he walked past the building. Funny short gray hair blowing in the breeze.

She jumped onto the bench beside her booster seat and bumped her plate, dumping chicken bites and fries all over the table and onto Mommy's plate.

"Bea! What are you doing?" Mommy lurched forward, corralling the food before it hit the floor.

Bea was so intent on seeing where he went that she didn't answer.

"Bea, sit down right now, or we'll go home."

She looked down at her now empty plate, food all over the table, over to Mommy's full plate, then up to Mommy's face.

"Hurry up and sit down. Now!" Mommy pointed to the bench, a mean frown on her face.

Bea stretched to see if she could see him.

Gone.

"Sit!"

She slumped and sat down but missed her booster seat, landing next to it on the bench. Her lips trembled, but one look at Mommy's face and she straightened up. She righted herself, feet on either side of the booster, and sat carefully. A french fry was on the bench beside her and she popped it in her mouth.

Mommy picked up Bea's food and dumped it back onto her plate. "What were you thinking?" Mommy looked out the window. "What was so interesting out there, that you had to upset the apple cart?"

"What?" Bea picked up a chicken strip and took a bite. "Apples, Mommy? Where?"

Mommy sighed. "I shouldn't use those words with you. You always take me literally." Mommy berated herself. "You are too smart for ... no, not going there. You are so smart." She tapped her drink cup. "If you eat all your food, you can have ice cream."

Bea jumped again, tipping the booster, but righting again. "I can?" She proceeded to cram French fries into her mouth.

"Not so fast." Mommy gasped. "Don't swallow your food whole. Take time to chew."

#

Katty shook her head, sucked on her soda. Empty. She popped her cup on the table and scanned the restaurant.

A man's eyes smiled at her over a coffee cup. The cup had advertising on it: Lacy's Plumbing — 1-800-Big-Drip.

She froze. She knew those eyes. Goosebumps skittered up the nape of her neck, sending shivers across her back.

He put the cup down and checked his watch.

Whew. Not who she thought.

She inspected him without looking too interested. Kind of good looking in a rough sort of way. Nice leather jacket. But those eyes. Reminded her of ... but seeing the whole face, she couldn't get a fix on who he looked like.

She could get used to those eyes looking at her over—

Bea choked.

"Bea, are you okay?" She rushed over beside Bea and thumped her back, grabbing for napkins. "Here. Spit it out."

Bea spit the food into the paper napkins, and Katty wiped her mouth.

"Can I help you?" A deep male voice vibrated behind Katty.

She turned.

Those eyes again.

"Is she okay? I noticed you jumped up and then ... " He smiled at Bea. "Are you okay, little girl?" He reached his finger out to tuck under her chin.

Bea hugged into Katty's side.

His voice sucked Katty in. She struggled to pull away. "Uh, I think she's okay. She choked." Katty wiped Bea's mouth again and stood. "She just got excited about ice cream and crammed food into her mouth."

"Ice cream." The man smiled. "I get excited about ice cream. Let me buy."

"No. It's okay. I was just waiting for her to finish her food. I can get it."

He reached into his wallet. "I'm glad she's okay." He pulled out a couple of twenties from a full wallet and dropped them on the table.

Katty stared at the money. She slowly picked it up and handed it back to the man. "Take it. I can get the ice cream."

"You sure? I'd love to get it for her and for you." He blinked down at her.

Argh. Those eyes.

Katty held out the money and pressed it into his hand. He squeezed and held on until Katty slipped her hand away. "Thanks ... anyway. Please take your money. We're fine. Aren't we Bea?"

#

Bea's eyes bounced back and forth between Mommy and the man.

He said something and Mommy stared at his face.

When Mommy talked to him, her face changed.

His bright blue eyes looked hard, like marbles, when he glanced down at her.

She shivered and hugged her middle. She didn't like those eyes. "Are you cold, Baby Bea?" Mommy reached down and ran her fingers along Bea's arms. "You've got goosebumps all over."

Bea shook her head, her eyes never leaving the man's face. "Let's go, Mommy. I'm tired." She climbed into Mommy's arms. "Please? Let's go home."

"You haven't had your ice cream yet." Mommy searched Bea's eyes. "Let's have your ice cream and then we can go." She picked up the pieces of chicken and dropped them onto Bea's plate and sat down beside her. "Would you like to join us?"

He smiled and bowed. "Don't mind if I do. Thank you." He sat across from them and cocked his head. "If I join you for ice cream, I can treat, right?"

"I suppose," said Mommy. "Just this once."

He looked a long time into Mommy's eyes.

Bea followed the conversation back and forth, from Mommy to the man and back again.

The man raised his hand, his eyes never leaving Mommy's, and snapped his fingers.

A waitress, clearing the table next to them, jerked her head up. "Yeah? Whatdaya want?"

The man slowly lowered his arm and locked onto the waitress' eyes. He still smiled, but he changed. His face changed. His eyes turned black.

The waitress popped over to their table. "Yes, sir?"

"We would like some ice cream, please," he said. He looked at Bea. "What kind would you like, little girl?"

Bea hid under Mommy's arm.

"Bea? Tell him." Deep sigh. "She likes vanilla, please."

"And for you?"

"I'll take chocolate."

The man raised his voice. "That's one vanilla and two chocolates in dishes. Thank you."

"Yes, sir."

Bea peeked from under Mommy's arm and watched the waitress scurry from their table, casting backward glances at them. The waitress bumped into another waitress who was carrying three filled plates spread across her arm. The dishes wobbled but none fell. Both waitresses breathed a sigh of relief.

So did Bea.

The man cleared his throat and smiled at Mommy. "Now, where were we?"

"Um, I'd like to start with names. What's yours?" Mommy blinked her eyes and smiled a funny smile.

"Oh, of course. I'm sorry. My name is Lex. Lex Forgé." He leaned closer. "And who might this young lady be?"

Mommy turned to Bea. "Tell him your name, honey." Mommy nudged her.

Bea hugged closer under Mommy's arm and peeked at the man.

"Sorry. She's kind of shy sometimes. This is Bea." Mommy nodded toward him. "Bea, say hello to Lex."

Bea peeked out and mouthed hello, and closed her eyes.

He burst out laughing. "How cute. And who might you be, Ma'am?"

The waitress cleared her throat and set down bowls of ice cream. "I think she had the vanilla and that leaves chocolate for the both of you, right?" She stood back, hands clasped in front of her.

He nodded to her. "Right. Thank you." He waved her away.

Mommy slid the bowl closer to Bea and handed her a spoon. "And yours?"

"My what?" Mommy picked up her spoon.

"Your name. What's your name? We told ours. Now it's your turn."

She cocked her head. "I don't usually give out my name."

"Aww. Come on." He pointed to the bowls. "We're having ice cream together."

"Okay. My name is Katty. Katelyn Randolph."

He held out his hand. "Pleased to make your acquaintance."

Mommy reached over the ice cream and shook his hand.

They held hands like that, arms stretched over the ice cream, for a long time.

Bea dropped her spoon onto the floor, the clatter breaking the spell.

"Oh, Bea. Now we have to get you a clean one." Katty looked up for the waitress, but she already stood beside the table, a spoon in her hand.

"Why ... thank you. You're so speedy."

Lex smiled as he stuck his spoon into his ice cream. He pulled out a huge bite, and let it drip back into the bowl.

Mommy fed Bea a bite, but Bea closed her mouth tight. "You don't want any right now? That's okay. Take a bite when you feel like it."

Mommy shook her head and slid her spoon into the bowl. She stirred the ice cream and watched the man.

He watched her back.

She loaded her spoon with a bite, brought it to her open mouth, closed her eyes, then licked her spoon. "Mmmm. Haven't had ice cream this good in a long time."

She looked at his. "Aren't you eating yours? It's yummy."

"I'm enjoying you eating yours. Even if little Bea can't eat hers." He twirled the spoon in his bowl then locked eyes with Bea.

His blue eyes turned cold again, dark, black. Marbles again.

Scary.

Bea fidgeted. "Mommy, I have to go potty."

"Really? I'm right in the middle of my ice cream. Can't you wait?"

Lex stared at Bea. She shivered and hid under Mommy's arm. "Mommy. I have to go now. I can't wait."

"She can go by herself, can't she?" His voice rumbled across the table.

Mommy hesitated. "Uh, no. She's too little." She turned to Bea. "Why are you hiding? You were fine before. Listen, let me finish mine and then we can go potty. Okay?"

Bea slid under Mommy's arm again.

Mommy dipped into the bowl and scooped up another bite. "Eat yours, Lex. It's melting. You don't want to waste it."

He stirred it and dipped the spoon for a bite, brought it to his mouth and licked. "It is good."

"There. You took a bite. Makes me feel like a pig when you don't eat. I'm gobbling mine down." She eyed Bea's. "You sure you don't want yours, Bea? It's going to melt."

Bea shook her head under Mommy's arm.

"Okay." Mommy sighed. She replaced the empty bowl with Bea's full one. "Somebody's got to eat this. Kind of melted though." She drizzled the ice cream from the spoon inches above the bowl.

Bea jerked on Mommy's sleeve. "Mommy, I have to go. Please?

I have to go potty." She glanced over at Lex. Something in his eyes made her shiver.

"I'd better take her. Sorry. We'll be right back." She scooted out of the booth and reached for Bea.

Lex smiled up at Mommy, then looked at Bea. "It was nice to share ice cream with you, Bea."

Bea stared at his full bowl, climbed out of the booth and scrambled in front of Mommy. She pulled Mommy along, away from the table and away from him.

CHAPTER THIRTY-FOUR

Clarence peered through the window of what looked like an old restaurant. Empty. Ceiling tiles littered the floor. Wallpaper peeled and trailed from the plaster. Litter and dirt obscured anything of merit. No apple pie there.

A screech high above startled him. Head tilted back, he searched the sky. That old bird.

Clarence shook his fist at it then realized it was circling. A huge swoop and back around, then a smaller circle and a smaller one. Smaller and smaller until it hovered right above him.

Clarence shook his head in wonder. "How can you do that? What do you want old bird? Why are you here?"

Screech!

The sound bounced off the buildings, making Clarence jump again. He relaxed as the bird flew away.

It flew north over the huge courthouse, circled twice, then out into the country. Probably had a mate somewhere. Funny old bird.

Back to the building. It had once been regal and solid. The brickwork testified to the gift of a true craftsman: fancy diamond patterns above the windows crisscrossed in an overlapping grid, ornate tiles installed alternately. Inside, light trails streaming between a gap in the neighboring buildings revealed dust particles floating in the air, creating squares of sunlight on old wooden floors.

Clarence snapped his fingers. The law office. He couldn't remember the names of the lawyers, but they were good folk. Dad had called on them more than once.

He checked the street for people or cars then rattled the

doorknob. Locked tight. He snuck around the block to the back alley and figured out which was the right building.

He gripped the old metal doorknob, but it fell off in his hand. Oh-oh. He tried to tap it into place, but it fell off again. Shrugging, he let it lie on the ground and pushed on the door.

Open.

He looked both ways then slipped inside.

It was pitch dark. He stretched his arms out in front of him and stumbled against something metal, then bumped into what felt like a chair.

Sliding his feet, he felt his way back to the door and pushed it open. He stood still while his eyes adjusted, listening. Short breaths echoed in his ears.

Old shelves became visible on one wall. A hallway led to the front of the building.

He inspected the floor, determined not to fall. Instantly the interior lit up, like someone had flipped the power on. Ornate sconces lit the hallway illuminating the walls; flocked wallpaper set off beautiful wood wainscoting below. Oriental rugs covered oak floors.

The shoes on the rug weren't joggers anymore, but dusty leather boots—kid size. Blue denim cuffed overalls drooped over the boots. Plaid flannel long-sleeved shirt tucked into the bib.

He grasped the collar in awe. He was a kid again. Prison loomed ahead of him not behind.

He'd read books about time travel where characters translated back in time and changed their destiny. Oh, to go back when Mom was still alive. Then hop to when Annie ...

Clarence followed the rugs into the front office where the receptionist sat, writing longhand onto a document. She looked up at him and smiled. "Did you find everything okay?"

Clarence held his hat by his side and bowed slightly, his head down. "Yes, ma'am. I did."

She pointed to a row of carved chairs along the far wall. "Have a seat. They should be done soon."

"Thank you, Ma'am." Clarence shuffled to a chair. Deep maroon velvet upholstery.

"You won't get it dirty." She pointed again. "Go ahead and make yourself at home."

"Uh, I'll just stand and ... " His eyes found a bookcase. "I'll just have a look at these books instead. If that's okay."

"Sure it's okay. Suit yourself."

"Thanks." Clarence read each title, tilting his head to the side. His fingers walked across the spine of each book.

"You can take one down and look at it."

He looked over his shoulder at the receptionist. "Thank you. I just might have to do that." He reached over and pulled one from the shelf. Smelled it.

"Take it to that table there."

Behind him stood a beautifully carved table with massive legs. Papers and file folders were stacked on one corner and a map took up most of the space, but he found room at one end.

He reverently opened the book one page at a time and scanned the words. Real cases. A case about a fire. A whole family of kids burned to death along with the father when he tried to rescue them, as the mother watched. Clarence shook his head.

Voices rose in volume, and a door opened somewhere in the back of the office.

Clarence turned to see his father shake hands with Mr. Clynder. "Thanks Ted. I appreciate your time and anything you can do."

"Sure Dawes. I'll be getting back in touch with you in a few days. Will that work?"

"You bet."

He patted Dad on the back. "I like what you're planning."

They nodded and turned toward the front of the office—eyes on Clarence.

"You reading law books, son?" Mr. Clynder pounded him on the shoulder. "Good way to start in the business, if I do say so myself." He grinned at Dad. "Is he going to be a woodpecker like you, or a lawyer like me?" He hung his thumb in his vest pocket and grinned. "What case are you on, son?"

"Well sir, this here fire case. Sounds real tough. Real bad."

Mr. Clynder nodded and paused. "Yes, that was bad. They tried to make it the mother's fault, but—"

"Yes sir." Clarence pointed to the book. "They proved it was the father's fault. Excuse me, sir, for interrupting. The mother was going to have another child. The father planned an escape route, but a beam blocked his way." Clarence glanced at both men. "How could a father do that to his kids?"

Just like a few blockheads he met up with in prison. In the future. Whew.

Mr. Clynder glanced at Dad.

"You seem to have a penchant for cases." He winked at Dad. "If your dad can't keep you busy, come on over and I'll use you."

Clarence's head popped up. "Really Dad? Could I do that? I'd like helping people out."

The men laughed.

"We'll see, Son. We'll ... "

Clarence closed the book, and a dust cloud billowed, obscuring the table. Dust danced in the sunlight streaming in through the front windows. Beautiful wallpaper no longer covered the walls but peeked through layers of peeling paint. Old bookshelves stood on the opposite wall, as before. But there was no desk. No receptionist. No table. No book. No case to study.

Wow. He was going crazy. Must have been his imagination ... but he remembered that happening. An old man going crazy—that's what he was.

Paper fragments and newspaper clippings floated into the sunbeam. Clarence chased them as they flitted and floated and caught one. He walked closer to the windows, holding it up to the sunlight. It was a newspaper clipping of a young girl with a sweet smile and bouncy curls and something about a library.

She looked vaguely familiar. He shoved a hand into his pocket, stirring the coins and fingering the toy ring. "Huh." As he shook his head, his stomach growled. Where had he seen her? He held it closer in direct light, and his heart lurched. He pressed it to his chest, his hand covered his mouth. He brought it back into the light to study once again and cupped it in the palm of both hands.

"Oh, my darling, my darling."

CHAPTER THIRTY-FIVE

"Mommy, I want to go home. I don't like that man. He can't have ice cream with us. Mommy, I want to go home."

Bea tried to explain things to Mommy while she used the bathroom. She finished and pulled up her panties and smoothed her dress down. "Mommy, I don't want to stay. I don't want to see him any more." Why wouldn't Mommy listen?

"Settle down, Bea. What is so awful about him?" Mommy held Bea up to the sink to wash her hands then used the toilet herself. "He's a nice man. He bought us ice cream. Or rather, he bought me some. I've never seen you not eat ice cream before. I know you're shy sometimes but not deathly afraid of anyone."

She washed her hands, checking her reflection in the mirror above the sink, tilting her head from side to side. Then closer in, her eye make-up. She pulled paper towels from the dispenser and dried her hands, still looking in the mirror, smacking her lips. Adjusted the clip in her hair. She smiled at herself.

Bea watched, eyes moving from the real Mommy to the Mommy reflected in the mirror.

Mommy's face changed into someone different. Somebody scary. Bea stared without answering, watching. Part of her was fascinated. Part terrified.

Mommy finished messing with her hair and face and looked down at Bea through the mirror. "What? What are you staring at? What's wrong? And why haven't you answered me?" Mommy whipped around. "Why aren't you answering me, Baby Bea?" She leaned down.

Bea backed away, eyes wide.

Mommy gasped. "You're afraid of me," she whispered and knelt in front of Bea. "You're afraid of me, Bea. Aren't you. Right now."

Bea nodded slowly, eyes never leaving Mommy's.

Mommy looked at the bathroom door, then back. "It's because of that man, isn't it."

Bea swallowed.

Mommy kept staring at the door. "He makes you scared, doesn't he." She sat back on her shoes. "You changed when he came over. You hid behind me the whole time and wouldn't eat ice cream."

Bea spoke for the first time. "You changed too, Mommy." She pointed at Mommy's heart.

"I didn't change."

Bea took a deep breath. "Yes you did, Mommy."

Mommy tilted her head. "Naw. Did I?"

Bea nodded. "You changed then. Now Mommy's back."

Mommy shook her head. "How?"

Bea started to cry.

"Honey. Baby Bea." Mommy gathered Bea into her arms. "There's something about that man. That Lex man. How can he change people? How did he change me?"

She held Bea away. "Why didn't he change you?" She put her fingers under Bea's chin and lifted her head. "Why didn't he change you?"

Real Mommy. Bea didn't move. She couldn't say anything. She couldn't take her eyes off Mommy.

"Wow. This is crazy. How can he have that kind of power over people? Over me?" Mommy stood up and checked her zipper. "We better go."

Bea flinched and shook her head.

"No, Bea. We won't go back to our table. We'll pay and leave. God give me strength to not look into those eyes." She sighed. "Those eyes." She stared at Bea. "Something's going on, huh."

Someone pounded on the door. "You done in there yet?"

Mommy opened the door and looked out toward their table. "He's not there."

She grabbed Bea's hand and pulled her past ladies waiting in line. She gathered their jackets from the booth as the waitress wandered over.

"Your man had to leave. He said to tell you to take the money. That you might need it someday." She chewed her gum on one side of her mouth and pointed at the two twenty dollar bills lying on the table under the silverware.

Mommy picked them up and shoved the money into the waitress's apron pocket. "He's not my man. And the money's yours." She closed the pocket and pressed her hand there.

The waitress gasped. "Really?" She patted the pocket. "I can have it? That's forty bucks."

"I said you could, didn't I?" Mommy helped Bea on with her jacket, zipped it up and slipped her own on. "Thanks for the service. You did a good job."

"Thanks." The waitress stopped chewing as her hand clenched her pocket. "Uh ... really. Thanks."

Mommy picked Bea up and pushed the door open.

Bea stared over Mommy's shoulder at the waitress.

The waitress stared back, still chewing her gum, hand still on her pocket.

She'd seen Mommy steal money before. Bea knew it was wrong. But she'd never seen Mommy give money away.

She snuggled her head on Mommy's shoulder. She patted Mommy's back. "Good Mommy."

"What Bea?" Mommy opened the car door.

Something fluttered inside Bea. "You're my good Mommy."

CHAPTER THIRTY-SIX

"I own this building, and he broke in." Pete Malovitch bent down and grasped the old doorknob. His property rights had been trampled—by a guy no better than a homeless man. "Look, Sheriff. Look at this. Broken. It's obvious he broke in."

Sheriff Dennison knelt beside Pete and examined the doorframe. "Pete, this door is so old a squirrel could get in." He tapped on the old wood. "And they probably do." He brushed in the dirt with his fingers and held up a screw. "How do you even know that doorknob came from this building?" He stood, hands on his hips. He looked left and right along the alley. "There's so much garbage along here, how can you tell what came from where? How do you know it was him?"

Pete stood and faced Sheriff, eye to eye. "Because I watched him break in, that's how."

"You what?" Sheriff scratched his chin. "From where?"

Pete pointed to his car parked behind the insurance building. "I saw him from my office window, came out back and hid behind my car." Pete smirked. "Saw the whole thing."

"All right, let's go in. Let's see what he's been up to."

Pete pushed the door open and they entered the dark backroom.

"Pete, this guy is harmless. He's just an old—"

"Harmless? What about that?" Pete pointed his flashlight at trunks lined up along one wall. "Looks like they've been moved. See the trail?" He shined the light along dust tracks. He lifted a lock. "And the lock has been hacked on this one."

Sheriff followed along, shining his own light on the drag marks.

Then the lock. "It's been sawed all right, but where would he get a hacksaw? He lives at the nursing home. The nurse said he was admitted with almost nothing to his name."

"Well, there ya go. He's looking for something. His kind don't have anything and they want everybody else's stuff." Finally getting somewhere. Pete opened the trunk. "Look. See? These are old insurance cases I've gone to court on. I bet he's lookin' for information, you know, to use against me. Didn't I hear he's a lawyer?"

"Pete. He's eighty years old. What would he have against you? And he just moved here. It seems contrived, somehow."

Pete drew up tall. "You callin' me a liar, Sheriff? You sayin' I rigged this? I've been here all my life, just like you. And yeah, he just moved here." He dug deeper under paperwork. "Look here. Here's the file on old cases. Looks like they've been tampered with."

He opened a file and stepped back to shine more light on the folder. "Well, looky here. It's an old case file. What's that old guy's name? Cal?"

Sheriff stepped closer. "Clarence. Clarence Timmelsen."

Pete handed the open file to Sheriff and tapped on a picture. "Isn't that him? Isn't that our guy? A few years younger, but I bet that's him."

Sheriff scanned the top newspaper article then sifted through the rest of the file. "Yes. This is Clarence. Look. Here's a picture of his dad back then. Looks just like Clarence now." He handed it back to Pete. "What's this doing here? Where'd you get all this?"

Pete shuffled the papers back in order. "All part of my dad's business before I took over. He was a lawyer and insurance agent. This is what that old man was after. Trying to cover stuff up." He pointed to the file. "This is the kind of man we have around our women and children, Sheriff. And if he's breaking into buildings, private property now, what's he going to do next, huh? I've seen him with that little girl and her mom in the park. Look on your database. Is he a child molester? Where'd he come from? Yeah, he grew up here, but where's he been the last sixty years? He was incarcerated. He's been in prison, for heaven sake. He killed his wife." Pete stepped back.

"I know that. I checked him out." Sheriff expelled a deep sigh. "Number one, I can't believe he'd hurt anyone now. Yes, the file speaks for itself. But, he served his time. Number two, maybe he did break in here, but what did he hurt?" He faced Pete. "He's just an old man in a nursing ... " He trailed off.

Pete grimaced. "Caught yourself, didn't ya? You thought of it before I did." He ramped it up. "Sheriff, what if he does something at the old people's home? What if he hurts someone there? I'd hate to think ... " He tapped the file, stirring up more dust. "You see what he did back then. What if he's been progressing all this time—getting deeper and deeper into crime to where nothing is sacred. No one is safe from someone like that. They stop at nothing." Pete looked out the front windows. "And he's right here. In this town. Right in our midst." He paused and pointed to the street. "Among our women and children."

"Okay. Enough drama, Pete. I'm going to need to check those files." Sheriff motioned to the room. "And access this building for investigation."

Drama? No. Justice. "You bet. I'm all about helping the law do their job." Pete handed over the box of files. "And feel free to check the rest of the trunk. I'm not sure what's in there, but my business is your business, Sheriff."

"Thanks, Pete. I appreciate your help in this."

"All in a days work." Pete shined his flashlight beam to guide Sheriff out.

Sheriff stepped into the bright alley and pulled the door closed.

Silence and darkness filled the space.

A cold rush of air brushed past Pete. He shivered and rubbed his arms.

Thoughts dropped into his mind. The puzzle was fitting together.

Pete stepped to a trunk shoved into a dark corner and opened it. He picked up a folder and walked to the window, checked the street, then flipped the folder open.

He reread a journal entry in his dad's own handwriting:

"Sunday ~ Today sealed the deal. Judge and I made sure, since Timmelsen was knocked out in the accident, he would never know the truth—that he was supposed to die, not Annie. But she was thrown from the car. The 'evidence' against him stuck, plus the testimony of well paid witnesses. Judge set it all up. Timmelsen will go to prison for life. Even if he goes before a parole board for good behavior, he'll never be free. Judge also passed down a decision that

Clarence will be sent to Osceola nursing home. Serves him right. Timmelsen was supposed to die and I was to marry Annie."

Pete slapped the folder shut. "All in a days work."

CHAPTER THIRTY-SEVEN

Sitting in his car, Lex tapped a starred contact on his phone and held it to his ear. "Hey, Phil baby. I found your kid."

"Oh, yeah?" Phil Daynton answered. "Is she pretty?"

"She looks just like you, man ... uh ... not to say you're pretty or anything." He clicked the blinker on and off. "She kept hiding under Mommy's arm. You think she's onto me?"

"Ha! You are scary."

"So Phil. What's the big deal about finding her?" He turned down the volume on the police scanner. "I have two or three kids that don't know where I am. They don't even know I exist. Why is this one so important?"

"None of your f-n business. This is a deal—a business deal— nothing else. The less you know, the better."

The inside of the Dive-Inn was visible from Lex's car. He had been careful to park where he couldn't be seen—behind a combine at the neighboring implement dealership.

Katty led Bea back to their booth. They were talking to the waitress.

"Naw," Lex said. "I'm invested. Spill it."

Phil coughed on the other end. "No, you don't understand. Just do the job you were hired for."

Lex started the car. "Screw you. I'm outa here. You can do this on your own."

"Okay. Don't run." Phil growled. "Long story, but the short version is that this little girl is the only kid I didn't eject. Katty got knocked up if I just looked at her, so I had 'em taken care of—know what I mean? She hid one from me, but I caught on and ended it myself."

"Eww. God, you're a demon." Lex smirked.

"But Katty started looking a little ... ragged, ya know? The drugs did their thing on her." Sound of a pop-top and a couple slurps. "Anyway, I left. But she musta been pregnant because the timing fits. She had our kid. I didn't know until her supplier told me."

"What are you gonna do once you get here?"

"What any self-respecting father would do. That's my kid, man. She's mine and I'm gonna raise her ... like any soft, fresh baby girl should be raised." He sucked another drink. "Got the picture?"

"Yeah, I get it. You are evil. Pure evil." Lex switched ears. "What about the mom? Where is she in this family picture?"

"That'll work itself out."

Lex eyed the gun on the floorboards. "Yeah. I think I know what you mean."

CHAPTER THIRTY-EIGHT

Clarence stood on tiptoes on the front stoop of the old town hall, peering through the little glass window in the door. He drummed his fingers against a door panel. Paint peeled from the wood, its crunchy texture under his fingers. He brushed some paint chips from his shirt and leaned in again to peer through the window.

No furniture or seating—all he could see was trash.

A hand clasped his shoulder. He flinched.

"I was afraid you'd jump if I spoke. You did anyway."

"Uh, yeah. You startled me." He snapped his fingers. "You're the guy from the library meeting ... Michael?" Clarence reached out his hand.

Michael shook Clarence's hand firmly and held his elbow at the same time. Guy hug.

"So, did your dad build this too?" Michael surveyed the structure.

Clarence tapped the old wood. "Yeah. There was that fire way back then and the town fathers or council, I guess they called themselves back then, used to meet in each other's homes before Dad built this. Pretty impressive back then. Now?" He nodded and picked at the paint. "Pretty sad."

"I have keys. You want to look around?" Michael jangled a key ring in front of Clarence's face.

Clarence backed up a step. "You have keys? You mean it?" He grinned. "I'd love to get in there. See if it holds any memories for me."

"Done deal." Michael inserted a key into the lock and it clicked.

"How did you happen to have the key? That's amazing."

"Oh, just a small thing. See," Michael blushed, "I happen to own this building and several around town. I can do whatever I want with them." He pushed the door open wide. "Including letting my friends see the place. Cool, huh."

Clarence barely heard Michael as he walked through the doorway. His natural eyes saw the dust, his natural foot kicked a board, his natural nose smelled old musty odors, but his spirit and memories experienced totally different scenes.

The swirling of dust particles around Clarence's knees sparked memories of the new building back then.

That day.

The day he and Annie married.

She looked extraordinary. Her hair was pulled back and up, but the ever-present ringlets trailed down around her neck and ears. Her brown eyes twinkled with excitement as she gazed into his. Delicate pert nose, full lips, tiny earrings sparkled from her ear lobes. Her flawless neck drew him, and as his eyes roamed over the rest of her, he let out a deep breath. Tears sprang to his eyes.

Her gown was white. That's all he remembered.

They married in the town hall and not a church, because her father was the judge and they wanted to be married by him—in his church, so to speak.

The hall was decorated with streamers draped all about. Very simple, but their every dream come true.

His dad was his best man and Annie's sister, Hattie, the maid of honor.

There was no procession, no band or organ. Annie's mother had hummed the wedding march, and they all joined in.

Clarence faced Annie, and the only words he really heard after the I do's were, "You may kiss your bride." The memory of that first kiss would last forever.

The guests were few, but they had made it a festive evening. Music had been provided by Clarence's dad and a neighbor man on the fiddle and guitar. Annie's mother had baked and decorated a beautiful cake. Those moments with his bride—his new wife—were sweeter than that cake by far.

When they caught each other's eyes, Clarence was moved to tears and Annie laughed. When she cried, he hugged her without thinking and instantly withdrew from her, aware of the judge's eyes on them, even now.

As they prepared to depart for their wedding night, his dad drew Clarence aside in the coatroom and hugged him. "Son, you're a man now, and I'm so proud of you as a son, but as a man too." He choked. "I know you got as fine a woman as your mother was, and I know she's in heaven cheering you both on." He grabbed Clarence and hugged him tight, slapping him on the back.

They parted and shook hands as the judge and Annie walked in. "Well, are we ready to consummate this marriage?" The judge held his arm around his embarrassed daughter, his other thumb hooked his black suspender.

Clarence stole a look at Annie.

She glanced at her shoes and swallowed.

"Come, come. You'll never give Dawes and me any grandchildren if you stay that shy." He slapped Clarence on the back. "Huh, Dawes."

"I reckon they'll get to that in their own time, sir," Dad said, his hand rubbing his son's shoulder. He spoke volumes with his touch, more than the judge did with his harsh words.

Clarence took a deep breath and held out his hand to Annie. She left her father's side, and the moment she slipped her hand into Clarence's, the dust swirled, leaving him once again in the dimly lit old town hall. Tiny particles followed the light from windows to floor.

Goosebumps.

Michael stood beside him.

"Woah, Michael, I'm sorry. I went back ... in ... time. I ... it all began here." He turned away and wiped his eyes. Faked a cough.

"Clarence, you okay? The dust and dirt getting to you? Maybe we should go," Michael said. "What if we get something cold to drink?" He checked his watch. "The Dive Inn is open and it's almost time for supper."

Clarence checked Michael up and down. "You are so tall. Were your parents tall?" He hadn't noticed before.

"Yeah. Everybody in my family is really tall. Some more than others." Michael held out his hands. "So, how about it? Supper?"

"Could we look around a little longer? Are there any lights or has the electricity been turned off?"

"Oh, I think it's on. Let me go and fiddle around. I'll be right back. Could be just a matter of needing a few light bulbs."

He left the room. Clarence spun around in a circle. "I sense you here, Annie. And when I'm here I feel like a young man. I feel like I did on that day, my Annie." He danced along the sunbeams, and dust sparkled in the sunlight as he held her. "I love you and miss you so." He slowed. "We were robbed of our long life and children filling our lives with laughter." A sob escaped as the lights flashed on, blinding him for a minute.

Michael walked into the room, smiling. "I hope this doesn't mess with your memories, seeing it like it is now with all the dust and dirt," he said. "I hope to get more done on this little project soon."

Clarence sneezed and coughed again. "What are your plans?"

Michael scanned the room. "I love old buildings. They have so much history and stories." He paused. "I want to make it like new, and maybe use it for my home, or offer it for sale as an office. I'm not sure." He stopped in front of Clarence. "Any ideas?"

Clarence nodded. "Does this town have a community place or fellowship hall? People don't get together anymore."

"Great idea, Clarence."

Clarence cleared his throat again. "Or a wedding chapel. Someplace where other couples could begin their lives together." He smiled, suddenly embarrassed. "Pretty silly, huh."

"No, Clarence. Now that you say that, I can see it." Michael walked to a wall close to where he was standing and rubbed at the wood. "It's got good bones, a good foundation. I'm sure cleaning and fixing it won't be a problem. Bring it back to its original beauty."

"Uh ... I could help."

Michael whipped around. "You'd do that? Really? With all your past experience of working with your dad?" He smiled. "I'd love that. But will you ... will it be—"

"You mean the nursing home?" He shook his head. "I run away from there all the time."

"I don't want any problems for you."

"I'm already in trouble with them." Clarence thought a minute. "Except one nurse. I think Carol truly cares. She is a gem if I've ever seen one." He held up a finger. "And I've seen one before her."

"If you're sure, because I'd love to have you teach me." Michael cocked his head. "Did you help him build this one, too?"

"I sure did." Clarence surveyed the room. "If I remember right, I put up the trim around the doors and windows. Plus staining and painting."

"There you go, then. Let's get at the plans." Michael checked the calendar on his phone. "Tomorrow?"

Clarence offered his hand. "Deal."

CHAPTER THIRTY-NINE

The next day, Bea sat in her car seat playing with Dolly. She murmured while she dressed Dolly in the same dress she had just taken off, caressing her brittle hair. "You're such a good dolly baby. I love my little baby. Your hair is so pretty. You look nice today in your new dress."

Bea held her close, closed her own eyes and hummed a tune that Mommy sang to her when she was a baby. She opened her eyes. Mommy had sung that song to her just last night. It had been a long time since Mommy sang to her. She smiled and rocked back and forth.

A large white van pulled up beside their car with lots of letters on it.

Bea eyed the letters. She already knew most of them. "H! Two Hs." She pointed at the letters and counted. "One, two. Letters and numbers. One, two, three." She looked at the sides and windows. "People riding in a car with lots of letters and numbers."

The van door slid open, and a leg stuck out.

Bea pretended not to stare and hugged Dolly, playing with her clothes. She snuck a peek at the leg coming out. "One leg, two legs. Two legs coming out."

Only there was just one leg.

The driver smiled at Bea as he lifted a wheelchair out of the back of the van and opened it.

Bea tried not to watch, but her eyes were drawn to an elderly woman with short gray curls and big eyeglasses.

The woman stretched her arm and grasped the arms of the wheelchair and stood.

Bea still only saw one leg. "One leg, two legs."

The lady swiveled on her one leg and sat down in the wheelchair. The driver adjusted the footrest.

Bea couldn't resist and stared—still waiting for the other leg to follow out of the van.

No leg.

She kicked her own legs. "One leg, two legs."

The driver wheeled the lady backwards to the curb.

"One leg."

The lady glanced up and grinned, waving.

Bea pushed into the back of her seat and peeked out of the corner of her eye. She squirmed and kicked, looking away, half-smiling.

The woman smiled and waved as the driver backed her up onto the sidewalk.

Bea stretched to see her and began to sing to Dolly. "Nice lady. One leg, no leg."

Mommy burst out of the store with her grocery bags and stepped off the sidewalk to let the woman be wheeled past. She ran back to the entrance door and held it open for them, smiling at Bea.

Bea watched Mommy hold the door and chattered. "One leg, one Mommy. One leg, one Dolly. One leg, one Bea." She pointed to herself.

Mommy stood aside to let other people through. She opened the door and tossed the bags onto the passenger seat and peeked around to Bea, reaching behind the seat to tickle her feet. "Hi Baby Bea. You okay?"

Bea nodded and giggled as she tried to kick away Mommy's tickling fingers.

Mommy got in and started the car.

Bea sang her new song. "One leg, one Mommy. One leg, one Dolly. One leg, one Bea."

"One Bea. Baby," Mommy added as she started backing out of her parking place.

Bea sang with Mommy as she kicked in her seat.

The man with the bird.

She stopped singing and bent forward in her car seat.

Mommy glanced in her rearview mirror. "Baby, sit back in your seat. Don't get me in trouble. Okay?"

"Okay." She kicked the back of Mommy's seat with her feet. "Mommy, that's the man."

"What man?" Mommy looked around the parking lot. "Quit kicking my seat. What man?"

"The man in the park."

"Where is he?"

"There." Bea pointed to the old man going into the grocery store.

When he opened the door, he looked back, like he knew they were talking about him. His eyes caught Bea's. He raised his eyebrows and winked.

She kicked harder and grinned.

He looked up and seemed to be watching something.

Bea looked up too, trying to see what he saw.

"There, Mommy. There's the bird he had with him that other day." Bea squirmed in the car seat, leaned into the window.

The hawk circled high above them, flying up, up, without flapping its wings.

The bird screeched and lifted higher and higher, still circling.

Bea pressed her hands against the glass.

The bird swooped between trees and the building and then up out of sight. When it dove back into sight again, she jumped.

The man stared at the bird then her, a smile on his face.

Bea kicked the back of Mommy's seat, swinging her legs.

"Bea! Quit kicking my seat." Mommy sighed. "Let's go home and eat. Ready?"

Bea shoved herself into the car seat and raised her hand to the man.

He waved back at her.

Mommy waved then gunned the car to the exit.

At home, Bea followed Mommy to the trailer, dragging a bag of apples along the sidewalk, Dolly tucked under one arm.

Mommy switched the heavy bags to one hand and inserted the key into the lock. "Huh. I'm sure I locked it." She let Bea in. "Bea. Really? Apples do not belong on the ground. Pick them up. I bought those for a treat and now they're gonna be bruised."

Bea lifted them as high as she could, but the bag still touched the ground.

"Here. Let me have them. You go in and help put stuff away."

Bea entered the trailer house, but stopped short. A man sat in the chair.

Mommy bumped into Bea, dropping the apples. "Bea. Come on. Move it. I gotta—"

Bea backed onto Mommy's foot.

"Ow. Bea!" Mommy dropped the groceries. "Oh God." She scooped Bea into her arms, crushing her close, cheek to cheek.

Mommy's eyes looked dark. This wasn't Mommy. But this Mommy wasn't mean or hurting.

This Mommy was shaking. Mommy was scared.

A deep voice boomed from within the trailer. "Well, hello, Katelyn. You're lookin' ... good."

The man stood up. "And who have we here?"

CHAPTER FORTY

That afternoon, Michael stopped at Hillcrest Homes. Visual layers of angels and demons overlapped the physical building and interior. Many beings towered above the roof and trees—some heads obscured by clouds. Angels surrounded the nursing home in lines except for a couple gaps. Angels nodded as he walked into the building; all the demons glared.

Michael stuck his head into the open office door and knocked on the counter. The angel behind the receptionist leaned down and nodded, his arm across his chest.

Michael nodded slightly in return.

Photos of smiling, toothless children, strung together by blue and pink ribbons, swagged on the partial wall of the cubicle. Sparkly streamers drooped with a deflated balloon; the message on the balloon, "Happy Birthday, Grandma," was still visible, only in a contorted font.

The receptionist didn't look up from her computer. "Yeah? Whadya want?" A small cross hung from a chain framed by a revealing neckline. Dark circles emphasized bags beneath her eyes that make-up couldn't hide and tiny lines traced her eyes and mouth, her forehead. Worry lines.

"I'm here for Clarence Timmelsen. Is he here?" Father's heart began to reveal the roots of the receptionist's pain. Michael glanced at the guardian behind her. His eyes revealed the rest.

She smirked. "Lemme check. Maybe. Maybe not. He might be in the park or downtown. Or ... at the grocery store. It's hard telling where he'll be these days." She glanced up at Michael, then right back down to her work. Slowly, her eyes inched up to Michael's full height. Eyes wide, her mouth dropped open. Breathless, she sputtered, "What ... can I help you with, M-Mr. ... Mr. ... may I have your ... name?"

He flashed his grin. The angel behind the receptionist sputtered. "Sure. My name is Michael, and I'm here for Clarence Timmelsen."

The receptionist didn't respond. Her mouth gaped. Her face went blank.

The angel behind her placed his hands on her shoulders.

Michael leaned in. "Ma'am? Excuse me, ma'am. Are you all right?" He waved his hand in front of her face. The smile might have been too much.

A nurse scooted around the corner. "Jane? I need you to call a family for me."

No answer.

"Jane? Are you ... " She noticed Michael and stopped. "Whoo-wee!" Elbow on the counter, her chin on her hand, she stared into his eyes. "Um, who do we have here, Jane?"

No response.

Another nurse rounded the doorway. "Jane, where are those files we talked about? I need ... "

Michael stepped back. The room was getting crowded with humans and angels and—

"Hello." The nurse looked from Michael to Jane. To Michael. "I'm Carol. Can I help you?"

Michael nodded to three huge angels surrounding her. He bent slowly. These three spent time closest to the Throne.

"I'm Michael." He held out his hand. "I'm here to pick up Clarence. Clarence Timmelsen? He agreed to give me some of his valuable time." He glanced at the nurse and receptionist, still standing like pillars of salt.

Carol shook his hand. "Girls. Um, girls?" She clapped her hands in front of the women.

"Oh. Oh, yes." Jane stretched.

The nurse moved her elbows from the counter. "I was just in here ... um. I know I came here for something." She pointed and nodded, ponytail bouncing. "I'll just go back to the nurse's station and ... " She waved to Michael. "It was nice ... meeting you, sir. You look nice ... uh ... you're a nice ... man."

He bowed his head and she backed out of the office.

Carol raised her eyebrows. "Sorry about that. I don't know what got into her. She must need to go on break. Low blood sugar."

She turned to Michael. "I'll show you Clarence's room. If he is going to work with you, you'll need to know what room he's in."

"Sure." He paused, looking down at Jane. "Have a great day. Thanks for the help." He waited for a response.

Her angel snapped his fingers.

Carol snapped her fingers too, and Jane jumped. "Oh my," Jane said. "I'm sorry Carol. I didn't see you."

"It's okay. I've got it covered." Carol started down the hall. "You seem to have made quite an impression with the office staff and the nursing staff to boot. I'm sure you are worthy of their worship, but ... " She closed a door to a resident room as they walked past, muffling the loud TV. "How is Clarence going to help you?"

"I purchased a building downtown, and Clarence happened to wander in."

He stepped aside for a horribly stooped man with a walker. A demon leaned on the man's back, glaring, positioned between the man and Michael.

Michael continued, following Carol, "We started talking and I learned he and his dad—especially his dad—had built it, so I asked if he'd be willing to help with the renovations. He agreed, and that's why I'm here." He hesitated. "And no, I am not worthy of their worship."

"Sure. It was just a comment. Not intended for truth." Carol pointed to a picture of Clarence beside a door as she knocked.

Two angels positioned one on each side of the door, genuflected as Michael approached. He nodded and they stood again. They were old friends and he barely contained himself from roughhousing with them, pounding them on the back, wrestling. He distracted himself by studying Clarence's photograph. His chest almost burst at seeing the angels assigned there. He toned down a grin.

"Clarence?" Michael entered the room and reached out his hand. He clasped Clarence's, pumping it up and down nodding at two more angels—one in each corner of the room. One had full weapons: a glowing carved sword, a shield bearing the mark of his rank, and helmet. They both bowed to Michael as he entered. He nodded, his eyes on Clarence. "How are you, Buddy? Ready to go?"

Clarence combed through his hair with his fingers then turned to Carol. "Did I tell you I got a job? I'm going out with Michael. We're working on his building."

"Okay." She cleared her throat. "At least you didn't sneak out. And at least you're supervised. That's more than I can say for the past week." She patted Clarence on the arm. "I think this man is a good influence on you, Clarence, so it's fine with me."

Michael's face grew hot. Embarrassment. Inhabiting a human body was tough. He never knew whether he would perspire, cry, or belch. Grew harder each day. Energy encouraged him from Father. He focused on the angels and the Word. He had known this assignment would be lengthy and difficult.

Clarence grabbed his jacket from the closet and closed the door behind him. He winked at Michael. "Ready?"

"I am if you are. Good to have you with me today." Michael winked back, eyes alerting the angels on post. Clarence's eyes twinkled today. Interesting day.

Carol checked her watch. "Are you going to be gone for meals?"

Michael shrugged. "We don't know yet. Is that okay?"

"Sure. I don't have a problem with that. Just make sure he gets fed and sits down once in a while. That he drinks some water. That's all I ask."

"Oh, I'll be okay." Clarence took off down the hall.

Michael nodded. "So, you're saying you want me to boss Clarence? Sure thing, Ma'am." He laughed. "I'd better catch up with him." He high-fived angels lining the hall as he passed. A demon ducked into a room, hissing and spitting, but an angel quickly brandished two swords, crossing them, binding the demon from wandering.

A tiny lady stopped Clarence in the hall. When Michael caught up to him, she was showing Clarence her mail.

Clarence reached for the papers. "This is your insurance?"

She gazed way up at Michael. Even though she appeared astounded, she didn't smile. Her eyes were red and swollen.

"Oh, Mrs. Hatly, this is Michael. Michael, this is Mrs. Hatly."

She barely nodded, her attention right back to Clarence. "I hoped since you're a lawyer, you might be able to figure this out. My insurance has always paid." She pointed to the document. "And now they refused." Her eyes filled with tears. "I don't know what to do. If they don't pay, I can't stay here." Her chin quivered. "I don't know where I'd go."

Clarence put his arm around her. "Can I hang onto these so I can figure this out?"

She nodded and wiped her eyes.

"I'm sure it's just a mistake." He looked up at Michael. "I'm going to help Michael today. Then I'll come back and sort this out." He folded the papers and slid them in the inside jacket pocket.

She patted Clarence's arm. "Thank you. You're such a gentleman."

He smiled and gently hugged her.

"You have a good day." She reached her hand to Michael. "Take care of my friend."

Michael leaned down, her tiny hand in his. "I will, Mrs. Hatly. If anyone can figure this out, Clarence can."

Outside, Michael slammed the door to his old red pickup and waited to start the truck until Clarence shut his.

An angel riding in the bed of the truck pounded on the top of the cab.

Carol and Jane waved from the entrance. Their angels crowded behind, imitating the humans. Michael clamped his lips shut and looked away from Clarence until he could talk without laughing. The nursing home was going to be interesting.

"They really like you, Michael." Clarence pointed. "Those women."

Michael laughed, but tried to fake a coughing fit.

"You okay?" Clarence patted him on the back.

He nodded, engrossed in clearing his throat.

"No, they really thought you were hot stuff. I saw how they made eyes at you. You had better look out, 'cause they'll be after you."

Michael rolled his eyes. "Naw. I'm not looking. They'll get tired of trying and not getting any response. Besides, they like you better."

"Ha. Like me better?" Clarence snorted. "No." He tapped his fingertips together, fidgeted in his seat. "Y-you should know something right now so you can dump me out if you want." He sucked in a deep breath. "I'm an ex-con." He faced Michael. "I spent the last sixty years in prison." He stared at his hands in his lap. "So if you can't handle that ... well ... tell me now and I'll get out of your truck."

Michael watched the trees wave and fan. "I know about you being in prison."

"You checked me out then."

Michael shrugged and nodded slowly. "You could say that."

Clarence nodded. "Okay. Just as long as we're on the same page. I don't want any surprises for you."

"No surprises." Michael started the truck and backed out. "How many years did you say?"

"Sixty."

Michael whistled. He drove out of the parking lot. "How'd you make it that long? I mean, didn't you want to break out a few times?" Some of his former angel comrades, now in chains, had to be wanting to break free.

Clarence huffed. "You bet I did." He glanced at Michael. "The first few years ... I guess I was ... in denial." He rubbed his thumbs together. "My wife was dead. I couldn't believe I'd ... I can't even remember the day she died," he blurted. "I guess I got knocked out." Silence. "So ... I just ... tried to stay out of trouble."

"But couldn't you get parole?" Michael shifted gears. Grinding. How did humans shift, listen and talk at the same time? No wonder they lost focus with the Commander.

"I tried, but hit wall after wall." Clarence turned away from Michael. "When I left prison a week ago—feels like forever now—the warden said the judge back then set it up to send me here to the nursing home."

"The judge?" They passed the grocery store as they drove up the steep hill. Downshift. Downshift. Should have gotten an automatic.

"My wife's father—that judge. If he set that up, I guess he made it so I'd never get paroled." He pounded his knee. "Damn, I got angry. Still am. I decided that nobody would ever run my life again. So I studied and got my law degree, but that didn't even help, because here I am." He shook his head. "Enough about me. You have family? Anyone?" Clarence adjusted the seat belt.

"I do, but in a different way than most. I have lots of family." A visual flashed in front of him, superimposed over the layout of the street: the host of heaven. He smiled. "Just not in the usual way." He turned a corner. "I'm a loner. It seems strange I'm sure, to you. But I just stick by myself."

Clarence looked away.

Michael glanced at him. "You got quiet. Did I say something wrong?"

Clarence shook his head. "No. You sound like me. I consider myself a loner too. It's not an easy life, but it's just how it is. I would have loved to have had someone, but ... it didn't ... "

Michael paused. "Is this going to be too hard for you Clarence? I mean working on the building where you were married? Too many memories?"

Clarence shot Michael a sharp look.

Oh-oh. Said too much. Did he tell me he'd been married at the town hall or—

Clarence shook his head vehemently and visibly relaxed. "No, I feel close to Annie when I'm there." He fiddled with the zipper on his jacket. "I feel so alive there, with all the memories. Even the memories of her father— the old bastard."

Michael chuckled. "I take it he wasn't an easy man to get along with." He parked in front of the building.

Angels surrounded it. Each angel was unique in dress, looks and weaponry. Every angel recognized Michael and nodded and bowed, or knelt. Angels lined the inside. Their anticipation, their excitement growing.

Clarence shook his head again. "No. I took his precious little girl away from him," he whispered.

That was pain in Clarence's voice. After sixty years.

"Well, here we are." Michael said. "Time to work."

Clarence stubbed his foot on the way through the door. He pointed. "First thing is to fix that."

"I'll add it to my growing list."

Clarence held out his hands. "Where's the broom?"

Michael laughed. "Here're all the cleaning supplies, tools, and building materials. Feel free to organize." He rummaged in the closet, bumped a bucket of old nails and tarnished hardware that clattered to the floor and grabbed a broom, dustpan and brush. "Here you go. Knock yourself out." He ignored the chuckling angel. Felt like his first time out of heaven.

Clarence set the dustpan and brush down in a corner and set to work. Swirls of dust particles danced in the sunlight as Michael opened windows.

"Too much air?"

Clarence stopped sweeping and bounced the broom on the floor. "Nope. It's okay. It's musty. Needs airing out." His eyes flitted around the room. "I wish you could have seen this place when it was all new. I can almost smell the fresh sawdust." He resumed sweeping. "I love that smell."

Michael began wiping walls and dusting cobwebs off the ceiling. "Did your dad do the electricity too?" He caught his finger on a rough corner. The pain from that splinter jolted him. Blood distracted him.

Clarence nodded. "Yup. Back then, you didn't subcontract out. You did it all. Some guys were better at it than others. Dad was better than most—at all of it." He stopped sweeping. "Was this anything after being the town hall? I mean any other business?"

Michael wiped his finger on his jeans. "I don't think so. Odd isn't it. That such a sturdy, well made building, was never used for anything else." He adjusted his ball cap. "Who owned it back then?"

"My father-in-law did. He owned half the town." Clarence tipped the dustpan. "Literally—half the town. He always joked in a cocky way, that he'd get the rest someday. I think he died doing just that." Clarence swept dirt into the pan. "Just stuff I'd hear in Chicago. I never came back. Until now."

Michael replaced a light bulb.

"You don't need a ladder for that, you're so tall." Clarence tapped the broom again. "You know where I grew up," he said, arms wide. "Here. Where'd you grow up?"

Michael opened a new box of light bulbs. "Well, I grew up around ... Idaho. We moved a lot. I don't remember much of my childhood. You're really lucky you remember so much. You remember your dad. You remember building this ... this building." He grinned.

"Yeah, and some of what I do remember, I don't want to remember." Clarence continued sweeping toward the back room. "But one thing is for sure."

Oh-oh. "What's that?"

"I don't remember this place being so dirty." He sneezed.

"God bless you!" Michael laughed. Two angels flew away on assignment. Michael bid them safety.

Clarence shuffled in and around the old junk, moving and

sweeping under chairs and tables. For a moment, it seemed like Clarence was interacting with something or someone. There was such grace to his movements as he swept the floorboards. Clarence closed his eyes and moved with the broom like he was holding someone in his arms.

Michael averted his eyes and smiled. His heart wanted to burst for Clarence as he traveled back in time to dance with his beloved wife. Those feelings seemed precious between a man and a woman, something Michael knew nothing about.

He quietly went about tasks: changing light bulbs, cleaning bathrooms, wiping down wood paneled walls. He paused at a window and stood for a time, relishing in the moment for Clarence.

The broom clunked to the floor.

Michael jumped and turned.

Clarence was nowhere in the room. The entrance door swung open.

"Clarence!" Michael hurried to the door. "Clarence?" He rushed around the corner. No Clarence. The old guy was fast.

The hawk circled directly above. It mounted ever so much higher on wind currents then dove to where Michael stood. The bird fluttered inches away from his face, screeching. The wind from its powerful wings stirred the invisible domain. Ripples encircled them. The power of the Father poured through time.

Then it spread its wings wide—eyes focused—and soared above the trees surrounding the old building.

Clarence was the target.

The bird flew higher.

Higher.

Michael nodded at the bird. Soon, old friend, soon.

CHAPTER FORTY-ONE

Sheriff Dennison shoved paperwork across the desk to Todd, a deputy, who frowned and said, "Sheriff, this doesn't seem right. He's just an old man. What did he do to deserve this?" He put his hat on, pushed it back, scratched and pulled it down tight. "He's already in a kind of jail, isn't he? Isn't that enough? I mean, what can he do from a nursing home?"

"I know." Denny rested his elbows on the desk. "But the background evidence is certainly there. I've spent the last couple days checking and rechecking—he spent his last sixty years in prison ... for killing his wife."

Todd's eyes popped. "He what?" Eyebrows arched as he whistled through his teeth. He shoved his ball hat up on his forehead. "He killed his wife? Like back then when they were young?" He shook his head. "For real?"

"According to all the files from Pete and the police database—for real." Denny shuffled papers. "I even called the prison this morning. It all checks out. And now with him breaking and entering, well ... we have to bring him in." He slowly stood up, groaning. Some days, he wasn't so fond of his job. "We have no choice. I don't like it any better than you, but we have to do what's right."

Todd nodded and pulled his hat down. "Okay. Where do I find him?" He picked up the papers and tapped them against the counter.

"Start at Hillcrest. Ask Carol—if she's there." He sighed. "Then start searching the town. Pete saw him at the park once. He's been at the grocery store. He's definitely leaving a trail."

"Okay, sir. I'm on it."

As Todd pushed out the door and headed to the squad car, Denny reached for the phone.

He'd better call Carol.

CHAPTER FORTY-TWO

Katty inched in front of Bea.

Every breath a gasp.

Prickles of fear crawled across her shoulders.

Bea climbed up Katty's legs. Her arms strangled Katty's neck.

"I said. Who do we have here?" Phil leaned forward in the old green recliner.

The room grew cold.

Katty's gut wrenched. "Phil. You're b-back." She slid another foot.

"Yeah, I'm back."

God he looked evil. Or she'd changed. His muscular good looks used to excite her.

She kicked a grocery bag, slid the other foot toward the kitchen.

Coughing, she edged toward the counter, Bea clinging. The knife she had used to cut an apple at breakfast was still in the sink. She let her arm dangle there, slid the knife along her skin under her sleeve and hid it behind her back, wincing.

"Whatcha thinkin' little darlin'?" he whispered in her ear, his hand on her shoulder.

Katty jumped. "I—I didn't hear you get up." She choked, his scent still raw in her memory. She shivered as his breath grazed her skin.

He slid his hand down her shoulder, to her elbow. "Who is this little filly? Introduce us."

Bea scrambled in Katty's arms, crawling away from him.

Katty struggled to hold her, shifted her to the other hip. The knife cut her arm. A rare surge of adrenaline spiked in Katty. A Mama Bear's rush to protect her young. She would have to die before she'd let him have her daughter!

Phil followed Bea. "Peek-a-boo!"

He bent to look at her. He snapped up to Katty's face, eye to eye. "She looks a lot like ... us." He grinned, his breath putrid, his voice syrupy. His eyes radiated all the vivid, horrendous memories of their past together: his brutal touch, cruel words, sadistic acts of violence. "I'm glad I couldn't find you ... I would have ... she wouldn't be here. What we couldn't do with her." One eyelid quivered. He cocked his head.

Katty hooked her arm around Bea's middle, got her balance, and bolted for the door.

Phil sprang and grabbed her. "Oh, no. Don't go. I want to get to know my ... daughter." Phil swung her to face him, gripping her shoulders. "Oh-h-h. You're trembling."

Slivers of terror clawed up Katty's back. She wanted to retch.

He ran his fingers up Bea's arm. "So soft and fresh." He looked directly into Bea's face.

Bea scrunched her eyes shut.

"Oh, she's shaking too. Like a little leaf." He reached under Bea's arms with both of his hands. "Come to Papa."

Katty flicked the knife from her sleeve into his gut and twisted it. Blood gushed and swirled.

The room morphed into their past bedroom. Phil had backed away from her, a bloody knife in his hand.

She screamed from then to now.

She tore Bea loose from him. Ran for the door, clutching Bea to her chest.

"Bitch! Bitch! Where do you think you're gonna go, huh?" he roared. "I found you this time. I can find you again."

CHAPTER FORTY-THREE

Hours after he had run out on Michael, Clarence found himself once again in front of the old town hall.

"Michael, you here? I want so much to believe." He ran his fingers through his hair. "I want you here. You make me feel like a good person." He tried the door.

Open.

He pushed the door and wiped his face with his shirtsleeve. What he saw amazed and scared him at the same time.

The room he entered was perfect. Just like when he and Dad had finished it. The wood paneling appeared new and smooth, clean and rich.

Michael couldn't have restored it that fast.

He rubbed the paneling up and down with his old weathered hand and shook his head.

A slight rustle behind him made him turn.

Someone was in the room with him.

Annie.

He gasped, put his hands to his face, and shuddered. His skin was different. Soft. Smooth. He held his hands out in front of his face. They appeared to be the hands of a young man. Strong, filled out, well muscled. No age spots. No wrinkles or thin skin with scattered bruises. Just the familiar scars.

He lowered his hands and beheld his bride.

She was as lovely as on their wedding day. But this time, she wore a skirt with a tucked-in blouse and an apron, blotched with white.

He peered closer at her face. White powder on one cheek. And the sweetest smile he had ever seen.

Satisfied. Happy.

A small child peeked from behind her skirt and shyly smiled at him.

Clarence dropped to his knees. He looked up at Annie. "Who is this? Is she ... ours?"

Annie smiled and nodded. She patted the little girl's head and gave her a gentle push.

He opened his arms and she tiptoed a step to him, a shy smile on her lips.

Annie gave her another pat toward Clarence.

The little girl stood inches from him.

Blue eyes to blue eyes.

She leaned into Clarence's shoulder.

He enveloped her in his arms. "Oh, my sweetie. Oh, my God." He cradled her, smoothed her unruly hair and cupped her chin. "You are so beautiful. You look just like your mamma. And you remind me of ... someone I've seen." He smiled up at Annie, then at the child. He laughed as he brushed the white powder from her cheek. "It's flour," he said. "Are you and Mommy baking?"

The child nodded, eyes twinkling.

There was a screech at the door, and the child ran behind Annie's skirts.

No one was there.

When Clarence turned back into the room, Annie was gone. So was their child.

He rushed to the spot where they had stood and fell to the floor. "No. No. No!" Sobbing, he pounded the floor, tears mixed with dust and dirt.

Gone. Again.

The floor transformed into old wood. Dirt in the corner where he had swept it. One new lightbulb.

He sat back on his haunches, hands on his legs. There was the broom he had left in the corner.

"But you were here, Annie. Where did you go? My darling. My Annie. And our child. Where did you go?" he cried. "Please come back. I'll change. I'll be better. Annie ... "

Silence.

Emptiness permeated Clarence as he sat on the dirty floor.

"Michael is even gone." He choked and hardly moved in the dust and the silence.

A horn from outside made him jump. Time had passed. The rays of the sun had lengthened.

He tried to stand, but only made it to his hands and knees. He pushed himself up and stumbled, crumpled, bending to his knees again. "How can I go on?"

Every cell of his body screamed when he slowly straightened.

Moments ago he had felt so young and alive. Now every minute of his age weighed him down.

Heaviness overwhelmed him. He stumbled and shuffled across the room to the door. He'd lost her again.

As he stepped out onto the stoop, the hawk screeched. The bird circled higher and higher, then tucked its wings and dove right for Clarence.

CHAPTER FORTY-FOUR

Katty shoved Bea into the back seat.

"Mommy!" Bea screamed and pointed. "He's coming!"

"Bea. Get in your car seat! NOW!" Katty jumped into the car and slammed her foot in the car door. Her eyes blurred. The pain knocked her back.

Holding his bleeding stomach, Phil stumbled from the threshold.

She shut the door again and found the keys, only to drop them.

He tripped down the steps and landed on the ground next to the car.

"Mommy! He's coming! Mommy go go!" Bea shrieked in her ear.

"Bea, get in your seat! Now!"

Katty fumbled along the floor, found the keys and managed to shove the right one into the ignition and crank it over.

The engine sputtered to life.

As she slammed it into reverse, Phil grabbed the door handle.

She yelled. "Hold on Bea!" She roared out of the driveway, catching sight of him rolling and tumbling—getting pummeled as the tires threw up loose gravel and dirt. The car swerved until she reached asphalt and the tires caught, spinning and squealing. They raced away.

Bea thudded across the back seat, wailing. "Mommy, Mommy, Mommy!"

"Oh my god! Oh my God!" Katty tore around the corner.

Behind her, Bea bumped something again. She sobbed and sobbed.

"Bea! Into the car seat!" Katty raced around another corner.

"I'm not slowing down, Baby! Gotta get away from that man." She glanced into the rearview mirror. "He'll never get his filthy hands on my little girl."

Bea climbed into the car seat and buckled. "Mommy?"

Katty tore around another corner. "He's never going to get you Bea. Never! Never going to use you like he used Mommy."

"Mommy, I buckled—"

A siren pierced the terror.

"No!" Katty gunned the engine. Tires screeched. She checked the rearview mirror as the car swerved wildly.

Blam!

Katty's head slammed into the steering wheel.

Bea's screams now, wove back through time to fuse with Katty's screams, then.

Terror forced Katty to a dilapidated old house and a dingy bedroom. Fear ripped open gruesome and terrifying memories. She had shrieked as she came to, struggled against ropes tying her down on their bed. Phil had backed away from the bed, holding a knife in his bloody hands.

Her blood.

Their baby's blood.

His eyes had spewed evil as he laughed. "Another one bites the dust."

Demons had swarmed with the hot blood. Became the blood. Hungry mouths, thirsty eyes. Their laughter rose to an intense pitch, twisting around her screams.

Their laughter had terrorized her dreams every night since.

Something pounded against metal.

Katty opened her eyes. Blood dripped from her forehead and nose.

Gravel and bricks pelted the car.

"Mommy?"

Bea? A baby lived!

The windshield was buckled. Steam hissed from the front of the car. The hood crumpled against a brick-fortified mailbox.

Katty pushed on the gas pedal.

It still ran!

"Oh. God." Her head throbbed. She blotted the blood with her sleeve and blinked, shaking her head.

"Oh my God! Bea!" She stretched, looking into the rear view mirror.

Bea sat in the car seat, eyes wet and red, stretching her arms toward Katty.

"Bea! Bea! You all right?" Tears mixed with blood. "Baby?" She jumped out and onto the backseat, grabbing at the twisted but buckled straps, face to face with her little girl. "You're strapped in? Oh my God! You're strapped in!"

Katty unbuckled Bea and crushed her to her chest.

CHAPTER FORTY-FIVE

Lex shifted closer to the driver's door. He was parked behind the implement company, near a row of green combines. From where he sat, he could keep tabs on the highway traffic, the park, the drive-inn. And if he craned his neck, he could check the employee parking spaces at the grocery store.

He tapped his trigger finger against the loaded gun, half listening to the police scanner on the seat beside him, half listening to the intercom from the implement company. Spring planting time.

An employee, dressed in typical work shirt and pants, opened the back door again. The guy had come out two other times: once to empty trash into the dumpster nearby and another to get something from his pickup. Each time, he had noticed Lex sitting there. He had waved the first time. The third time, he just came out and busied himself with some old machinery parts lying against the building, rearranged them a couple times and looked directly at Lex.

Hurry up Phil. Get your kid and let's get outa here.

Lex wasn't sure if he wanted a kid hanging around. And he was pretty sure Phil wasn't going to get Father of the Year. More like—

Static crackled from the scanner. Lex turned up the volume. "Caucasian male transported to ER. Life-threatening stab wound to the abdomen. Mega loss of blood."

Time spent as an orderly a few years back would come in handy after all.

Lex leaned forward. "Phil baby? Is that you? What did you do?" He started the car. "You let a puny woman get to you?"

Backing away from the farm equipment, he started to flip off the employee, but at the last minute thought better of it. Might need this little hide-away again. He waved and held up his beer, grinning.

The man laughed and waved back.

This town was A-okay.

CHAPTER FORTY-SIX

Clarence balked when the deputy pushed him toward the open cell door. He strained against the handcuffs.

"It's just until we figure this all out sir ... uh, Mr. Timmelsen. They'll bring supper in a little bit."

Clarence stared at the bars. He barely heard the words.

"Sir?" Todd stepped in front of Clarence and pulled him along.

Clarence stumbled.

Bars. He had spent sixty years behind bars. But these cell bars and window bars marched toward him like the brooms in that old movie they had shown in prison. That part had terrified most of the inmates. Old childhood monsters chasing them down.

The deputy's radio sputtered. "Todd, you on supper break?"

Todd glanced at Clarence. "Naw. No time."

"Get to ER. A white male seems suspicious—bleeding profusely. Lawn service guy dropped him off. Said he was delirious. He was talking about killing a woman if he'd ever got his hands on her."

"Roger that." Todd replaced his radio. "You won't be here for long, Sir. Just until Sheriff can clear some things up."

Clarence's feet planted just outside the cell door. "No." His legs crumpled.

The deputy caught him before he fell and heaved him to the cot.

He sank down as the deputy unlocked the cuffs and closed the cell door.

The radio broke in. "Todd to ER!"

"On it."

The lock clicked and Clarence jumped. Bars were everywhere—in front of him, in back of him.

Clarence shivered, stared at his hands and rubbed where the cuffs had pinched.

Handcuffs.

Bars.

Again.

CHAPTER FORTY-SEVEN

Lex hid behind the entrance door in the ER hallway, waiting for his chance to rescue Phil. That buffoon deputy needed to go away. Somehow. He squeezed his arm against the gun holster inside his jacket.

The deputy spoke into a radio. "Sheriff? Todd here. They're examining him now."

Lex squinted. What a dweeb. The dork thought he'd contained Phil Daynton?

"Good. Stay with him. Don't leave his side. I don't care what you have to see in that ER, ya hear me?"

"Yes, Sir." The deputy pushed the door open and hesitated just inside. A nurse rushed past him, carrying bloody linens. She threw them in a laundry hamper just outside the room.

He swallowed and paled.

Ahh. Deputy Dork was squeamish.

She turned to go back into the emergency room and grinned, holding up an emesis basin. "Need this? You are the fastest case of green I've ever seen."

Lex slid behind the hamper. Easy does it.

Dork, white as hospital sheets, shuffled past the gurney to Phil's head.

Love to see him spill his guts.

Medical personnel rushed around the room. A doctor entered and assessed the patient.

"No pulse. Shockers. Get the paddles." The doctor fired orders as fast as he could talk. "Start the IV. He's lost a lot of blood."

Beep, beep, beep. Buzz. Whirr.

Staff hurried in and out of the room.

Lex had broken Phil out of worse places. Ha. Phil could even fake death.

"Watch the levels, people. Okay. Looks like surgery. Gotta go in and patch him up. Prep him."

"No way he's going to make it through this. He's lost too much blood."

"He's shutting down. Get him to surgery, STAT!"

Lex peeked around the hamper. The deputy was gonna hurl. Sweat soaked through his shirt. His eyes watered and crossed. He swooned, his head slammed against a counter and he was down for the count.

Good boy.

Personnel hustled the big deputy out a side door and onto a gurney.

Except for one old nurse.

Hand on his gun, he skimmed around the hamper and decked the nurse across her forehead.

He scooped Phil up. "God, you've gained weight."

Phil's eyes popped open. A grin spread across his face.

CHAPTER FORTY-EIGHT

Clarence shivered, though fully dressed and covered with a blanket. He stared through the window far above. More bars.

The concrete block wall was just like prison. Nicer facilities here, at least. It struck him that this cell should have felt familiar—like home. He had lived his whole adult life in a cell. Even though these walls were devoid of his years of artwork, scratches and hash marks, it was still a cell with bars and concrete.

He pulled the blanket over his head.

He didn't belong here. The thought shook him. If not here, and not Hillcrest, he was homeless.

The office door scraped open. A crack of light beamed toward him.

He tensed, barely making out a silhouette. The shadows shifted, and a person walked to Clarence's cell, hands resting on the bars.

"Clarence?"

He held his breath.

"Clarence? You asleep?"

He raised up on his elbow. "Who is it?" He shielded his eyes against the light. "Who's there?"

"Sheriff Dennison." He jingled keys. "I need to talk to you. I'm going to unlock your cell and come in. Is that okay?"

Clarence nodded. "Yeah. Sure. You're the sheriff. You can—"

Keys jingled, and once again, there was the click of a lock.

Clarence struggled to get up, but the sheriff gently pushed him back down.

"Please don't. I'll sit on the floor." Sheriff Dennison eased himself to the concrete. "I can't go home without talking to you."

Clarence rose up again. "Sheriff, you don't have to. I know what I am. I know—"

"Shhh." Sheriff shook his head. "I didn't want to bring you in. You've done your time." He whistled under his breath. "Sixty years. Damn."

Clarence blinked. Sixty years—

"There was pressure from some people in the community to lock you up. I brought you in, just as much to appease them, as to keep them from harming you. I want you to know I'll do everything I can to protect you and your rights."

"Rights." Clarence choked on a laugh. "I have no rights. You said it yourself. Sixty years in prison and now I've been shipped off to a nursing home. What rights do I have?"

Sheriff Dennison stared at the floor. His jaw worked back and forth. After a long moment, he looked Clarence in the eye. "If I read the law correctly, you start over as a new, totally cleared citizen." He cocked his head. "But I did get to read in your file—you're a lawyer? You studied while you were in prison? That ought to help establish you as a cleared citizen. Rehabilitated."

Clarence stared at the bars. "People don't see me that way. All they see is ex-con."

"I'm the sheriff, not them. They can have an opinion, but ultimately, it is up to me and the court. And right now, I'm going to let you rest while I do the paperwork, then we'll transfer you back to Hillcrest."

Clarence closed his eyes. "Yeah. From prison to the old people's home, to here, back to the old people's home. I have never had any say over my own life since I was ... back ... a kid of twenty. Sixty years. Dad tried to visit me, but that bastard judge disallowed even that."

"Who was the judge? I haven't had a chance to go that far in your records."

"Percy Green." Clarence wished he could forget his father-in-law. "I can still see his face—set on revenge." But could he blame the man, after what Clarence had done to sweet Annie? Sweet, sweet

Annie. Clarence rolled away from the sheriff. "I wish he'd shot me instead. All this'd be over. I'd be dead." He covered his face with the blanket. Jaw tight. Hands clenched.

The cot shifted as the sheriff stood. Then the faint click of the door. Just one click. No click of the lock.

He pulled the blanket tighter around his head and squeezed his eyes shut.

CHAPTER FORTY-NINE

Dennison glanced up from his desk and looked out through the office windows as Todd, his head bandaged, escorted a wild-looking brown-haired woman and a female toddler from the squad car. The woman appeared to be in her late twenties—hard to tell. Rough looking.

Once indoors, the woman shook Todd's hand from her arm. Blood streaked from her nose to her chin. One sleeve was bloody. "I don't need to be here. I can—"

Todd gave her a gentle shove toward the desk. "Ma'am, you just drove into a brick mailbox. You don't have a choice."

The woman limped to the counter, carrying the child. The child was bleeding from a cut on her arm. The side of her face might be bruised. Eyes were red.

Denny hustled to the door of his office. "Todd. Hospital?" He pointed to them.

"No hospital," the woman demanded, shaking her head. "No way!"

Denny walked to her. "This your daughter?" He looked her over, then the child. "Ma'am, your daughter is bleeding and needs to be looked at. You need to be checked, too."

"No." Her head high. "No hospital. Please, just let us stay here." The woman stumbled.

Drunk?

He frowned at Todd. "Did you test her? Is she ... "

He shook his head. "Traumatized. Been babbling about some guy that came back. Keeps saying he can't have her daughter." He

197

shook his head. "She wasn't even going to let me drive her here until I got another deputy to follow us in her car. It's beat up, but drivable."

Denny exhaled. "Sit here and let us get your information. What's your name, Ma'am?"

She stood stiffly beside the chair. "Randolph," she said. "Katelyn Randolph. This is Beatrice."

Denny reached for a box of tissue, placed it beside her and checked her nose. "That might be broken, Katelyn."

"Katty." The woman started weeping and sat, squeezing the child against her.

Beatrice shuddered but stared, first at Denny, then Todd.

Denny picked up a document on his desk and handed it to Todd. "You okay to transport the prisoner back home? I'll cover this."

"I'm fine." Todd picked up the paper and looked it over. "Right away." He disappeared through the door toward the cell block.

Denny pulled several tissues from the box and thrust them into Katty's hand. "Tell me what happened."

She gulped and gently blew her nose. "He's evil. He used to ... " She looked at Denny, at the dispatcher seated close by, and then back at Denny. She blew a breath out, raised her chin and said, "I think I killed him. Just now. I think I killed him."

Denny straightened. Serious domestic violence. First the guy with the stab wound. Now ...

He grabbed a scratch pad and pen. "Where, Ma'am? What's your address?"

"212 Frederick Street."

Trailer court. He pulled an empty chair closer and sat. Betcha.

"What if I killed him? You can't take my baby from me. She's all I have."

Denny shook his head. "Slow down. We won't let anything happen to you or your daughter. She looks like she's been through enough."

Beatrice hugged into her mommy, pulling away from him. Poor kid.

The cell block door opened. Todd stepped through first, his hand at the old man's elbow.

The little girl raised her head as Clarence walked into the room.

His hands were cuffed behind his back, head down. He didn't look left or right, just at his feet as he shuffled past.

"Mommy!" Little Beatrice peeked from under her mommy's arm. "Mommy. That's him."

Denny flinched. Was he wrong about Clarence? "That's him?" He leaned down. "Beatrice, who? Who are you talking about?"

The girl hid behind Katty, but a tiny finger pointed toward Clarence.

"Clarence?"

The man stopped.

Denny said it again. "Clarence?"

"What?" Clarence lifted his head.

"Wait a minute, Todd." Denny stood, holding up a finger. "Child, you know this man?" He should have checked the sex offender list.

The girl wiped her nose on Katty's shirt. She nodded and quickly ducked under her mommy's arm.

"Clarence, you know this little girl?" Denny pointed at the child.

He looked at Denny. Then at Katty.

The child peeked out.

His eyes softened. "What happened to you, Little One?"

Katty Randolph perked up at last. "Bea, he's the man with the hawk, isn't he? And at the park?"

"Are you okay, Little One?" Clarence almost whispered.

Beatrice—Bea—nodded and rotated in her mommy's lap, facing Clarence. Fearlessly. No, more than that. Eagerly. Gladly.

"Well, I'll be." Denny whistled. Whew. "How did you meet these two?"

Clarence opened his mouth to speak, cleared his throat and started again in his raspy voice. "We didn't—officially. We ... just ... happen to see each other some days." He stepped closer. "Don't we Sweetheart? You're the best thing in my day."

Bea nodded and relaxed against her mommy's shoulder. She hopped to the floor and touched Clarence's handcuffs, eyebrows raised.

Denny half smiled. "Uh, Todd. I think we can do without those."

Todd unlocked them and clipped them onto his belt.

Clarence rubbed his wrists, gazing at Katty, then Bea, then at Denny. "Are they," he cleared his throat, "are they okay?"

"Boy, we are totally messing with the Privacy Act here." Denny shook his head. "We haven't been able to get a statement from them."

He shook his head again then folded his arms across his chest. "Uh, Clarence. With your law degree, you think you might be able to help the department out once in a while?"

Clarence stared at Denny. He blinked and his face relaxed. "Um, you mean ... if you think that's okay." He nodded.

The dispatcher's radio started squawking. "Sheriff." She turned to Denny. "They lost him. Like the guy and his partner just disappeared."

Todd pounded the counter. "I don't see how he can even move, he's lost so much blood."

Denny glanced at Katty.

Katty shivered. "He's still alive," she whispered. She pulled Bea onto her lap.

"Tell Jim to stay on it. Find 'em." Denny turned to Clarence again. "Well, Clarence? Ready to open your law books?"

CHAPTER FIFTY

Lisha tucked the hand-crocheted afghan around Mrs. Hatly's knees. "There you are. Take a snuggle nap before dinner." She checked the call light and clipped it to the blanket, then pushed the chair around so Mrs. Hatly could monitor the hall activity. "Anything else?"

"There he goes. He's back. Was he really in jail?" Mrs. Hatly pointed down the hall.

Lisha pivoted just in time to see Clarence, escorted by a deputy, turn the corner down another hall. "Well, the lost is found. Or the dead has a'risen. And ... I'm not supposed to say he was in jail, Mrs. Hatly." Lisha folded her arms across her chest. "You said it. I didn't." Still, she leaned into the hall to catch a glimpse of them.

"I hope he's all right." Mrs. Hatly pulled the afghan up on her chest, tucking her arms underneath. "He's such a nice man, that Clarence. He dressed me one day. I was naked as a jailbird, uh, a jaybird, in one of my spells," she chuckled, "and he walked up to me, covered me with my robe and kissed me on the cheek." She shivered. "He's exciting."

Lisha's eyes popped. She edged out the door as Mrs. Hatly's head drooped to her chest with a quiet snore, a sweet smile on her face.

Lisha lifted her white jacket and fanned her face as she strode off down the hall. Mrs. Hatly naked? Yeah. It happened from time to time. Clarence exciting? Not in that way, fo sho.

Harold stood guard at his door, hands braced on his walker. "A bad penny always comes back."

"Harold. That's not nice."

"Probably better than what you're saying right now." Harold stared her down.

"I ... like ... him. Clarence, I mean." She backed up face-to-face.

He shook his head at her. "I've seen you walking behind him, doing your little act."

Lisha bounced, eyes squinted, shoulders shrugged. "Whatchu mean, my little act?"

He chuckled. "Busted aren't you? You mimic him: how he talks down to you, how he points his fingers, his tone of voice. I'm surprised he hasn't heard you, much less Carol or another nurse." He rolled his shoulders and hips, imitating her perfectly.

Lisha pursed her lips, eyebrows arched high. She slowly brought her hands to her hips, one hip bumped to a new high. "You don't miss nuthin' do ya, Mr. Harold?"

He smirked and puffed out a satisfied breath. "It's my job."

She sauntered to the living room and helped two residents untangle their wheelchairs. "You two been racin' again?"

One chuckled. The other snored.

Two ladies sat side-by-side on the sofa, chattering loudly. "There's that man." One pointed at Clarence. "I told the nurse, he has to go back to jail or prison or wherever he came from."

The other leaned forward, her fingers cupped her ear. "What's that?"

"I said," she yelled, "I told the nurse that man has to go back to prison."

"You're so right. We don't need his kind here in our home." She peered at her friend over large round glasses, and leaned in closer, talking just as loud. "He might rape one of us."

The other woman gasped, hand over her mouth, shuddering.

Lisha held her breath and turned to see Clarence stop abruptly. TV's weren't blaring loud enough to cover that up.

He dropped his head, shaking it. His hands balled into fists.

The deputy said something to him Lisha couldn't hear, patted his back and moved him forward.

Carol crossed her line of vision.

Lisha raced after her into the nurses station. "Carol."

She glanced up. "Lisha, I'm busy. This whole place is in a turmoil right now."

"Thas what I wants to talk to you about." She placed her hands on her wide hips. "Our jailbird."

Carol snapped her head up, glanced over the counter at the residents then stared into Lisha's eyes. "Our jailbird?"

Oh-oh.

"Lisha, I don't ever want to hear that come out of your mouth again. Besides, he was only there a couple of hours."

"Yes, Ma'am." Lisha ducked.

"Now. Was there something important you wanted to talk to me about?"

"Yes." Lisha straightened. "There is." She leaned in closer. "The little old ladies are afraid he's gonna ... you know. And the men want to shoot him, or have him castrated. It's awful for someone to have spent their life in prison, only to be sent to this heavenly home for ... the elderly."

Carol smirked. "Did I just hear angels singing?"

Ouch.

"Gah. I'm sorry, Lisha. I'm—"

The deputy clicked past the nurse's station and tipped his hat. "Ladies." He stopped and leaned over the counter, checking his surroundings. Lisha spotted his name badge: Todd Cochran. Bandage sticking out from under his cap. "He's harmless. He may wander the town a bit, but he wouldn't hurt a flea or a little old lady." Todd glanced down the hall.

Lisha acted surprised. "Oh, we weren't talking about him. We were just—"

"Talking about him." Carol finished Lisha's sentence. "Thanks Todd. We both needed a little reminder," she turned toward Lisha, "that we, as staff, treat all our residents, and each other, as guests. And that they deserve the utmost," she straightened, "respect."

Lisha, her shoulders back, mouthed every word along with Carol.

"Good. Glad to hear." Todd tapped the counter. "He's been through hell and back. He could use some kindness."

"But, I heard he was a lawyer. If he was in prison all this time, he couldn't be a lawyer." Lisha shrugged.

"He is a full-fledged attorney—passed the bar exam and everything. He went to college while in prison and got his law degree."

Lisha glanced at Carol.

"Wow," Carol whispered.

"In prison?" Lisha said.

Todd dipped his head. "Yeah, I know. If I made half as good a use of my time on this earth." He adjusted his cap. "Well, speaking of time, I'd best be going back to work—saving lives and all that stuff."

Lisha stood next to Carol, watching Todd walk away for a full minute then turned to face her. She didn't speak.

Neither did Carol.

Lisha chewed on the inside of her cheek as she chewed on what Todd had just told them. "Well, at least he didn't just watch the boob tube and make drug deals while he was in the slammer."

Carol pretended to smack Lisha. "You goof." She sighed, looking down the hall toward Clarence's room. "I'm surprised too." She frowned. "I guess I better ... go down ... see how he is." She scratched her head. "What do you say to a—"

"Jailbird?"

CHAPTER FIFTY-ONE

"Shut-up. You need to shut-up so nobody will hear you." Lex parked behind the combines and grabbed a bag from beside him. He jumped into the back seat beside Phil. "God, she got you good."

The wound gapped. The doctor had only gotten a couple stitches started at one end. "You are one lucky son-of-a-bitch that I used to work at a hospital."

Phil coughed. "So like you're ... a doctor ... now?" He coughed again, and the wound opened more.

"Hell, yeah." Lex opened the bag and pulled out a bottle of medicinal whiskey and some peroxide. "Used to clean up the ER with this stuff."

Phil opened his eyes. "Whiskey?"

Lex laughed. "Peroxide on the ER counters. Whiskey for my health."

Phil broke out laughing, ended up coughing. Blood seeped.

Lex opened the whiskey, lifted Phil's head and poured it into his mouth.

Phil coughed, but swallowed it down. "Burnin' Baby." He dropped his head onto the seat. "Heal me, Doc."

"God, you're burning up." Lex took a swig of whiskey, wiped his hand on his jeans and braced himself. He poured peroxide into the wound.

Phil writhed, groaning. He pushed the bottle away and threw up. More blood.

"Hold still." Lex slugged him and all was quiet.

Except for a gasp from outside the car.

Lex jumped out.

There stood the John Deere employee gaping at Phil.

"Dude. Just in time." Lex reached into the car and pulled out a couple beers propped next to the gun. "Let's just be honest here, son. You didn't see a thing." He handed him a beer, tipped his own, glanced behind him at the gun. "Agreed?"

The employee didn't move a muscle, just his bulging eyes. At the gun, Phil, then at Lex and nodded slightly. He popped the top and sucked the beer down. He walked away, tossing the empty can into the weeds.

"Smart man." Lex dug in the sack and pulled out bandages and proceeded to patch Phil up.

CHAPTER FIFTY-TWO

Carol knocked on Clarence's door. "Clarence, you in there? You ready for some supper soon?" Fake happy voice.

She slowly pushed the door open.

Fully clothed, Clarence curled on his bed, facing the wall.

"I know you're not asleep, Clarence." She closed the door. "We have to talk." She tiptoed to the bed.

Barely discernible breathing. Holding his breath?

"Please let me help you."

His shoulders twitched.

"If we play it your way, I have no recourse but to call the home office. And they won't deal with you like I'd like to." She gathered steam. "I'd like to treat you with respect—to honor you—to honor what you have done and given in your life. But the home office? They'll send you to a psych ward."

She edged around the end of his bed. "You're a lawyer and you've been in prison. You know what lockdown is. You might never have been inside a psych ward, but you've heard the key turn in a lock." She sighed. "Then you're alone with your demons. You know what's involved, don't you Clarence?"

He shifted on the bed, shoes tapped against each other.

"I'm not trying to scare you," Carol said. "I realize you don't scare easily, but I'm trying to get you to see what I'm up against. At a certain point, it will be out of my hands."

Clarence's shoulders began to shake. He broke out in sobs, fist at his mouth.

A knock came at the door. Lisha stuck her head in. "They're serving. Is he ... ?"

Carol shook her head. The door closed.

A deep ragged sigh arose from the bed, and Clarence wiped his face. He peeked at Carol and shuddered. He rolled to his back, exhaled deeply and sat up on the edge of his bed, elbows on his knees and face in the palms of his hands.

Carol looked everywhere but at him. Nothing on the walls—only a calendar offered by the nursing home. Nothing on the table, except the utilitarian lamp provided by Hillcrest Homes. No cozy afghan draped over the chair. No decorative pillows or knickknacks. The only decoration was his picture outside his door taken upon admittance—she'd taken it herself. Oh, and that scarf with uneven fringe. Even Carol knew a dropped stitch—like someone had hurried to get it done. Somebody made it for him.

What had happened to his family, if he ever had any? No friends came or called, except for that tall guy, Michael Whatshisname.

Clarence consumed her thoughts now almost as much as Joe. How could she help him get back to peace, instead of insanity and unforgiveness. How could she help him come to grips with his past and find hope for his future—however long that was?

He glanced at her and shook his head. A last tear tracked down that wrinkled cheek.

Carol sat in the chair and gazed out the repaired window. Some bars were down. She peeked back at Clarence.

He looked out the window, too. His breathing settled.

Leaves outside danced in the breeze, twirling about each other. Birds twittered.

At last Carol checked her watch and rose. "Just a warning—Miss Henningway has you on her schedule."

He wiped his face.

With her hand on the door, she thought of Joe. She couldn't help him, but could she help Clarence?

CHAPTER FIFTY-THREE

An hour later, Clarence clapped his hand over his mouth. Laughing in Pete's face would not go well.

"You son-of-a—" Pete Malovitch jumped out of the chair.

Miss Henningway rushed to shut the door to her office at Hillcrest Homes. "Pete sit down and shut up. People will hear you. They're heading down for supper!"

Pete leaned over the insurance adjuster sitting between him and Clarence. He poked Clarence's chest. "You are such a bastard. You need to get your f-n nose out of other people's business."

"Now, Mr. Malovitch. Let's keep this civil." The adjuster pushed back his Brylcreem hair. "I'm not sure where the claim payments went, but I'm so thankful Mr. Timmelsen here, found the error."

"Someone just checked the wrong box or something, Mr. ... "

"Mr. Dekker." The adjuster held out his hand to Clarence.

"Mr. Dekker." Clarence shook his hand. "I wonder where the money ended up?" He wiped the grin away and folded his hands in his lap.

"You and Mrs. Hatly will have your payments reinstated. And there are others." He opened his briefcase, removing several documents. "A Mr. Adams. Mr. Otto. Mrs. Walters." He glanced at Miss Henningway. "I must meet with them today. This must be settled immediately."

Clarence snickered. "I'm afraid you'll have to go two blocks east to find them."

Pete growled.

Miss Henningway drilled Clarence with her eyes.

"Ahh. They're on an outing? I'll wait." He crossed his arms. "It's good for the elderly to get fresh air."

Clarence snorted. "They're getting fresh air, that's for sure." He leaned forward, ready to push out of the chair. "They're at the cemetery. They're dead."

Mr. Dekker gasped. He chattered as he spilled the contents of a file folder onto the floor. "D-dead?" He bumped his head on the desk when he bent to retrieve them.

Miss Henningway groaned. "No. They live here. Just down that hall." She pointed.

Mr. Dekker turned to Clarence. "How do you know this?"

"Googled it."

"What?" Pete's voice cracked.

Clarence nodded at Miss Henningway. "I just borrowed one of your computers—they're pretty cool." He stood. "One of your employees helped me."

He picked up a pile of papers he'd been hiding. "Oh, and Harold. He lives here. He's a detective and a pretty good one. He helped me get the files." He handed them to Mr. Dekker. "It's all here. The dead people, Mrs. Hatly and me."

He eased behind his chair. "Now if you'll excuse me, I'm sure you can take it from here. I have to get to the dining room before they shut it down." He ran for the door and down the hall.

Pete's gonna kill someone.

Dining room. He could hide behind the wheelchairs.

Pete burst into the room. "Where is that son-of-a ... ?" He shook off two aides and Jane, the office receptionist. "Take your hands off me! Where is that bastard Timmelsen?"

Clarence hid behind Mrs. Bernadine, who was in a reclining wheelchair. Oatmeal drooled out of one side of her mouth.

He patted her arm.

She chewed and eyed him.

"It's okay, Mrs. Bernadine." He had never really talked to her, but the way her eyes focused, she was all there. She got it.

"Sir, you will not disturb our residents." Jane hooked Pete's arm with hers and yanked him back down the hall.

He swung her around and slammed her into the wall, knocking over a cart loaded with plastic water glasses.

Residents screamed. Several aides backed wheelchairs away. A dietary aide carrying a tray loaded with fruit bowls stepped on a rolling glass and tumbled to the floor, applesauce splattering.

Clarence walked toward Pete, his fists clenched. "What do you mean coming in here and scaring these good people?"

"How'd you get out of jail?" Pete stomped toward Clarence. "I had you put away."

"What?" Clarence's voice broke. "That was you?"

Jane, sprawled on the floor, yelled into her phone. "Hillcrest." She nodded. "Pete Malovitch." She tapped the screen. "Cops are on the way."

"Good. They can put you back in jail, Timmelsen."

"What do you have against me? I did my time."

"You have no right poking your nose in other people's business." Pete roared. "You ... you ruined my life!" Pete rushed Clarence, his hands clenched.

Someone shoved a walker in front of Pete and he fell flat into the applesauce.

Harold!

Tottering, he grinned, his bib still around his neck. He leaned on the walker like a world-class Samurai warrior having just finished battle.

Pete scrambled to his feet, wiping his hands on his shirt, just as two deputies skidded beside him.

Pete pointed at Clarence. "Deputies. Put that man in jail!"

Jane pointed at Pete. "No! This is the man. Get him out of here!"

Pete ran toward Clarence but Mrs. Hatly appeared out of nowhere and rammed him with her wheelchair. She pushed her glasses up on her nose, eyes twinkling.

A deputy shoved Pete down, clicked handcuffs on him and dragged him upright.

"You can't get away with this. I have evidence. Sheriff Dennison knows all about it." Pete jerked at the handcuffs. "Timmelsen's a liar and a cheat. He's a murderer!" The deputies dragged him out.

Pete cussed and yelled down the hall.

Clarence walked past Mrs. Bernadine, patted her arm, and pushed out the exit.

Movement to his right made him turn his head. The cops locked

Pete in the squad car, but behind them, at the far end of the parking lot, Miss Henningway scurried to her vehicle, a bulging bag in her hand. Purse slung over her shoulder.

Making a run for it, eh?

The hawk screeched in the distance.

One other thing Clarence had to do. This was not going to end well.

CHAPTER FIFTY-FOUR

Minutes later, Mindy burst into laughter. "You can't hurt me anymore, Clarence. You are a funny man and I love you."

Silence in the grocery store. Mindy swallowed. Said too much again.

Clarence's eyes bugged out. He coughed, leaning on the counter.

Mindy giggled. "I love you, Clarence. You are like my Grandpa. Mean and wild."

Clarence threw the money down, picked up his candy bar and walked out.

A lady paid for milk and Mindy gave her change back. John bagged it and walked to the door.

Clarence slipped back in and waited in the corner, sidestepping away from John.

John pushed the door open. "You come back to insult Mindy again? You need another candy bar to push in her face?"

Clarence didn't say a word, but waited inside the door.

The woman followed John outside.

Mindy watched them through the window, Clarence visible in her peripheral vision.

Clarence cleared his throat.

Mindy glanced up. "Nice lady."

Clarence faked a cough. He stepped forward and cleared his throat again.

John opened the door and walked inside.

Mindy looked at Clarence directly. "Is there something else you need, Clarence?"

"I'm sorry." He turned, bumped into John and pushed the door open so fast, the candy bar slipped from his fingers. He burst through the doorway and never looked back.

She picked up the candy and pushed the door open. "Clarence. Your candy bar."

He kept on walking.

Mindy crumpled. She looked up at John then back at Clarence hurrying away.

CHAPTER FIFTY-FIVE

"I really appreciate your hospitality, Deputy. Your little cop car world is fascinating. All the gadgets and everything. What kid wouldn't want to be a cop nowadays?" Pete held out his cuffed hands.

The deputy hesitated, but unlocked them.

"Here's a little something for your trouble. And I'm sorry I cut loose back at the nursing home in front of all those sweet elderly folks." He counted out two hundred dollars and pulled the cash from his wallet. Those fake policies were coming in handy today.

"You can find your own way home, Pete." The deputy patted his pocket. "And we won't tell anyone about our little deal. Sheriff frowns on—"

"Bribery?" Pete shrugged. "It's not so much a bribe, but a donation to the Stalwart Defenders of our little burg." He shoved his wallet into his pocket.

The police radio broke in. "Sheriff, this guy's crazy. I had him, I swear. He bleeds all over like he's dying and the next minute he kicks me in the gut and gets away."

Sheriff let loose an unusual string of words over the radio.

"An escapee?" Pete brushed off his shirt and adjusted his belt.

"Oh." The deputy looked up and down the street. "Some guy was after the gal inside."

Pete followed his gaze. A younger woman stood talking to Sheriff. Timmelsen's friend and her kid from the park. She and Timmelsen had seemed pretty tight. She appeared beat up. Pete folded his arms across his chest and yawned. "Yeah?"

"Well, evidently they have some history, because she knifed him and got away."

"What does he want with that bitch?" Pete tipped his head toward the building. "She looks like somebody you'd run like hell from."

The deputy laughed and stepped closer to Pete, his face cocked away from the building. "It's his kid. Bet he wants the little girl."

Pete pounded his open hand on his chest. "No. She's so innocent. I've seen her. Very pretty."

The deputy glanced at the building, then quickly away. "I hear tell Sheriff's got the old man helping—you know the one from prison. He's helping get her free of all past charges."

Pete nodded. "Oh, he's slick, that's for sure." His blood wanted to boil at how slick Timmelsen was. Pete took a step away. "Well, won't keep you anymore. I can walk to my agency. It's only a block away."

The radio sputtered again. "He's got an accomplice. Guy's driving a 1991 Buick LaSabre, white."

The deputy waved and jumped into the car. "Duty calls."

Pete saluted him and started a slow jog through the alley and hit the backdoor of his building. Probably should keep the place locked up. He opened a safe, pulled out his 9mm Ruger. Always loaded. He shoved it inside the front of his pants and pulled his shirt out over it.

Maybe he and that runaway guy should join forces.

Get his little girl for him.

And put Timmelsen back where he belonged.

CHAPTER FIFTY-SIX

Katty shifted the car into drive. The deputy had said it'd be okay. Gotta get out of town. If Phil found them again ...

"You okay Baby Bea?"

Bea kicked the back of Katty's seat.

"I don't even care if you kick my seat anymore, Bea." Katty pulled away from the stop sign. "I don't know where to go. We can't go to the trailer." She blew out a deep breath. "I don't even ... I don't know." She wiped her cheek.

"Mommy?"

"What, Baby?"

"Mommy, I see those little lights again. The sparkly ones. They're all around me."

"Bea? Are you all right? You hit your head when we slammed into the mailbox."

"Mommy. The Lights are back."

Katty pulled over. She turned in time to see Bea's face surrounded by light specks, reflected in Bea's brown eyes.

Bea kicked her feet. "Mommy, they tickle." Her eyes widened. "They're around you, too."

One flew close to Katty's face. She began to weep. She slowly held out her hand and they hovered just above her fingers. She swallowed. Another gently landed on her head.

Bea giggled.

The lights filled the back seat, framing Bea's face.

"Mommy." She kicked. "That other Mommy's gone."

"What?"

"That ... mean Mommy's gone." Bea wiped her eyes. "All I see is you, Mommy."

CHAPTER FIFTY–SEVEN

Pete faked a swagger as he cut across the alley behind his agency. He jumped into his black late-model pickup. It was a stand in for the luxury car he kept hidden in his garage at home just for out-of-town trips.

How was he going to find those guys? He didn't even know names. But he knew the vehicle—a white Buick. There were only maybe twenty of those in town, mostly driven by little old ladies. He'd written the insurance policies.

He drove down the alley, crossed the street and into the next alley. Cars parked there were awaiting miracle work of the body shop. The town had three body shops which meant claims, which meant opportunity. He had deals with two of the shops: find a clunker, file a claim, and split the money. Business was good.

Wait. Was that the car? He drove closer.

Gah! Mrs. Mason. Go home.

He drove behind the lumberyard.

There. Behind the implement dealership. Damn. He backed up and drove the other way. The stupid road didn't go through. F-n small towns.

He pulled his gun out and slowly pulled in close to the back of the car, blocking it. He'd hidden here himself a couple times, to get out of the office when he needed a drink.

If he could just get to the driver's side without them noticing.

He opened his door and the buzzer sounded. Damn!

A man sat up in the front seat of the car. He had a gun.

Pete rushed to the door. "Hold it. Put your gun down." He pushed his Ruger in the man's face. "I have a deal in mind you won't want to miss."

The driver didn't put his gun down but held it pointed at Phil's gut. The guy on the back seat appeared unconscious. Maybe this wasn't such a good idea. His eyes opened and something unearthly hit Pete, making him stumble backwards.

The guy leaned up with a groan. "What kind a deal? Who are you?"

"I want old man Timmelsen out of town. Or dead." Get it together Malovitch. Pete cocked his gun and pointed it at the man. "And I hear you want the little girl and her mom."

"Just the girl." The guy grimaced. "What's in it for you?"

"Revenge. Pure revenge."

CHAPTER FIFTY-EIGHT

Clarence glanced up when the screech grew louder. "Where are you, old bird?" He strained to get a good look at the sky. "Too many trees."

He rolled out from under the huge old spruce. "Ouch, I'll be picking needles out of my butt for a long time." From his vantage point on the ground, the tree stretched up forever, touching the sky.

The hawk circled way above. "Hey, bird. What are you doing old fellow?"

The hawk screeched and circled, flying higher and higher, then dove, floating on the wind currents, wings gracefully outstretched, curling at each tip.

"You are magnificent, you old bird."

"And so are you, Clarence."

He rolled onto his hands and knees and looked up into Carol's face.

"What are you doing here?" He pushed himself off the ground, brushing his knees and hands, scattering spruce needles. "How did you find me?"

Carol chuckled, then pointed to the sky, following the hawk in his flight pattern. "Your old bird told me. Right over the tree. I looked everywhere, but it wasn't until I heard him screech that I took notice." She pointed skyward. "He was right over your tree, if I can call it yours."

Carol scanned the park. "There. Let's sit awhile, shall we?"

"What? Before I stand in front of the firing squad? You heard what happened." Head hanging, shoulders slumped, he followed her to a bench. "A little reprieve before I die?"

She plopped down. "Stop. I'm exhausted from trying to keep up with you. Where do you get your energy to run away? I know it's not the food. You taking vitamins?"

"You ought to know. You give me my pills. Everyday."

"Ha. You mean every day that you haven't already run away. When you're not there, I have to chart that you refused your meds. Or that you were unavailable. How is a resident unavailable in a nursing home?"

"I see your dilemma."

"No you don't. You have no clue. We are in so much trouble with the home office. Miss Henningway left. That place is in such turmoil."

She sat back and sighed. "I see why you come here." She pointed. "That old slide is huge. They don't build them like that anymore." She craned her neck. "It is quiet here. You can smell the outdoors and not ... well, you know what we smell in the nursing home. The sounds here are wonderful, especially your bird." She shifted on the bench. "Except this bench is hard."

He pointed to the tree and grinned. "It's pretty soft under that tree. Except the needles poke."

Carol chuckled. "You deserve to get poked."

"I suppose I do." He shook his head. "I know I haven't been easy to get along with."

"No. You haven't."

He picked at the flaking paint on the bench. He cleared his throat. "I ... " He coughed. "I'm ... sorry."

"You mean that, don't you?" She faced him. "You really mean that."

"When you sat with me in my room? I ... well ... " He picked at a leaf that had floated its way down. "You are a good woman, Carol. You remind me of someone I once knew. She was a beautiful, wonderful woman, so full of promise, so ready to burst into life."

He stopped and chewed on his inner cheek. "You remind me of her. She was my—"

A rustle in the tree above distracted him then the hawk broke free of a branch.

Goosebumps.

It flew low to the ground, picking up speed, tucking wings close to its body as it dodged trees, banking left and right.

"Wow," Carol gasped. "There is something ... divine about that bird. Like it knows more than we do. I've never seen anything like it."

Clarence swallowed, his leg twitching. "I know. When I first came here, he would hover outside my window and peck at the glass. I've never heard of a hawk doing that." He chuckled. "That was before he broke in. I began to be able to feel when he was out there. He would wait until I came to the window."

The bird soared up, catching the air current and lifted higher until it flew seemingly into the sun.

"It always seems to be drawing me somewhere." He whispered and shielded his eyes.

"I feel drawn too. I don't know what it means for me." Carol looked at Clarence. "Do you know what it means for you?"

He nodded.

Carol stood and checked her watch. "I have to get back. You coming?"

He reached out and clasped her hand. "I'm not sure." He looked at the hawk. "I think I need to find a little girl and her mommy."

CHAPTER FIFTY-NINE

Katty pushed Bea in the grocery cart. Her heart pounded. "We need things to snack on. Quick and easy." She grabbed two bags of potato chips, one bonus bag of pretzels. Jitters told her to run. "What do you want, Bea? Cereal?"

At the word, cereal, Bea's head popped up. "Please, Mommy? Please? Cheerios? Honey Nut Cheerios? Please?" Bea kicked her feet. "And roni and cheese, Mommy." She pointed. "That one!"

Katty rubbed her temples. No headache please—not today. "No, I think we'd better have liver or ... " She whispered to Bea, nose to nose. "We have to buy stuff we can eat in the car, okay? Not sure we can go ... back. For awhile." She looked into Bea's eyes. "Remember?"

Bea nodded her head up and down, a solemn expression in her eyes. Big girl. "Yeah, Mommy. Okay."

"How about ... chicken in the can? Wish we could get soup," Katty said, then stared ahead. "Could we do soup? Nah." She focused on the shelf. "Beans." She tossed in a couple cans. "Baby hot dogs. What's it say? Vienna sausages. Whatever." She cleared the shelf, two cans at a time. "Protein." She handed one to Bea.

"One." Bea looked into the cart. "Two. Three. Lots."

Katty pushed the cart to the end of the aisle.

"Well, hello ladies." Phil jumped in front of them.

Katty froze.

Bea stretched to see behind her. "Mommy?" Bea grabbed at Katty's shirt, climbing and pawing.

Buckled in.

Phil's skin was wet. His eyes were glassy. "I love to see the females get excited when I'm around." His eyes traveled over both Katty and Bea. "What brings you out today?" He brushed Bea's hair out of her face and held out both hands to her. "Come to Daddy."

Bea frantically clawed at Katty. Goosebumps covered her arms.

Katty fumbled at the safety buckle. Her hands shook. Stuck. She tried to steer the cart away, but Phil grabbed it and held tight. She'd never seen his eyes so black. His pale face glistened.

"I just want to say hello. I don't want to hurt you or anything." He opened his jacket, glowering.

Katty gaped at the bloody mess; the belly wound was only half stitched. She stumbled a step and then shoved the cart into his midsection.

He doubled over.

She wrenched the cart back again and almost tipped it over.

Bea screamed and clutched at her.

His hands gripped the cart, like vise grips. He straightened slowly. Growling. Grinning.

Katty hugged Bea's head into her chest, taking another step back.

He followed—only the cart between them.

"I just want to be friendly." Phil rammed the cart into Katty with such force she flew backwards—feet in the air—into a tall display, knocking over cans of soup.

Bea shrieked and kicked.

Phil yanked the cart toward him and leaned over it, stroking Bea's hair. "You are so pretty, little one."

Katty shoved at the rolling cans, trying to stand.

"You look an awful lot like someone I know very well." His feet shifted. "An awful lot." He leaned toward a glass freezer door. "Well, hot damn." He bent toward Bea. "You look like me!" He screamed the last word.

Katty struggled to get up. She kicked the cans aside and lunged for Bea.

Clarence rushed Phil.

"Clarence!" Katty yelled. "Help!"

Lex jumped Clarence, wrenching his arms.

#

Bea!

He had to get to Bea!

"Let me go, you bastard." Clarence kicked behind him, trying to break free.

Katty's attacker faced him, inches away. He looked dead, smelled worse. His eyes—nothing in prison could have prepared Clarence for those eyes. Black circles ringed glassy eyeballs and something ghastly flitted in their depths.

Terror crawled up the back of Clarence's neck.

"Old man." The man growled and looked at Bea, then back at Clarence. "Oh. Isn't that sweet? Is this Grandpa?"

He patted the top of Clarence's head. "Every little girl needs a grandpa." He punched Clarence hard in the gut.

"Phil! No!" Katty yelled.

Clarence doubled over, struggled against his captor, but he never looked away. Stay focused! That, he had learned in prison.

Katty quickly unbuckled Bea, grabbed her out of the shopping cart and started down the aisle.

Good girl.

"Little Bitch. Bitch," Phil roared. "You can't get away. I'll always find you." He tripped on a can, but found his footing and started after Katty.

Clarence stomped his heel hard into his captor's foot. He pulled a hand loose and shoved it into the guy's face, grabbed his nose and twisted. Stabbed his fingers into eye sockets. The guy let loose of Clarence's other arm, growling in pain. Clarence dove at Phil and tackled him. They both landed on rolling cans. Phil kicked, but Clarence held onto Phil's belt.

Something hard and cold shoved into the back of Clarence's neck.

He held on, a death grip. He would not let go, even if Phil dragged him to hell. He would not let go.

"Thought you could outsmart me, huh, Clarence Timmelsen." That voice! Still sprawled and clutching Phil's belt, Clarence cranked his head far enough around to see ...

Pete Malovitch!

He held a black Ruger. Deadly. He cocked it. "Let him go." He popped Clarence on the head with the butt.

Clarence shuddered at the pain, releasing Phil.

"Go get your bitch, Phil." Pete's voice was low and deadly. "I'll be right with you, after I take care of this jailbird."

Pete seized Clarence, twisting his ear hard. "Pretty tough for an old man, aren't you. I never should have underestimated you son-of-a-bitch." He rapped Clarence's head again.

Clarence's eyes watered. Room spun.

"You should have died in that a crash long ago, you bastard. Not Annie. Dad was supposed to marry her, instead of my stupid mom. He and Judge had it all set up. Brakes in those old cars were always going out. Judge paid a lot of people. Paid a jury. But she was killed, so he set you up!" He pounded Clarence's head again and laughed in his ear. "Sixty years for a crime you didn't do."

Clarence shivered and choked. Pete's words echoed. The words were there, but slowed down, each syllable dragging.

"And now you die for it, bastard." He aimed the gun at Clarence's ear. "Now you d—"

Blam!

Blood spattered Clarence's cheek.

He gasped.

His ears rang.

The grip on his arm went limp.

Pete fell over cans, landing hard.

Terrified, Clarence felt his head. Confused, he looked up.

Sheriff Dennison pointed a gun at the ceiling. Two Deputies ran up the aisle and trained their guns on Pete.

Clarence crawled to his feet and stumbled up the aisle. "Bea."

CHAPTER SIXTY

At the end of the aisle Clarence turned the corner to a scene he would never forget. Katty lay unconscious, a nasty bruise on her right temple. Still breathing.

Bea was nowhere.

Mindy and John sat back to back, tied up behind the check stand, silver tape stretched over their mouths. They motioned with their heads; eyes urged him out the door.

Drops of blood led him.

When he stepped outside, the hawk screeched. It vibrated in his every cell. It must have been circling until he came outside. The clouds were ignited by the waning sun, purples and blues the backdrop.

"Lead me, old friend. Where is Bea?"

The bird circled, screeching louder. Clarence struggled to follow. His eyes blurred.

He started to cross the highway. A semi blasted its horn, roaring past. He stumbled on the train tracks. Hand railings on the bridge pulled him along, over the creek.

"Old bird, where are you?" His eyes watered. It was futile to look under every tree and bush. He could hardly go on. He rubbed the back of his head. Wet. Blood.

Movement. Just a flash, like a reflection from the traffic on the highway or the sun reflecting off a pop can. It seemed to hover in midair.

The hawk flew in tighter circles until it floated right above the flicker.

Then he saw her and ran.

Perched at the top of the huge old metal slide was tiny Bea, shaking in terror. Her mouth was taped with duct tape. Her arms were outstretched, hands taped to the metal sides of the uppermost deck. She couldn't move. She stared at him, pleaded with her swollen eyes, screamed in spite of the tape.

The hawk dove at him, knocking him off his feet. "You dumb bird!"

Until he saw.

Phil crouched below the slide, almost hidden by dry bushes and vines trailing up the slide supports. He had gathered kindling and trash and started a fire directly below Bea. His eyes blazed. "If I can't have her, she'll be a burned up sacrifice by the time you get to her," he yelled.

Bea bounced up and down, wailing.

Gunshot.

Clarence turned. Three squad cars sped across the highway toward them. Sheriff Dennison leaned out his window, a gun in his hand.

The hawk screeched from above.

Something flashed into Clarence's mind from way back—a moment of clarity from his childhood. His mother's voice floated from his past. "My Father." She had always called Him "My Father," like He was only hers.

Clarence blinked, squeezing tears onto his cheeks. "My Father." He'd almost reached the slide.

The fire crackled up the vines on the slide poles.

Phil took off running.

Clarence stumbled. A Keep Off sign lay crumpled on the ground. He put his foot on the ladder's lowest rung.

Bea's face was wet and red. She pulled and struggled against the tape, squeaking his name.

He gripped the metal railings and managed another step.

The railings were already hot—hot through his scars.

He plodded up the ladder between burning vines.

A small flame ignited on his sleeve.

He batted at it and kept climbing.

"Which art in Heaven."

Another rung.

"Hallowed be Thy name."

One more. The railings were burning his hands now.

"Thy kingdom come. Thy will be done, on earth, as it is in heaven."

His eyes stung from heat and smoke, but they never left Bea's. It was almost like she was in a different world. He could see her screaming, crying, jumping, but all he could hear was his mother's voice. "Give us this day our daily bread. And forgive us our trespasses as we forgive those who trespass against us."

His foot slipped on a rung. Shoes must be melting.

"And lead us not into temptation, but deliver us from evil."

Bea.

He ripped melting tape from the slide deck.

She hugged his neck and clung to him.

He pushed through the opening, onto the slide itself—the wooden side railings burning.

Shutting his eyes and enfolding Bea in his arms, he launched.

His feet hit ground.

Strong arms and Sheriff Dennison's voice: "Gotcha, Clarence."

A siren wailed, and red lights flashed through his eyelids.

Hands lowered him onto a soft surface, but he clung to Bea.

"For Thine is the Kingdom, and the Power, and the Glory."

In his arms—Bea finished with him. Her tiny, hoarse voice with his ragged one: "Amen."

CHAPTER SIXTY-ONE

Clarence opened his eyes.

Blinding light.

He rubbed his cheeks. Tape. Or bandages?

Whispering voices.

Beeping.

Beeping.

BEEPING!

Clarence shuddered. "Stop that noise!"

Silence.

A bird screeched.

"Clarence? He's loosing consciousness—"

Screech.

Clarence ducked as the bird swooped, headed straight for him. He braced himself, covered his head. The flap of powerful wings and rustle of feathers was nothing compared to the screech that drilled his senses. The sound raged through his veins, vibrated to his core.

He straightened and shook his fist. "What are you doing, old bird? Why are you trying to kill me?"

The bird circled higher and higher, then dove at him again.

Clarence ran across the street to an old house.

A woman, getting out of a car in the garage, yelled and dropped her bag of groceries.

He skirted around the house to the alley behind and stumbled through the backyard. Fear prickled up the back of his neck. He tripped in a tire rut and tumbled.

Another screech sent chills. He pushed himself up and shuffled to the next street. Stopped to find his bearings.

Nothing. He recognized nothing.

Lost.

The hawk screeched again and dove, driving him across the street.

Concrete turned to gravel.

He shuffled and stumbled over a sidewalk, across that street, into another yard, through a fence.

Until he found himself outside of town.

Open road.

Shelter belt of trees in the distance.

He rotated in the middle of the dirt road.

Trees along fence lines, fields of crops, old abandoned buildings.

Nothing he recognized.

And town was more than a mile away.

He hollered at the sky, shaking his fist, wishing he could reach the hawk and knock it to the ground. "You dumb bird. I am going to be in so much trouble. Carol will call the cops herself, this time. They'll put me in lockdown or the psych ward."

The bird circled back and dove again, driving Clarence even farther from town. Stumbling, exhausted, he fell to his knees and gasped for breath.

Then he saw it.

An old, old car rumbled toward him, stirring up dust. He could hear the rough, uneven sound of the engine—an old engine.

Dusky streams of purple, orange and dark blue broke up the western sky. Dad had always said this was a dangerous time of day to drive. Hard to see animals out hunting. Hard to see people walking along the road.

Like he was now.

He scrambled off his knees and tripped into the ditch, careful to keep sight of the car.

Out of the corner of his eye, he spied a deer sprinting across the field, running toward the road.

Clarence yelled, "Look out!" He pointed to the deer.

The driver couldn't see the animal.

He was laughing with the passenger, a young woman.

Clarence froze.

He knew this place.

He knew the car.

He knew the driver.

"No. No! Look up!" Clarence pointed and waved his arms. "It was the deer! Oh, God. It was a deer and not ... Oh God."

Clarence crumpled to his knees and watched in horror as the car plowed into the deer.

It swerved out of control, off the road, throwing the passenger—his Annie—into the ditch.

The car rolled over her with a sickening thud.

Clarence screamed and screamed, pounding at the air. "Oh God, not again. Not ... this ... again."

He tried to stand, but fell to the ground and lay sobbing. "It wasn't me. It was a deer. We hit a deer. Oh my Annie, you knew I would never hurt you. Oh my Annie forgive me."

He lay in the ditch for what might have been minutes—to him, eternity. Sobbing.

Until he felt a hand on his shoulder. He started and jumped. Raised his head.

Michael.

In full-dress angel costume. Wings and all.

"Michael. You ... " Clarence pushed up on both elbows looking toward the car ... and Annie's body.

There was only a ditch. Filled with weeds and debris, trash. A plum thicket.

No car.

No Annie.

He sobbed into his hands once more as Michael hovered behind him, hand still on his shoulder.

Clarence wiped his face on his sleeves. "So, you're back, huh? I thought you'd left me." He could barely look Michael in the eye.

Michael smiled, but didn't answer.

Clarence stared for a long time into the sunset. Sighed deeply. "I didn't kill her." He searched Michael's eyes this time. "Annie. I didn't kill her."

Michael shook his head.

"She was pregnant, wasn't she? There was a baby." Clarence wiped his face.

Michael slowly, gently nodded. "Yes, my friend. She's precious. Sits on the lap of Mighty One."

Clarence glanced from Michael to the fading sky. A ragged breath escaped.

So many questions answered.

CHAPTER SIXTY-TWO

Blinding light.

Beeping.

Clarence felt his face. Bandages covered his eyes.

Hard plastic over his nose and mouth. He ripped it off.

"Uh-uh, Jailbird. Not on my watch."

Raspy voice.

Someone pulled something over his head and pressed plastic over his nose and mouth.

He ripped it off and tossed it. Landed somewhere with a splot.

Giggles.

Someone grabbed his wrist. "Just checking your pulse."

He groaned. Phew! What was that smell?

"Is he in pain?" A soft voice. Who?

"Probably. He's mad about the oxygen mask and that I'm messing with him." The nurse leaned close. "You are one lucky son-of—"

Bea! He grabbed at her. "Where's Bea?"

He ripped bandages from his eyes and rubbed them. Flowers lined a high shelf and window ledge. Flowers? Sunlight streamed through the blinds at the window.

He blinked again, his eyes watering.

Michael.

"Michael. You're here."

The mask was pushed back on.

Clarence patted his face. He yanked it off over his head and tried to sit up.

"Oh no you don't, mister. Down. And this stays on until I say so."

The nurse pushed him flat. "Who is Michael?"

"He's my friend." Clarence coughed and pointed. "Michael, you fraud. You're an angel."

Michael smiled.

"Put the mask back on, Jailbird." She adjusted the side elastic bands tightly.

Clarence pushed up the mask. "You called me Jailbird."

"Well, that's what you are, aren't you?" Her hands on her hips. "You spent time in prison, escape from the nursing home, I hear. Then visit the jail. The name fits." She pushed him down on the bed again.

The top of a little head appeared above the edge of the bed.

"Is this who you're looking for?" The nurse lifted little Bea onto the bed.

Her eyes were watering, too. A bandage covered one wrist and her mouth and cheeks were red where the duct tape had been. She wore a hospital gown and some of her hair frizzled to the side of her head.

But she was smiling.

"Bea." He raised an arm, and she nestled onto his chest, her head next to his.

"Bea," he cried, and patted her. "Oh, oh. Ow." Bandages on his own hands. He held one up and looked at the nurse again.

She frowned. "Burned. Both of them. Burns on top of burns. Hopefully they will heal ... in time ... with treatment."

He swallowed the lump in his throat.

"Need a drink of water? You need to keep up your fluids. And ... " She almost chuckled, but cleared her throat instead. "And your backside is burned a little too."

Ohhh.

Bea raised her head. "What's a backside?"

Katty leaned in, bandage on her cheek. "It's your butt." She patted Bea's. "This." Her face softened. Eyes lingered in Clarence's. "You. You saved my baby daughter."

She continued to pat Bea. Her face crumpled. "How can I ... ?" Her chin quivered. She choked and leaned over Bea, hugging them both.

He gulped. His cheeks were wet. His tears and hers.

She stood, wiping her cheeks. "I got you wet." Laughing, she grabbed a tissue and blotted his.

Clarence breathed out one contented sigh.

"My Father," Bea said.

He lifted his head. "Where did you learn that?"

"From you." She tapped his chest. "Who art in shaven." She raised her head. "Does God shave? Are you my grandpa?"

The nurse leaned in with a tall plastic lidded cup, a straw pointed at him. "Drink up, Jailbird."

He watched Bea as he drank. Ahhh.

The longer he looked at her, the stronger something rose in him: memories of Annie kissing his fingers and praying over his hands, so long ago, and ... her love for him. He hadn't experienced that kind of love since.

Until now.

"Where's your bird?" Bea's eyelashes fluttered. Sleepy girl. Been through so much.

"Sweetie. Its ... uh outside." Laughter bubbled up in Clarence. "My bird is outside flying high." He reached for her hand.

Someone knocked at the door.

"Where's that Clarence? I gots to find him for Mrs. Hatly, here. Is there room for a wheelchair?"

Lisha. In all her ... glory. Big teeth and all. Still in her uniform. What a woman.

He caught himself smiling at her.

Mrs. Hatly. Oh, she was cute.

She stood from her wheelchair and barely came above the level of the bed. Bea could be taller. But those twinkling eyes. She patted his arm and kissed his cheek. And Bea's. Wiped her eyes and his.

He blinked.

The distinct creak of a walker. Harold. "Had to see my buddy." He reached over Bea and patted Clarence's shoulder. He clasped Clarence's arm.

Carol stepped from behind Harold. Tears in her eyes. She leaned over Bea and hugged him. "I'm so proud of you, Clarence."

Clarence's throat constricted. His vision blurred. "You're my special angel, Carol." He nodded at Michael.

A radio sputtered from somewhere. Sheriff Denny leaned from

behind Carol. "Clarence. I'm so glad you're okay. You're a tough man."

"Tough for my age."

"No." Sheriff focused on Clarence and saluted. "You're a tough and brave soldier for any age."

Clarence glanced at Bea nestled in beside him, almost asleep. "Did you ... did you get 'em?"

Sheriff dipped his head. "Not yet." He squinted and slowly shook his head. "It's like they disappeared. But ... we'll find them."

Lisha spoke up. "Hey, whatever happened to your friend?" She grinned. Damn she had teeth. "You know. Tall, dark and gorgeous."

Clarence chuckled and winked at Michael. "Oh, he's around."

Michael nodded back and winked.

Someone touched Clarence's arm.

A huge bouquet of flowers quivered in front of him. Stunning. A head peaked from behind it.

"Randy?" Clarence tried to sit up.

"Down boy." Randy gripped his arm. "I told you I'd come back to see you. Never thought it'd be so soon."

He put the bouquet on the shelf and revealed something from behind his back. "Brought you a treat. We all know how hospital food can be."

A kid's meal from McDonald's.

Clarence laughed.

Bea roused and scrambled to her knees. "A Happy Meal!"

"Want some Bea?" Clarence nodded toward it.

"Yeah." She sat up and opened the box and popped a chicken nugget in his mouth. And one in hers.

Harold reached around and pulled out a French fry for him and Mrs. Hatly.

Bea handed a nugget to Mommy.

The nurse moved to the other side of the bed and pushed the straw into Clarence's mouth.

Out of the corner of Clarence's eye, Michael bowed his head.

Clarence paused and bowed his, one eye open.

Michael's head slowly lifted, his eyes directed to heaven. Powerful wings slowly appeared and unfurled. He raised his arms and blinding light seemed to meet him, pulling him to full stature.

Clarence started to weep.

Bea dropped her nugget into the box and snuggled back down onto Clarence's chest. "He's so pretty," she whispered.

Lisha made a joke and the room erupted in laughter. All unaware of the miracle taking place.

"Can you see him, too?" Clarence whispered and watched where Bea's eyes traveled, holding her close.

"Your angel? Yup." She watched until her eyes slowly closed. She quickly opened them, looked at Michael, smiled at Clarence and her eyes fluttered closed again.

Harold stuttered, forgetting the punch line to a joke.

More laughter.

Clarence pressed his stubbled cheek against Bea's head. He softly wept as Michael disappeared.

Ahhh. Family.

End

AUTHOR NOTES

When I first wrote Released, I was preparing to write it in NaNoW-riMo (National Novel Writing Month). It's a great way to puke out a rough draft. 50,000 words in the month of November, every November. I made the 50,000 words that year and several after. I always plan to start preparing at least in September but especially in October. Yeah. I freaked when it hit October 28 and I was putting the Halloween candy out. Panic. So I took the easy way out: setting—Osceola, Nebraska—where I live, main character's name—Clarence, my dad's name. Whew! That's done! (I don't think he will care—he's in heaven!)

Our local nursing home is NOT Hillcrest Homes! The sights and smells I wrote about aren't in any way reflected in our own nursing home. The people—staff or residents in the BOOK—are NOT in any way like the REAL, precious people actually living and working in our local nursing home!

Any resemblance to local people is purely coincidental. I love our town and people.

This book is mostly written from an ex-con's point of view. Clarence sees EVERYTHING in a negative manner, from the tattered wallpaper in his room to the smells. Nothing is going to please him because he'd rather be dead!

Oh ... and Clarence is me.

Gasp.

Anger? Yup. Bitterness? Yup. Stubbornness? Whew. Yes. I was imprisoned by my own emotions, but now I'm free because of the saving Grace of Jesus Christ. Is anybody reading this still imprisoned by emotions? Let's talk. Email me. Contact page on my website. I'll answer.

Things I learned during this process?

1) You can print a whole manuscript after the little x appears above the PGBK cartridge telling you to replace the cartridge. There's a whole lotta ink still in there! Just a little trivia. *Smiling*

2) Never give up. The enemy, the voices, procrastination will hammer you. They'll tell you the story is stupid. Or people will laugh. Or the worst: people will never read it. It'll lie like a lump somewhere in a digital backyard. But the more you dig in, the stronger you get. I use 2 Corinthians 10:5. I speak it out loud to those voices. "I bring THAT thought captive to surrender to the obedience of Jesus." Maybe even stomp my foot. It helps.

Then I sit down (because I stand up and shout at the voices sometimes) and write. Grinning. It's kinda fun to be crazy.

I use that verse like a thought filter. Think coffee maker. Put the filter in, the coffee in. Pour the water in and hit start. What comes out is hot, smellin' good. Tastes good.

Stay with me—I bring that thought to Jesus and let Him put it through His thought filter. In other words, it has to pass through HIM. When it comes out, it is pure, hot and strong.

Just like good coffee.

"Jesus said to him, I am the Way and the Truth and the Life; no one comes to the Father except by (through) Me."

John 14:6 Amplified Version

ACKNOWLEDGEMENTS

Writing a book becomes a family/community endeavor. Like a building, the foundation has to come first—otherwise it will all collapse. My thanks goes to NaNoWriMo. Without you, I never would have gotten a rough draft finished! (Plus other rough drafts, to be published down the road a bit.)

Thanks to my Prayer Warriors. When hit by fear or frustration, I'd send an email. Peace would roll over me. I could hear God and made decisions. I still made mistakes, but because of your encouragement, I got back up. You are a Lifeline.

Thanks to Kathy Tyers Gillin, my editor. Because of you I can publish with a smile. (Grinning at what was. Smiling at what is.) You took my mess and made it readable—hopefully something powerful in people's lives. I enjoyed every email, every comment. Even "Eek!"

Thanks to Jane Dixon-Smith, my book designer, who designed the inside and outside. I love this cover! From the first email you sent, I could tell it would be fun to work with you. You are patient to put up with my insecurities. Very talented and gracious.

My critique group. We have jumped from one place to another and will continue to do so as our lives evolve! One thing always stays the same: we shred each other's manuscripts with love! Red pens allowed!

Thank you Layne Gissler. I had no idea what I was doing in writing about prisons or ex-cons or … well, thanks for letting me pick your brain and for setting me straight on things. I appreciate the job you do.

Thank you Marla for being my Deputy consultant. Thanks for all you do that we don't see.

I am blessed to have a family photographer who is a professional! Lori, thank you for always accommodating me and finding just the right pose to hide a few things and enhance a few! Plus it's fun!

My beta readers: Jan, Sheila, Pastor Al, Layne, Lori, Jo and Cassie. Some are family, all are friends. Thanks for the time you gave to this project. I asked you to be brutal. Some of you were. Ahem! (Grinning.) Thank you!

Judy Krysl, thank you for getting me on the road with the cover design. We both believe that God's timing is perfect! I enjoyed working with you. And THANK YOU for naming the book! (In the first sample of the book cover, Judy threw up a name to hold the title place. "Released." God brought that word everywhere to confirm that this was the title of my book.) Thank you. Thank you!

I'm a novice at writing all these inside-the-book pages, but I feel thanks goes to McDonald's as a setting in an early chapter. Using your restaurant made my job easier as everyone has been to McDonald's! http://www.mcdonalds.com/us/en/home.html.

There were several scenes where I used TV commercials and Progressive fit super well. I love those commercials! https://www.progressive.com. And the game show, Wheel of Fortune helped me find a comical and solid way to get Clarence down a hall to his room. http://www.wheeloffortune.com.

I also want to thank the many authors who have gone before me in this incredible journey of indie publishing. All have been helpful and open about what has worked for them. It is an amazing journey and with the many opportunities available today, both digitally and print-on-demand (POD), it is an exciting time to write!

Yay, God!

THANK YOU READER

Thanks for reading Released. I identified with Clarence. I hope you did too, because there are more books about him coming soon!

Look for other titles: short stories, novels, kids' books in the future.

You can keep updated by email if you go to:
www.bonnielacy.com

Sign up for free stories. I have a whole slew of them!

Also email bonnielacy@bonnielacy.com
for news on upcoming books, projects and my writing life.

If you like Released or any future works by me, please take time to leave a review where you bought the book. When I buy books or goods, I always read the reviews before I buy. Maybe you do too. It helps you find what you like. It helps me sell my work!

Thanks so much!

Made in the USA
Charleston, SC
06 August 2015